W9-BBN-981

J C Sweeney

The Men That God Made Mad

The Men That God Made Mad

A NOVEL OF IRELAND'S EASTER RISING

BY

W. A. Ballinger

G. P. PUTNAM'S SONS
NEW YORK

Copyright © 1966, 1969 by W. A. Ballinger

All rights reserved. This book, or parts thereof, may
not be reproduced in any form without permission.
Published simultaneously in the Dominion of Canada
by Longmans Canada Limited, Toronto.

Library of Congress Catalog Card Number: 69–18163

PRINTED IN THE UNITED STATES OF AMERICA

For the great Gaels of Ireland
  Are the men that God made mad,
For all their wars are merry,
  And all their songs are sad.

G. K. CHESTERTON
"Ballad of the White Horse"

Part One

I write it out in a verse—
MacDonagh and MacBride
And Connolly and Pearse
Now and in time to be,
Wherever green is worn,
Are changed, changed utterly:
A terrible beauty is born.

> W. B. YEATS
> "Easter 1916"

1. Easter Monday

"AT the G.P.O. . . . Charge!"

As James Connolly gave the order there was an awed moment of incredulity in the hearts of his motley army. Was this how moments of destiny came—in the heart of a city, before the incurious eyes of the usual Sackville Street strollers, beneath the tower that enshrined Horatio Lord Nelson and without so much as the cry of a bugle to hearten a man? Was this the way to take Dublin and free Ireland? In that instant many a man felt his heart quail for the sheer downright nonglory of it all.

Then the moment's indecision was gone and the first man to break the ranks was followed by all the rest.

Dark green hand-stitched uniforms and civilian clothes with a yellow brassard about the arm; rifles and shotguns, pikes and clubs, bayonets and aged swords. Weapons stabbed the air, and comrades were in deadly peril from the frantic enthusiasm of comrades as the charge surged across the pavement and through the sparse crowd who had, perhaps, something slightly out of the usual in this Easter Day demonstration that seemed at first sight so like so many more.

The well-bred Palladian front of the G.P.O. seemed to raise its pediments in horror, and the figures of Hibernia, Mercury and Fidelity appeared more than ordinarily graven as the column swept beneath them and into the broad, marble-floored elegance of the post office.

Bewildered staff stood frozen in their positions behind the

9

mahogany counters, seeing but not taking in the mob which had so suddenly shattered the calm of their occupation.

A pike rammed a British officer in the rear as he composed a telegram at the counter. As civil war swept up around her, a woman was still demanding stamps from an ice-faced civil servant.

"Everybody out!" roared James Connolly. "Out, out!"

His bandy legs were splendid in highly polished leggings, and he wore the uniform of a commandant general. His husky roar startled even his own men into obedience, and some of them had started to the exits under the impression that the operation was off. Their officers had to bar the way to them while the post office workers and the general public now flowed in a frightened, bewildered and resentful stream toward the street beyond.

Outside, they did not move away but gathered in the street, staring back toward the sidewalk, still only half-believing that what had happened was so.

Then the great sheets of plate glass of the windows began to shatter from within, smashed outward enthusiastically by the rifle butts of the Citizen Army. There was the rumble of desks being dragged to form barricades.

And as they dodged the shards of glass the crowd knew it was true, all true.

Fascinated, they looked up to see climbing across the pediment and the molded Arms of England the distant shapes of Volunteers who made for the foot of the flagpole.

Jerkily a green bundle made its way aloft to be broken out and flutter sedately in the gentle breeze.

Green bunting with a golden harp in its center flaunted above the Arms of England, and across the flag was stitched the legend: IRISH REPUBLIC.

Half of Dublin was at its lunch and it was Easter Monday, 1916.

The Kilcroom detachment was well to the front when the charge began. Declan O'Donovan was among the first men through the stately doors, which was fitting since Declan was always a swift man on his legs for all the size of him.

Certainly, despite Terence McKeon's very strict orders, he was not with the Kilcroom detachment as they marched into the G.P.O. They marched in very neat and soldierlike, McKeon at the head with his hand on his Peter the Painter Mauser, the German officer's handgun which had been immortalized by the anarchist Peter the Painter at the siege of Sydney Street in London, and his boots polished till the glow was like the moon over Claddagh. A compact group, a well-trained group, professionals almost.

Peadar Casey's heart, he bringing up the rear, beat with a pride he tried to fight down as he compared the Kilcroom men with the others. It was not for him or any of them to feel pride like this, to feel themselves above anyone or better than anyone. They were all soldiers for Ireland, fighters for freedom. And yet the little demon of pride could not be restrained, whispering in his ear that the rest were a rabble compared with Kilcroom.

Slap-bang in the middle of the post office Terence McKeon brought them to a halt. Their heels clacked fiercely down on the marble floor. They stood very still, shoulders well back and their single-shot Martinis at the identical angle of slope.

"Order . . . arms!"

The butts slammed the marble together, and all around the confusion of the big room eyes swung toward the precision of the sound as if there were those afraid that the British had marched into their midst.

McKeon stood his group easy and marched over to Connolly. His salute quivered like a guardsman's.

"Kilcroom detachment awaiting orders, sir."

Curiously the commandant general's eyes scanned him, tak-

ing in the freshly pressed heather-green uniform of the Volunteers, the polished boots, the rigid military stance.

"That would be Captain McKeon, eh? That's a smart bunch
with you. Will they stand fire?"

"They've stood it, sir . . . and given it back. The Long
Road Corner—Gilligan's Corner—sir."

McKeon's gray-green eyes did not blink, though he was
thinking that surely Connolly must have heard of the fight at
Gilligan's Corner. Was there anyone in Ireland who had not
heard of Gilligan's Corner and the fight there?

Connolly nodded abruptly.

"Take the back, Captain McKeon. I'll leave the guard of
our rear in your hands."

Casually he waved a dismissing hand and turned to greet the
O'Rahilly and Sean T. O'Kelly, who was to be president of
Ireland thereafter but was then engaged in bringing some flags
from headquarters at Liberty Hall.

McKeon's temper was flaring inside him as he marched his
group down the long, imposing corridors to the rear of the
vast building.

It was not that he resented being given the back of the
building to guard—it was the way it had been done, the casual
way.

Until that moment, he raged silently, *he hadn't even
thought of the rear. The place could have been left wide open
for a counterattack.*

Inefficient. Unreasonable. These were the words that fought
in his mind. Terence McKeon was a man who loved matters
to be carried out efficiently. And he liked them to be carried
out for a due and proper reason.

It was not that he was cold, a machine mind. But he was
only too well aware of the faults of his people, of the wild,
undisciplined enthusiasm that could collapse as swiftly into
the depths of that strangely cynical despair which is the

birthright of the Gael. "Sure I knew it would be no good, anyway," a man would say as he died bravely and uselessly, victim of a lack of planning and a lack of reason.

And in this today, thought McKeon, there had been enough lack of planning and an utter lack of reason.

It was on . . . it was off . . . it was on again . . . it was off again. It was little wonder that half the Volunteers stayed at home or at their work or in the pubs or wherever they might find themselves that historic day, that instead of the five thousand men the plans had called for to take Dublin, only a few hundred actually took arms.

Had not the president of the Volunteers, Professor John MacNeill, in dispute with his colleagues, inserted a notice in the Sunday *Independent* of the previous day stating: "No parades, marches, or other movement of Irish Volunteers will take place"?

It was a hell of a way to run a revolution, and Terence McKeon's tidy, rational, schoolmaster's soul was in more revolt than the city.

Yet he took his men to the rear of the post office and positioned them carefully where they would have the best field of fire—and the best cover from the counterattack that surely could not be long delayed. The taste of failure to come was strong in his mouth, the taste of death.

For it was not reasonable that this half-organized, ramshackle, heroic revolt could succeed. They were dead men, he thought, he and all the lads he had brought from Kilcroom.

Now, and for the only time in his life, he had doubts. Not of the Cause or of the men that led the Cause—but of their methods, of their helpless, hopeless, slapdash unreason. They were, God save them all, so bloody Irish.

The lads from Kilcroom, he thought. He had brought these lads—and he thought of them as lads, though half of them out-aged him—here to be butchered. For he had no doubt that butchered they would be.

It was unreasonable to suppose otherwise than that the British would wipe them out in short order. And he had brought them. It had been his cogent reasoning, his long, careful speeches in the field behind McCarthy's Rocks that had brought them.

And to their death.

And yet in this Terence McKeon was wrong. History had brought the men from Kilcroom—history and Declan O'Donovan.

The day when Declan stood forward in the field and waved his hat and said: "If Terence goes, sure no one will stay in Kilcroom"—that was the day when it was decided. Declan led and the men followed, and that was the way it had always been in Kilcroom.

From far back in the building there was the sound of a shot, and McKeon's men stood to their arms. But needlessly. The shot had been fired within the building.

Upstairs, on the second floor, had been a section of British troops under a sergeant and corporal. They were there to guard the telegraph room, and when the Volunteers surged up the stairs they were met by leveled rifles.

One shot was fired from a Volunteer's gun and the Scots sergeant dropped.

"Don't shoot!" the corporal called. "We've no ammunition."

And so, incredibly, it proved. A detachment of troops to protect the nerve center of the capital—in a time of mounting tension—but not a single round for a single rifle.

If he had known, Terence McKeon might have taken heart. It would have shown him that, unprepared and random as his own organization might seem, the enemy was no better.

But of the wounded sergeant and the empty rifles McKeon knew nothing. He knew only that he was a man short.

"Where's Declan?" he demanded.

"He was one of the first in," Peadar Casey gritted. Peadar, whose hard, dark face was fanatically alive with the pride of what they were doing. "He'll maybe be nailing the colors to the mast."

"Get him," McKeon ordered sharply. "Find him and bring him. His place is here."

Casey doubled away and had no trouble finding Declan. Hardly anyone in Dublin would have found trouble seeking him.

Declan had pulled himself up into one of the glassless windows and was declaiming to the crowd outside, declaiming and singing, improvising:

Oh, Mary, this Dublin's a wonderful sight,
With the English all running about in a fright.
They've lost this fair city, I'm thankful to say,
It's Ireland's alone now on this Easter day. . . .

There was a good deal more to the same strain, not brilliant versifying but spontaneous and very much to the liking of the crowd without and those of the Volunteers within who could spare a moment. They were grinning at the songster as they heaved the barricades into position and prepared their defense positions.

Casey heard James Connolly's Ulster accent demand: "Who's the song thrush?"

"One of the Kilcroom crowd," answered Patrick Henry Pearse, president of the provisional government. "A lively lad."

"There'll be time enough for singing when the shooting's over," Connolly snorted brusquely.

Casey tugged at Declan's leg.

15

"Come down outa that, you eejit!" he hissed. "The captain wants you."

With a last flamboyant gesture to the crowd beneath, Declan leaped down lightly into the post office.

"If the captain wants me, he will have me," his baritone voice declared loudly. "Declan O'Donovan was never the man to hang back when he was wanted."

Casey's face tightened as he steadied O'Donovan for an instant. The reek of whiskey was strong about the big man. This early in the day. Drunk on this historic day, the Day of Liberation. He could have killed the big man there and then. Could he take nothing seriously? The People's Cause fairly launched, and this great, laughing playboy had to make a sport of it. He was as bad as all those that the real revolution —the socialist revolution—would surely oust. Maybe he was even worse. For he had no background of wealth to excuse him.

A scurrying girl came fleeing down the corridor, one of the last of the telegraphic assistants.

Declan's arm scooped her up in a flurry of kicking legs and fluttering underskirt.

"A kiss for a soldier of Ireland," he boomed and planted his laughing lips fairly on hers.

She squealed as he put her down, and scampered off to freedom. Sourly Casey thought there had been a hint of pleasure in that squeal. There usually was when Declan kissed them.

"Get to your post!" he snarled.

"Aye, aye, Lieutenant, sir. Declan hears and obeys."

He gave an absurd parody of a salute and began to march like an exaggerated guardsman.

Peadar Casey said nothing more but marched behind him, thinking sour thoughts.

McKeon saw them coming, and the irritation he had felt

at O'Donovan's absence was tempered as always by the pleasure the sight of the man always gave him. O'Donovan in a room was like a fire in the hearth, and his presence there would be more than a simple matter of another rifle.

The reproofs he had mustered died unsaid on his tongue, and instead he said brusquely, but not harshly, "Declan, take the corner window, will you?"

As he spoke he glanced at his watch. He was listening intently, listening for the blast as the powder magazine at Dublin Castle blew up. He listened in vain, for though indeed the rebels had entered the castle, there had been no key for the magazine door. If he had known this, known that the lack of a key had prevented the destruction of the symbol of England's power, his lip might have curled more and his thoughts about unreason and incompetence have been harsher still.

In the far distance a few rifle and pistol shots crackled. And for the moment that was all there was of revolt on this Easter Monday in 1916. The quiet before the storm, the quiet that gave a man time to think, to think how it had begun and to wonder how it would end.

He looked around at the intent faces at the windows, at the crouched bodies, at Declan O'Donovan and Peadar Casey and all the others he had led there from Kilcroom. What was in their hearts? What was in their minds? Fear? Glory? The knowledge that the die had been irrevocably cast?

How many of them knew they were doomed, that this whole raggle-taggle, off-again-on-again rebellion had as little chance of success as a snowball in hell?

Terence McKeon knew. And though he knew, he was not afraid. It had been necessary. On its failure success could still be built.

But how many from Kilcroom would live to see it? How many would go back down the winding roads of Cork they had left in such high spirits?

17

2. The Collector

"Failure is the only real foundation for success. You'll never get to the top till you've been to the bottom."

Those words had been said to Terence McKeon by his mother, that enigmatic woman who trailed the shades of former beauty about her like a Donegal shawl. They were paradoxical on first hearing, and yet they had the whole truth of life in them, he thought—of Irish life at least. Ireland dearly loved a failure, a man or a cause, and this had to be so or this wonderful people with all their talents, their genius even, would have ruled the world.

If success had been their love and they had wooed it thoroughly, there would have been no contrast. Success existed only against the darkness of defeat.

McKeon remembered the words as he stood in the post office on that fated Easter and saw clearly the disasters that must lie ahead. And yet on those disasters what successes might yet be built?

Terence McKeon had known the taste of disaster before this.

"Well, you've seen the old State House, you've seen Harvard, you've seen Radcliffe, you've gawped at the Washington portraits, and you've stood on the very quay where the Boston Tea Party lit the torch of freedom bright. You've done your schoolmasterly duty, I'd say, wouldn't you?"

The electric landaulet purred silently through Boston's

streets, the rich scent of leather, the roses in the silver holders and his own cigar overwhelmed almost by Moira Burke's perfume, applied with enthusiasm rather than discretion.

She sat beside Terence McKeon in the rear of the car. A dazzling, free-spoken hoyden with glinting, restless dark eyes and lips whose rich red was the result of no artifice, McKeon was sure, from the frequency with which she licked them.

"My prospects of seeing Boston again are rather remote," he answered a little stiffly. "It was my duty to see as much as I could so as to tell my class all about the cradle of freedom when I get home."

Moira laughed deliciously, a light, tinkling laugh.

"You speak like a dry old stick, and I'll bet you ain't more than maybe a couple of years older than me."

"Maybe," he agreed as stiffly as before but inwardly cursing his own ineptitude, his almost secluded life with his mother. This was a time when he would have even surrendered his mission and all it meant to have the light insouciance of a man-about-town. Or even more appropriately, he thought, if he could now have something of Declan O'Donovan's way with women. The bold Declan would never have been embarrassed by an encounter like this. Declan would have reveled in it . . . and so would the girl.

"Maybe," she echoed in a gruff voice. "Is there never a touch of the Blarney about ye at all, Mr. Terence McKeon of Kilcroom in the County Cork?"

Oddly, her affected accent was more like a Belfast woman's than a Southern Irish girl's. But he had noticed that this eastern American city with its chilly spring had more in common with Ireland's north than its south. Boston might be, as they claimed, the second city of Ireland, but for all its Holy Cross Cathedral it was a Protestant city. The Southern Irish had been moving in only over the last half-century, whereas its early history was all very much Nonconformist.

"I'm sorry. I'm afraid I've never really—" He was conscious that he was blushing. She did not laugh.

"I'm sorry too. I shouldn't be teasing you. Papa would have my skin if he knew. Teasing a hero of Ireland."

Big Jim Burke would not have dreamed of touching his daughter, McKeon was quite certain. The plump businessman who was his host in Boston stood totally in awe of the motherless girl and could deny her nothing. The expensive landaulet in which they were being driven was Moira's own. So, in effect, was the driver.

"As I said, you've seen everything. So what would you like to do now? I have a sailboat if you'd like to go to sea. We could go down the bay. There's a good breeze."

"Oh, I doubt if I'd have time for that. I've still a few collectors to see. And then there's this reception your father has been so kind—"

"I fear that County Cork is not living up to its advertisements. And Papa had given me such glowing reports. Very well."

She rapped on the window behind the driver's head.

"Home, Sean," she ordered.

Terence McKeon had never felt so thoroughly embarrassed in his life. No doubt, he thought sourly, if he had been reared in some big house, accustomed to the airs and graces of society, he would have been able to carry off a situation like this with aplomb. Instead it seemed he had contrived to insult his host's daughter. Or if not insult, at least displease.

And yet it was certainly true that he had work to do before the party Big Jim Burke had arranged for him that night.

McKeon's mission in America was simple enough. It was to collect funds for the Brotherhood. There existed already a collecting organization in Boston and New York, Irishmen resident in the cities, members of the Brotherhood, who made weekly collections from their compatriots, a quarter here, a dollar there. McKeon had covered New York already, with its big Irish population. Now he was doing Boston, making the rounds of the collectors, encouraging them, urging them to greater efforts.

Terence McKeon had been chosen for the mission because of his undoubted probity. Others had gone before him who had not returned with as much as had been expected. There were suspicions that at least part of the funds might have been diverted. To check on past returns was also part of McKeon's work, little though he liked the idea of spying, even at second hand, on any Brother.

To date it seemed to him there was no evidence of any defalcation. The figures given by his predecessors tallied with those of the local collectors.

"The fact is, mister," a barman had told him bluntly as he handed over his own contribution, "that folks is not so easy to touch now. They see the money going out all the time. They don't see any action for it. Hell, they'd get more action playing the ponies."

"We're training," McKeon assured him. "All over Ireland we've got men training. When the time comes we'll strike."

"Folks is saying the time to strike is now. England's at war. From over here it looks like now is the time. Hell, if you miss this chance you'll never get another."

"Do you want us to go out and fight the English soldiers with our bare hands? Well, then, man. We've got to have the money first. We've got to buy guns. Don't worry, you'll see full value for your dollars in good time."

The barman had quailed a little at the cold savagery behind McKeon's eyes.

"Sure, sure, Ireland will be free yet. But I'd like to see it in me Da's day. He has a great notion to go back there before he dies . . . and he hasn't long."

Moira Burke's temper was recovered by the time they got

back to the big house in its own grounds that stood as a memorial to her father's industry.

He had been a plasterer's laborer when he left Kilcroom. Now he was a millionaire, they said, a building contractor with fingers in a dozen pies.

"Jim Burke," his mother had said as he packed to leave for the States. "You're sure to see him. He's a big man now over there."

His Uncle Eustace had put it differently: "Them Burkes were never any good. Sure I remember him when he hadn't got an arse to his britches."

Now he wore a well-cut frock coat with a gold Albert looping across his well-filled stomach. He had bristling, sandy hair, watery, green-blue eyes and a lower lip which trembled faintly but continuously from some nervous tic.

"Thank the Lord you're back, Moira," he greeted her. "I can get no sense out of them ones in the kitchen. Will you go and tell them what's to do with the dinner? Master, will you come and take a drink with me?"

"Be sure it's only one," Moira warned as she flounced from the ornately paneled entrance hall to the kitchen. "The master has people to see still."

Burke took McKeon through to his own study, book-lined with impressive volumes which were probably never read. There were some decanters and Waterford glasses on a side table. Solemnly Burke poured.

"I needn't ask if it's Irish you'd want. Lord, master, but it's a business, this socializing. These duds. I'd as soon be back in me oul' dungarees. But ye have to do it. Ye have to do it. It's expected."

The doom of Ireland, McKeon thought. "It's expected." How did his fiery, irresponsible race ever become so overlaid with the burdens of respectability? And yet his own cause depended too on "it's expected." Men joined the Volunteers or the Brotherhood or the Citizen Army because it was "expected." Over here they subscribed to the funds because "it's expected."

"Society sets its own patterns," he answered Burke weightily. "If you want to succeed or be accepted even you have to conform."

He glanced down at his own clothes: neat, a little shabby but clean and made of good material, exactly what was expected from a master. A schoolmaster.

"And the girl there," Burke continued to complain. "Oh, she's a worry, a terrible worry. If only her poor dear mother, God rest her soul and may she rest in eternal peace, if she was here! But I'm not a man knows much of women. I wish she'd get herself married and have someone else do the worrying, but she's not the marrying kind either. . . . Were we back home in Cork she'd have been married this year back and no nonsense about it. But now, here . . . I tell you, it's not Ireland, Mr. McKeon. It's not Ireland."

He walked back to the table and poured himself another drink. McKeon had scarcely sipped his. Drink had never appealed to him, though his mother always kept a bottle in the house and sometimes they took a glass of hot toddy at bedtime.

"You have someone else to see? You'll not be late back, I hope. I'll have some important people. . . . Our crowd, you know. Honey Fitz—you'll have heard of him—Joe Kennedy, big and getting bigger. Kelly. . . . He's a Dubliner really, shipping. I think we'll have a pleasant little surprise for you. I'm sure you'll like it. A drink?"

"Perhaps I'd better finish my calls." McKeon put down his glass and rose.

Moira came into the hall as McKeon left. There was some flour on her nose and a trace of jam—or could it have been blood?—on the silk sleeve of her dress.

23

"See you tonight," she told him as he made for the door. "Tonight."

She giggled curiously as he left.

"Hagan?" the girl said. "I guess there's no Hagan here. Or any other Irish. I'm a Polack myself. Or at least my Pa was."

She leaned against the doorpost and smiled. A tall, buxom girl with blond hair and deep blue eyes. She was just beginning to get fat.

"I'm sorry to have troubled you."

"It's no trouble. Won't you come in? I'm on my own, more's the pity."

Terence McKeon had no doubt at all that her regrets were financial rather than social, though he had not to his knowledge met a prostitute before.

"No, no. I mean, I'm sorry . . . I . . . I have to find Mr. Hagan."

He was blushing again and knew it.

The girl laughed but in a kindly way, seeing his embarrassment and understanding it.

"Try the police," she advised. "Or maybe the morgues. If you're out of luck, you could always come back here, honey. I won't be going anywhere."

She laughed again as he descended the steep, narrow stairs to the street below that wound through this part of the old city.

McKeon was disturbed by the encounter. The memory of the girl lingered in his mind: the full figure hardly concealed by the partly buttoned shirtwaist, the red lips, the laughter that scorned the world and its conventions and implied a deep, friendly understanding of man and his ways.

As he went back to the Burke house in a cab he found the image of this drab and the image of Moira Burke confusing themselves in his mind.

*   *   *

The orchestra was playing outside in the long drawing room with its dangling crystal chandeliers and its gently gyrating dancers.

A fat, short man with a vast cigar in his mouth had nudged McKeon in the ribs and indicated the bell.

"Three hundred million dollars on the hoof this little lot represents," he declared. "Three hundred million dollars. On the hoof. That's something to think about, young man."

Now most of that money was represented by the group in Burke's study: second-generation Americans but Irishmen still.

"We'll not waste your time, Mr. McKeon," said Kelly, the shipping man. "You may have wondered why you've had no contributions from us. We wanted to know how the rest of our people were contributing—and we're here to say we'll match dollar for dollar. Every cent you've collected this trip we'll double."

McKeon's words spoke thanks. In his mind there was some reserve. Their generosity was only going to amount to about three thousand dollars a head—which would be about the cost of this reception.

"There's just a wee thing, though," Burke put in. "You see, there's some of us. . . . Well, business is that complicated. We wouldn't like the English to get wind of our donation."

"They could hurt our trade," another man expatiated. "They're big customers in oil, meat, steel, of course. The war—"

"I understand. Your donation will not be acknowledged publicly."

"We'd go farther than that. What we give we'll give in cash. No checks. The English have their spies in the banks. Cash tells no tales where it's been. . . . Now, how much is it?"

"Twenty-seven thousand four hundred and three dollars and seventy-five cents," McKeon answered, face bland but an acid contempt in his mind. Did there have to be a gombeen-man at the heart of every Irishman? Or was it only wealth that corrupted? Oh, it made sense, certainly, to conceal from the English that they were supporting intended rebels. It would be bad for business.

One of the others began to count out the money in hundred-dollar bills, loving the feel of every note, parting with it reluctantly.

"We'll see the Dublin papers," said Burke. "Where you announce what a good trip you had over here. The acknowledgment of the total there will be all the receipt we'll be needing."

Or in other words, McKeon thought, *don't try any tricks, me boyo. We know how much you should turn over. We'll see you do.*

Afterward there was the dinner, supper rather, some patriotic speeches and some drinking. McKeon took more than he had intended in an effort to dispel the gloom that seemed to be settling on him. He wanted nothing more now than to get away, to get back to Ireland, to Kilcroom, to a life with meaning. Here the whole purpose of existence blurred.

During the meal from time to time he saw Burke throwing an anxious glance at his daughter, seated almost opposite McKeon. Moira was flushed, irrepressible, half-drunk. One or two of the other women were casting sidelong looks at her. They would have plenty to talk about later.

After supper the night seemed endless, but at last McKeon found his way to bed. He had just begun to undress and was on the point of emptying his pocket of the money they had given him and packing it away in the special satchel he had brought with him—handmade by Muldoon, the saddler in Kilcroom.

The door opened suddenly and Moira Burke swayed in, a bottle of champagne held unsteadily in her hand.

He stared at her in astonished silence as she held a finger to her lips.

"Drinkies," she whispered. "I'm not letting a hero of Ireland go sober to his bed—or lonely either."

She giggled in silent appreciation of her wit. She was wearing a dressing gown, a frilly, high-necked garment in pink satin.

When she sat on the bed and held up the bottle, the garment parted across her knees, and if she was wearing anything under the dressing gown it was very short indeed.

"Come on then," she whispered. "Be responsive."

Terence McKeon felt the blood thumping furiously through him at the sight of the woman and with the knowledge of the offer she was making.

She laughed softly, threw her head back and stared up at him through narrowed eyes. Her scent was strong, as strong as it had been in the electric car. The redness of her lips had the rich allure of freshly picked rose petals. She radiated desire.

And Terence McKeon could feel his own body answering that call, the urgent tingling in his loins, the thickness in his throat, the overwhelming wish to succumb.

If he had had two more drinks, one more drink maybe, it would have been enough. But his mind was in control of his body.

"Miss Burke," he said as stiffly as he had ever spoken, "I think this is very improper. I am a guest in your father's house, and to take advantage would be—"

"Yes, teacher," she tittered. "Oh, give over with your sermonizing, will you, for God's sake! Are you a man at all? God, it isn't often Moira Burke has to ask twice for what she wants."

She made a sort of half-lunge at him and he skipped back, conscious of the ludicrous figure he must be cutting. She

27

laughed aloud and he had a vision of the whole household storming in. Anger came at last to his aid.

"I must ask you to leave this room at once or—"

"Or . . . or what? Would the big, handsome, strong master beat the ickle-bitsy girl? Go on then, if that's your mood."

With a sudden agile twist she turned and knelt over the bed, pulling up her dressing gown in the same movement.

And for a terrifying instant, gazing at the pale, offered buttocks, McKeon felt desire almost overwhelm his anger, felt his body quiver and try to thrust forward.

It seemed to him he had been standing there for minutes or hours, but in fact the girl had scarcely turned before he too was turning, snatching at his coat and running from the room as if the devil chased him.

In the next room that he was aware of inhabiting he wakened with a thumping head, a bruised body . . . and twenty-seven thousand four hundred and four dollars the poorer.

3. The Blackout

"I thought you were coming round," he heard a girl's voice from an immense distance. "I thought I saw you move. Would you like a cup of coffee or would you prefer a cure? I've got some bourbon here—"

The voice wavered away into the distance as memory came back patchily.

Moira Burke . . . leaving the house, wandering down into the dock area. A ship was unloading cargo, winches clattering; he remembered the distinctive clatter of the winches. He had heard it often enough around the quays of Cork.

And there had been a bar open to cater to the longshoremen. Why should he gravitate to a bar, he who hardly drank? Yet he had sat there in a corner and the fear . . . it was fear, no less, that Moira Burke had inspired in him, fear of himself and of her . . . the fear had passed gradually as the whiskey warmed him.

He had been talking there in the bar with someone. Who? What had been the words? Himself declaiming? Lecturing? There was obscurity there. A face in the bar. Now an ache in the head.

A face in the bar with a bright smile beneath a sweep of mustache. A courtly manner. A touch of a brogue and a deferential interest in him. A good fellow, he remembered. And no doubt he had brought him back to the Burke house.

Except that the voice did not sound like Moira Burke's and the bed where he lay lacked the comfort of his bed in

Burke's big house. And after the way he had left Moira she would scarcely be tending him so tenderly. Unbidden, the vision of his last sight of her sprang into his mind, and he gave a little groan.

"I have some ice and it might do your head some good, honey. My Pa always hit the bottle when he'd been on the bottle. If he could get the stuff, that is, and had the price of it. It pulled him together okay."

The room had no familiarity at all when Terence McKeon contrived to blink open an eye. It was a bedroom, and he lay in a double bed. This was a small room, cheap, untidy. Above his head a lithograph hung a little askew on the wall. At the foot of the bed was a chest of drawers doing duty also as a dressing table. Toilet things littered it. Beside him on a low table was a chamber with the handle broken off. His jacket hung on the back of a chair, but he still wore his trousers though they were down to his ankles. He thought he had his shoes on.

There was a door beside the chest of drawers and beyond the door a folding screen. From behind it came the sound of a gas jet. Beyond the screen was a window, and it seemed to him from the angle of the sun's rays that it must be close to evening.

"How long have I been . . . asleep?"

"All the livelong day, kiddo."

The girl carried a steaming teapot as she came out from behind the screen, and as he saw her he recognized her. He knew now where he was.

"Miss—" he faltered.

"Slansky's the name. Call me Hilda."

What drunken impulse had brought him back to this whore? He felt unclean, totally ashamed of himself, as he sat up slowly and took the tea she offered.

"You don't seem a drinking man like most of the Micks,"

she said shrewdly. "So I didn't give you any bourbon in it. But I'll have some myself. Whiskey and coffee go together, I always think."

He sipped at the tea and tried not to cringe inwardly. What had he done? How had he come there?

He felt the panic of the virtuous man who has erred inexplicably. It seemed to him that his parish priest's ironic, accusing eyes were on him.

"Excuses are easy," Father Roche used to say. "Anyone can make excuses."

The girl wore only a slip. There was only one bed in the room. Therefore he must have spent the night with her. And he knew exactly what Father Roche would have thought of *that*. *That* might be all right when sanctified by the marriage ceremony and strictly for the purposes of propagation. But the lower half of the body was to be taken as not in the best of taste. It was an unfortunate oversight on God's part that he had not seen fit to make the business of sex a good deal more delicate. But then, he could hardly think of everything.

"You sure as hell hung one on last night," Hilda Slansky confided. "I never knew anyone come as full."

She laughed at the memory.

"You stood there in that doorway, hardly able to stand, and not a word could I get out of you. That big lump on your head and blood down your face . . . I hardly knew you."

"I said nothing at all?"

What had brought him here? What submerged desires had the drink brought out?

"Not a peep, honey. Not a word."

By now the girl was seated confidentially on the edge of the bed. A grimy white slip was patently her only garment. But McKeon felt too ill to be in the slightest moved by this partial nudity.

"You just stood there swaying on your feet with a silly

31

smile on your face. Naturally I thought you were a customer, and then I knew you by that suit . . . though to tell the truth it was that dirty— Anyway, I said to you to come in and you went out flat across the bed and never stirred no more. So I took off your coat and tried for the trousers, only I couldn't get the shoes off as they were tied in funny knots. So I left them on and pulled you over the bed. And there you lay all night."

She gazed at him curiously.

"You sure tied it on last night and no mistake."

An immeasurable weight lifted from McKeon's heart.

"I just . . . slept?"

"You weren't fit for anything else, honey." She laughed raucously. "Many more of your sort and I'd begin to think something was wrong with me."

Her words were the best cure McKeon could have had.

"If you'll be so kind as to turn your back I'll get dressed."

"Turn my back! For Chrissakes, I've seen all of you there is, barring a bit of your ankles and your feet."

Just the same, still laughing, she turned. Thankfully Terence McKeon pulled up his trousers and swung from the bed. Specks of fluff covered the dark gray serge, and he brushed vainly at them. Then he tied his tie, pulled on his coat and shrugged himself into some semblance of normality.

"Well," he began, "you've been very kind, Miss Slansky—"

"Oh, it's no more than I'd have done for any poor bastard. What's wrong?"

The girl's eyes widened as she saw Terence McKeon's hands flutter to his inside pocket, saw him literally change his personality in one brief instant.

His face became a savage, frozen, unpitying mask, and he stepped suddenly forward and seized her in an embrace which had nothing of lust, nothing of pleasure, in it.

32

"The money," he demanded in a voice as rough as the back of a file. "What have you done with the money?"

That it was gone he had realized in the first instant his hands began to check. The money had made a solid, sizable wad in his pocket, and its absence could not be evaded.

His hands had closed almost automatically around the girl's throat though never before in his life had he touched a woman in anger. They were squeezing, thumbing in against the windpipe.

The money. Ireland's money. The sinews of war for freedom. The money he had been sent to collect. . . .

What sort of a traitor had he made himself to lose that money? And it was his own inner reproaches that made him tighten his grip still harder.

Unconsciously he had driven the girl backward until she fell on the bed, bent across it with her slip riding up her belly and his own body pressed against her nakedness in a travesty of passion.

Her mouth was gaping silently, her face puffing, eyes starting out from their sockets. Legs and arms and body were quivering spasmodically.

Perhaps just in time Terence McKeon released his grip as the first surge of rage was replaced by shame. But his eyes still held a frozen threat, and his voice rasped out the questions at her.

"The money?" he insisted. "What have you done with the money?"

It was a good two minutes before she was capable of answering, her voice hoarse with pain.

"What money? Hell, mister, I never took money from no one, not in my life. What the fug do you take me for, anyway?"

A spark of indignation was quenched almost instantly by his hand on her throat again. Now his voice was totally calm, soft and cold, and more frightening than it had been before.

"In my pocket were almost thirty thousand dollars, woman, money collected for Ireland's fight for freedom. That money is there no longer. Let you now give it to me peaceably and with no further ado. For I will tell you, woman, that your life is not worth a moment's purchase if you fail."

"I swear by the cross!" she moaned. "I took no money. I took no money. Would I have kept you here if I'd taken the money? Couldn't I have thrown you down the stairs, drunk to the wide as you were? Why would I sit round waiting for you to come to? For Chrissakes, have some sense, you stupid Mick!"

Hilda Slansky was so patently telling the truth that Mc-Keon released her and stood back, face pinched and pale from the intensity and confusion of his emotions.

"You're quite right," he said in his normal voice. "I had no call either to attack you or accuse you. You must forgive me."

He beat suddenly and savagely at his temples with his fists.

"My God, what a traitor I am myself! What a man to send out on a job like this! A few drinks and—"

The girl rubbed her throat gingerly and ruefully but without rancor.

"Hell, a man's entitled to a few drinks now and then. All the same, it wasn't wise to be carrying a roll. Around these docks no one carries more than he needs. There's guys down here would slip you a Mickey for a roll a tenth of what you were carrying."

"A Mickey?"

"A Mickey Finn. Boy, oh, boy, you're an innocent! The old knockout drops. Sleep water—"

"Ah! You mean my drink might have been drugged?"

"Oh, you're catching on quick. I'd say you've been hocused dead to rights. For that kind of money you're lucky they didn't kill you as well. Maybe that's how you got the lump on the head—left for dead in the gutter somewhere. Lucky they didn't tip you in the dock."

She stood up and pulled down her slip. The concern remained in her eyes.

"Ireland's money, you said? Are you what the Irish here call a collector?"

"I was . . . I'm not fit to bear that name now. I'm . . . I'm. . . . There are no words to describe how contemptible I am. A betrayer of a trust, a sacred trust. A—"

"Don't be a jerk. Calling yourself names won't help."

McKeon paced urgently up and down the room with the thoughts in his mind as uncontrolled as if he were a headless chicken.

"It'd be more to the point to think about getting it back," the girl observed dryly. "For your own sake at least. Do you have any idea where you were, who you spoke to?"

McKeon shuddered painfully. "A blank. The night's a blank. I was in a saloon somewhere . . . I was talking to a man. I think I'd know him if I saw him—"

The girl was pulling on her outdoor clothes.

"Wait here. Maybe I can find something. And maybe not."

"I'll come with you—"

"No, siree. Look, mister, you're a stranger this end of town. I can find out where you were—but nobody's going to talk when you're about. You haven't been much use to anyone this far."

Crushed by his burden of guilt, McKeon sat alone in the room after the girl had gone. Her last words had emphasized his uselessness. He had lost the money. He did not even know how. He had become grossly drunk—Mickey Finn or not. How his mother's lip would have curled in her gentle, biting disdain!

What should he do? What could he do? Go back? But how could he face his mother, face Ireland, face Kilcroom with the knowledge of his failure? It would be better to die.

A spark of anger flickered in his mind as he remembered Moira Burke. If she had not . . . had not done what she did he would not have hastened to the town, would not have drunk himself stupid.

Terence, his mother's voice warned. *Only a coward puts the blame of his own actions on another.*

He ground his knuckles into his temples and groaned in his despair. He must find a church, he thought. Confession would help. Perhaps confession would be the only help he could get. To pour out his folly in the anonymity of a confessional. . . .

The stairs outside creaked, and a moment later the girl came in.

"You're a jerk right enough," she greeted him. "A stranger in the town and you have to pick the roughest, dirtiest, toughest, crookedest saloon on the waterfront. Boy, oh, boy! You're lucky you have a whole throat let alone an empty pocket. You'd be dead this minute only for Dapper Tashy. They're real dock rats in the Russian's place where you were —Polacks and blacks and bums from whatever. They'd cut a throat as soon as—"

"Dapper Tashy? Who's he?"

"He's the man who took your money . . . near as I could find out."

4. The Game

"Your hundred . . . and up two."

The smoke clung in a dense cloud beneath the ceiling of the narrow, long hotel room. The sustained tension in the atmosphere was almost as palpable.

There were five players around the card table and a dozen or so of the inevitable kibbitzers.

Terence McKeon had found the Big Game. He had found, also, the man he sought. Dapper Tashy sat on the other side of the table, and McKeon recognized him as soon as he entered, the broad elegant sweep of mustache reaching out to greased sideburns, the crinkled, glinting dark hair, the perpetual, gleaming smile around the thin stogie. And he remembered the voice as he raised the pot. This was the man he had met in the Russian's and the man who had almost certainly given him the drug. This, surely, was the man who had robbed him.

Two crisp hundred-dollar bills fluttered from Tashy's slim, pale fingers, and the gambler's eyes examined his companions to see who would play along.

It seemed now to McKeon that he could recall more of the previous night's events. He could remember the conversation with the affable stranger, even remember the man warning him not to flash the roll from which he had been paying for his round of drinks. Then there had been a blur in which that soft voice told the barman: "I'll see him home. Don't worry."

And then the blankness.

"That him, then?" demanded Brady, a wizened, gray man in a baggy suit at McKeon's side.

"That's him," McKeon agreed.

He felt the beginnings of relief. Once his mind had begun to work properly again in the prostitute's room he had realized the need for assistance in the search for the man who had robbed him. Brady was a Brotherhood collector, a man also with various vague connections in many fields, a fixer, a contact man, one who knew what was happening wherever it happened in Boston. He knew Dapper Tashy. And it had taken less than an hour for him to find where he was.

Tashy, he had told McKeon, was a gambler by trade or profession, a man whose home was a suitcase in a lodging house. He was Irish, as McKeon remembered vaguely. And when a man like that had money he would have but one thought: to gamble. For to the gambler money is not for spending, for use. Money is for playing with.

"Well, let's get the police," McKeon murmured. "Let's get the money and get out of this."

Brady looked up at him in astonishment and scorn.

"Are you out of your mind? Police?"

"Why not?"

"For a start the police wouldn't touch this game. Finigan, who runs it, is a cousin of Captain Hogan. Hogan gets his payoff every week. Then you'd have to prove that Dapper robbed you. You don't have the numbers of the notes, do you? I thought not. Police!"

McKeon was taken aback. It had seemed to him that it would be merely a matter of finding Dapper Tashy, calling in the police and recovering his money. Now life grew more complicated.

"Two pair," said Tashy at the table. "Queens and—"

"Threes," an unemotional voice responded.

A podgy hand scooped the pool away. McKeon felt a catch

at his heart as he saw the notes gathered carelessly. His notes. The Brotherhood's notes. Ireland's money.

"The word is"—Brady had circulated among the other watchers—"the Dapper is dropping it in large lumps. They put him five grand down."

So that even if the police came, even if they would arrest Tashy, even if the processes of law could be speeded up, Dapper Tashy would still not be able to return all he had stolen.

"He'll get it back, probably," Brady murmured. "The Dapper plays a good hand of poker. The cards have run badly so far. But unless they clean him right out he'll come back. So maybe you should wait till he's back on top again. Then—"

"Then what?"

Brady smiled dryly, revealing yellowed, broken teeth.

"That's up to you. The only way you'll get that money is to take it."

Terence McKeon chewed on his lower lip. Knock Tashy on the head as he left the game? The idea had its attractions. But could he be sure of success?

Hilda Slansky knew Dapper Tashy. "He pimped on me for a while," she had said. "When he's low in funds he'll still come for a sawbuck."

With her life McKeon was not then concerned. "He's tough enough in a fight. He'd use a knife in a flash. You'll have to watch him."

McKeon tried to see himself dealing with a man like that. Regretfully he dismissed the idea. A schoolmaster was not built for brawling, not this one. A gun then? But that would be to go far beyond the confines of the law. McKeon tried to think of any point at which he had an advantage over the gambler. The answer came swiftly.

"Can I join the game?" he asked softly.

"You play poker?" Brady was startled.

"I have. It's a simple game basically. So far as I can see the only way of getting back the money is to win it."

"That's a hard school. You'll need a big stake."

"I'll get it," McKeon promised. "I'll have to go and get it. Will I be able to come in again all right?"

"So you're back, my fine Cork silver tongue? I didn't think you would be."

Moira Burke was again not strictly sober. Now that he knew her, McKeon could interpret the signs—the faint slackness about the mouth, the eyes which were wider, less sharply focused than they should have been. Looking at her now it was possible to see her as she would be in a few years' time, to see her and pity her.

"I had to come back for my things," he answered coldly.

"They're waiting in the hall. We'd have sent them on. Or do you not trust us that far?"

They were in the drawing room now, Moira in an elegant crimson velvet evening gown, Terence McKeon still bearing faintly the traces of the gutter despite his efforts to clean himself up.

"You have had an accident, it appears," she drawled in that nasal Boston accent.

McKeon nodded stiffly.

"Nothing serious. Now, it is necessary for me to collect my things and leave, paying my respects first to your father."

"You'll have to go to Philadelphia for that," she smiled. "A contract there. But I'll tell him. 'Mr. McKeon presents his compliments and regrets that he had to depart without—' "

"Thank you, Moira." He rose from the silk upholstered chair with its pattern of moss roses. "If you would be so kind. Now—"

40

She tinkled a little bell with a languid finger, and a young maid came in.

"Mr. McKeon would like his baggage."

Terence McKeon bowed stiffly and followed the maid. He was back in less than two minutes.

"The satchel," he demanded harshly. "Where is the satchel?"

Moira Burke rose and smiled with an acid sweetness.

"The satchel? Now, let me think—"

"No games, Moira, if you please. Where is the satchel?"

She pretended to frown, then gave a tinkling laugh.

"Why, of course. You were less than careful with your satchel, Mr. McKeon. You left it unlocked. It was brought to me and I observed it to be full of money. It seemed that I should take care of it, lest the servants be accused of—"

"Let me have it, please."

"It is in my room." She started toward the door.

"Please send for it."

"That would never do at all, Mr. McKeon. That would be exposing the servants to temptation. If you want your precious satchel, you must come and get it."

Terence McKeon followed her to the door and up the broad staircase beyond. What thoughts stirred in the beautiful head before him, what past frustrations had created the turmoil of desire which racked the girl? Only one question remained in his own head—what would he do?

The girl's bedroom was exactly as he would have expected: lavishly furnished with deep-piled carpeting and silken wall hangings. A canopied four-poster stood in the center of the room, its baroque posts gilded with Cupids and the underside of the canopy a great, glinting Venetian mirror. Peripherally McKeon wondered what Big Jim Burke would think of this room. But Burke, he decided, would never dare invade his daughter's empire.

"A drink for the master?" Moira cooed.

"I've come for the satchel, as you know, Moira. Give it to me, and I'll bother you no more."

"Ah, fie now, Master McKeon! This is not gallant. When a lady commands, a gentleman obeys."

"I am no gentleman, Miss Burke. Kindly give me the satchel."

"Not till you have taken wine with me, shown that any differences we may have had are forgotten and forgiven."

Now, McKeon thought, she had given up playing at being an Irish maid. She was now the great lady, the courtier. He felt weary.

"Very well," he agreed ungraciously and took the sherry that she offered.

Almost half of it was gone before he recognized the underlying taste and felt the almost familiar reeling of his senses. He felt an ultimate humiliation of failure as he realized that yet again he had been drugged.

The girl's laughter tinkled merrily in his ears as he swayed, and then she threw herself at him, bearing him back onto the bed with strange, shrill little cries twittering birdlike in her throat.

And yet, after all, he had taken only half the drink. He had recognized it for what it was in time—if he could yet free himself of it.

With floundering, frantic gestures he threw the girl aside, forced fingers down his throat, felt his degradation reach a nadir as he fouled the deep pile of the carpet.

His consciousness had not been driven from him completely. He still had the strength at least to rise, swaying, and gaze at the girl who lay now waiting for him on the bed, eyes mocking and yet lustful, fingers fluttering up and down the length of her now naked body.

"You should be ashamed of yourself, Moira," he said

hoarsely. "But . . . my concern is with my satchel. You have mocked me enough. Now let me go."

"When I am ready. When I have done with you. Otherwise perhaps I will call for the servants. What would Ireland think of her soldier who assaulted his host's daughter? And the Boston courts would take a bleak view. Come, master, come and learn there are more matters than you teach."

Her finger beckoned imperiously. Her whole body seemed to arch toward him. At last Terence McKeon was powerless to resist.

And as he started forward he had the numbed feeling that after all he no longer wanted to resist.

Her shapely arms drew him down on her, guided his hands into caresses his mind at last agreed to, enveloped him in scented wave after wave of desire made corporeal. Her voice crooned endearments, and her fingers undressed him deftly while her eyes watched remotely the reflection in the mirror above of the increasing convolutions on the bed beneath.

When it was over at last and they lay still, she said: "Your satchel is in that wardrobe yonder, schoolmaster. Now, when you wish, you may take it and go."

Terence McKeon could think of no reply.

And when he rose at last and tidied himself, he could only flush deeply at her final taunt: "I'm sure men have suffered worse for Ireland."

5. T for Traitor

The absence of guilty sensations within himself surprised Terence McKeon as he sat at the card table, eyeing his hand. He forced himself to consider what his mother would have thought and said about the interlude with Moira. She might not have disapproved. But if she had, her disapproval would have been emphatic.

Yet even the sharpest evocation of his mother's disapproval failed to rouse any real sensation of guilt in his mind. Other courses of action might have been possible without his actually having bedded the girl. Yet he had failed to think of another action.

And he was not sorry, he was astounded to learn of himself. Guilt there might be. But he had enjoyed the deed.

The nine and four of hearts, the three of spades and the jack of diamonds made no sort of hand to build on. He threw in and waited for the next deal.

The man they called the Swede drew two cards which, on form, suggested three of a kind or at worst a double open-ended run or flush. The Swede was cautious, McKeon had noted. Mull, a thin, precise man who had a flavor of iodoform like a doctor, took one card and was almost certainly trying to fill a run. Dapper Tashy himself took three, probably drawing to a pair. The dealer, a gloomy man who was never called anything but Hank, followed McKeon's example and threw in.

The Swede kept his opening bet cautious. Mull gave it a hefty raise and Tashy saw the bet.

Where did his mother stand in the matter of other women, McKeon wondered as the hand went on without him. Broad-minded she was, of course, in speech at any rate. But there was no denying that his father had left her when their son was still a child. And why should a man leave a woman who was undeniably beautiful, more than usually intelligent and educated? Why should he leave unless there was some lack of satisfaction in the matters beneath the waistline? Unconventional his mother might be in the matters of speech and of those black cigars she smoked. But did that unconventionality conceal some basic, unsuspected flaws? Was it a defense lest the world suspect what really went on within her?

Dapper Tashy swept up the pot, and from the look of the wad to which he added the notes he was now winning pretty heavily. McKeon picked up his own cards slowly. A jack, a queen, another jack, a three and a third jack. He felt a thrill of excitement. It was his best hand so far.

The pot was opened by the man to his right, Hank. McKeon hesitated over whether to raise or not and decided not to. His hesitation could as well be interpreted as whether to stay in the game. Mull and Tashy stayed in the hand, Tashy raising the bet by fifty dollars. Everyone took two cards apiece.

Terence McKeon looked at his pickup: the queen of spades and the ace of diamonds. If he had kept the queen he would have had a full house. But the odds against improving three of a kind by drawing two cards were eight and a half to one. The odds against improving by taking only one card were fourteen to one. Terence McKeon had throughout this game been playing strictly to the mathematical probabilities.

His mind was doing a series of subconscious calculations.

All his opponents had drawn two cards. If all had started with threes then the odds were that his three would be best. On the other hand, the chances would be only two and a fraction against one other opponent having filled a full house.

Mathematically, McKeon decided, his chances were as good as anyone's. This could be his chance to start hitting Dapper Tashy.

When the bet came to him he went in with a thousand dollars. No one dropped out. Mull saw the bet after the Swede had raised two hundred and fifty. Dapper Tashy went in with another five hundred and Hank dropped out.

McKeon saw Tashy and raised another thousand. It did not then strike him as extraordinary that for his first game of poker he should be playing for these immense stakes. It had been a day of extraordinary happenings. He had been knocked on the head, robbed, had his first woman and doubted for the first time his mother's total wisdom and integrity.

In any case, poker had at one time interested him as an abstraction, a mathematical concept. Though in Kilcroom he taught English, history and elementary arithmetic, as a student the concepts and principles of gambling had interested him. He had tried to find in the Celtic races' addiction to gambling a clue to their other natures. The gambler, he had deduced, played with a submerged desire to lose, to pit himself against the ultimate fate. He paid no regard to the mathematical probabilities. As the gambler eventually lost totally so did the Irish lose in the larger gamble of life.

He had in fact written a small monograph on the subject which had never been printed or indeed read by anyone else save his mother. His explorations into the odds concerned remained fresh in his memory. It seemed quite natural that now he should be putting his theory to the test with money which was not his own, whose loss must mean the destruction of his self-respect and quite probably the loss of his life.

Afterward he came to the conclusion that his mind had probably been affected temporarily by the blow on his head. Now, though, his brain had never seemed clearer.

Mull dropped out on the next raise and so did the Swede. For the first time since he had joined the game, Terence McKeon was in direct conflict with Dapper Tashy.

Five thousand of Ireland's dollars were in the pot—that is, five thousand of McKeon's Irish dollars—when Tashy saw him.

Three jacks were not good enough. Dapper Tashy had filled a flush. Unemotionally he scooped the pot toward him, and the tension eased.

"I figured you for a house," Tashy remarked and lit another cigar.

He did not then give, and had not since McKeon entered given, any sign of recognition. Did Tashy not know him? Or did he hope that McKeon, bemused by dope and drink and a knock on the head, had failed to remember him? Or was he bluffing in life as easily as he did on the poker table?

It seemed impossible that he could not remember a man he had drugged and robbed. But it was reasonable that he might believe McKeon did not remember him. Save that the coincidence of McKeon turning up in the big game was a long-stretched one.

On probability it seemed to Terence McKeon that Dapper Tashy not only knew him but guessed the purpose of his presence.

The kibitzers were murmuring about the big hand as McKeon dealt. For himself there was nothing in it. He threw in and gave the others their draws.

Dapper Tashy won again, and Mull began to show signs of his patience cracking. McKeon hoped he had enough money to stay with the game. He wanted no one to leave now. He thought he knew their games. The equation must not be disturbed.

Tashy lost on the next hand, then won a small pot. The Swede won twice running, then Hank came in with a full house against a straight and a flush. There was heavy betting, though McKeon had thrown in his two pairs early.

He had lost by now almost eight thousand dollars. Tashy, he estimated, was about ten thousand to the good. The others were not quite breaking even.

Someone had sent for chicken sandwiches, and the crusts were stuffed in the ashtrays. Burning butts sent up wisps of toastlike scent, and ever after when he smelled toast Terence McKeon would remember this game.

The tension was mounting now. The Swede snarled at Tashy once when the latter was slow in putting in his money to the pot.

"It's cash makes bets, Dapper, not words."

"All right—so here it comes. And with another five."

They were betting in hundreds all the time now.

And Terence McKeon continued to lose. Ten thousand dollars of his new money followed the old. What a collector he was being!

Sometimes a watcher would leave the room for a drink, relief or to bring back a friend. Among the watchers the excitement was even more intense than at the table.

At last McKeon began to win. He had a succession of good hands. And more important he had good hands going along with him—but not good enough. When he was holding a full house his opponents had threes and flushes. They had to bet.

Twice Dapper Tashy tested him out with bluffs, jumping his raise to the maximum in the hope that McKeon would check in.

Each time McKeon saw. Each time Tashy was holding a busted flush.

On the second such hand Tashy's aplomb was at least a little shaken. He had just dropped eight thousand dollars.

"It takes an Irishman to do it to an Irishman," he quipped uneasily.

McKeon said nothing. But a chord of memory twanged. On their first meeting Tashy had said a lot about being Irish. He had been very worried lest anyone else in the bar should see McKeon's roll of notes.

"That's Ireland's money—and I don't want to see it come to any harm."

McKeon remembered—and fought back the first sparks of anger. He must continue to play as he had done so far: coldly, unemotionally, mathematically.

And if his run continued he would win. He would do what he had come to do.

Chance came sooner than he had hoped.

On Hank's deal McKeon picked up a hand containing ten, jack, queen and king of diamonds plus the eight of clubs. He discarded the club. Any diamond would give him a flush. The ace would give him an unbeatable royal flush. The nine would be almost as good. Any other ace or nine would give him a straight. Odds against filling either a straight or a flush were thirty-eight to nine and thirty-nine to eight. For the straight flush, of course, the odds soared. Nonetheless, it was a hand with good potentials.

Mull took two cards and might have three of a kind. The Swede took one and could be trying to fill to two pairs. Or a flush or straight. Dapper Tashy took three, presumably keeping a pair. Hank took one and showed his usual disgust with it.

Terence McKeon, as had been his habit throughout, added his drawn card to those in his hand, made a deck of the five cards, then spread them only enough to see the corner of the card he had drawn.

He looked quickly, and his heart sang a little hymn of praise while his face, he trusted, showed nothing.

He had drawn the nine of diamonds. He had a straight flush. It was almost inconceivable that with this hand he should not win. Only a royal flush could beat him.

At once it was apparent that there were good cards all around the table. By the time the betting had come back to McKeon there was eight thousand in the pot and the raises were coming in two thousands.

Mull had been losing steadily for a spell before this. Now abruptly his face crumpled.

"This one I'd like to raise five—anyone take my marker for that?"

A stony silence was his answer.

"Hell, I've took markers before this. Look, I'll give you security. I've got a shipload of timber going out tomorrow from right here in Boston. I'll assign it."

"At poker," Tashy said, "it's for cash. On the nail."

Mull looked as if he were about to weep. "God rot you all," he cried. "I fill to fours and—"

He threw down four sevens and an eight and with his face puckering turned away from the table, stumped to the door and paused there, reluctant actually to leave until he knew who won the pot. He would be a man who picked at scabs, McKeon thought. At least he would know a corresponding relief when he learned that he would not have won in any case.

At the table no one spoke. Unemotionally the Swede raised McKeon two thousand. Tashy raised it five and Hank threw in, speaking for once.

"Maybe I'll be sorry. It don't seem a good day for houses."

He leaned back in his chair. Terence McKeon did some rapid arithmetic and some hasty character study.

The Swede had drawn a single card and might have a straight flush. He might have fours. He might have nothing.

He had plenty of money left. How good did he think Mc-Keon's hand was?

And Tashy? This time all the professional gambler's experience could not suppress an inner excitement. His hand was very, very good. McKeon had no doubt about that.

This was the moment of decision. This hand could recoup all that he had lost. It could also lose all that he had.

"I'll raise it ten thousand dollars," he said harshly and pushed the money into the center of the table.

The Swede began to sweat. He mopped at his forehead, opened his mouth a couple of times, then clamped his jaws tight.

Abruptly he threw in his hand and slumped in his chair.

"Someone bring me a shot of bourbon," he demanded hoarsely.

Now it was up to Dapper Tashy, and the gambler's eyes locked with McKeon's across the table. At this moment there was no doubt that this had become a personal duel. There was no doubt also that Tashy recognized McKeon and knew why he had come there.

Greed and hatred and triumph were all in his face.

"I'll see you," he repeated. "Put them down face upward."

Terence McKeon did not stir.

"What are you waiting for?" Tashy demanded.

"You're the one who said 'at poker it's for cash,' " McKeon answered woodenly.

"What the hell! It's only a formality," Tashy raged.

"So be formal," snapped Mull from the door.

Angrily Tashy pushed out the notes across the table. "Now I'll see you."

"That doesn't look like ten thousand dollars to me," McKeon answered mildly.

Hank counted the notes. "Two and a half grand shy," he announced.

Tashy almost gibbered with rage now, and his hands searched his pockets. He found another fifteen hundred.

"There!" he snarled. "Now show me that hand."

"You're still a thousand short," McKeon refused. "I understand that this is strictly a cash game."

Tashy's lips drew back into a thin, colorless, rubber line.

"So you'll take a marker," he snapped.

"So I won't."

Tashy looked around at the others with desperation in his eyes.

"A thousand bucks. Who'll take my marker? Look, I'll give you two for one . . . three for one . . . Goddamn it, I'll give anyone ten for one! Nine thousand dollars clear profit for the use of a grand for a minute! Hank. Swede. You there, Mull, don't you want to make yourself a buck?"

Silence sat as heavily in the room as a glacier in its bed.

Terence McKeon said nothing but casually began to draw the money toward him.

"What the hell are you at, you bastard?"

"I've made my bet. It hasn't been taken. I'm taking the pot. That's the rule."

Tashy began to rant then, an unintelligible stream of words frothing from his mouth. Then he grabbed at the remaining money on the table.

"Nine grand of that's mine. I couldn't cover. The bet wasn't on."

McKeon looked mildly surprised.

"Money that goes into a pot stays there. That's the usual rule."

"He's right," Hank growled. "Hell, if anyone could take his money out—"

Tashy slumped back in his chair in total defeat.

"Four aces," he gritted. "Four aces and I couldn't bet up to them."

"Maybe you're lucky." McKeon answered him mildly enough. "You couldn't have beaten a straight flush anyway."

He tipped over his hand, and in the room was a shocked silence. King, queen, jack, ten of diamonds . . . and the nine of hearts. McKeon stared in disbelief. He had been betting on a simple straight, not a straight flush. He had bet confidently in the sure knowledge of a virtually unbeatable hand. What quirk of wishful thinking had made him mistake the nine of hearts for that of diamonds?

Suddenly he was sweating, shivering, almost unable to gather up the money.

And the crowd, kibitzers and players both, were roaring their laughter, even those who had lost to that unwitting bluff. All, that is, save Dapper Tashy.

"Look, to show there's no ill feeling, how's about a drink, McKeon? You beat me the hard way, but I guess a man who can't lose shouldn't be playing poker."

Dapper Tashy was at his most affable again.

"A drink?" McKeon answered. "I'd enjoy one. But won't the bars be closed by now?"

Dawn was reddening the sky with the promise of a good day. McKeon was still keyed up with the tension of the game. His money was safely lodged in the hotel's safe, and this, he suspected, was known to Tashy. Did the man really hope to be able to dupe McKeon twice?

In any case, McKeon was not sorry to have been accosted outside the hotel. He had not finished with Tashy yet.

There was the matter of the theft, the matter of the drug, the matter of the knock on the head. He had left the Burke home with the intention of redressing all those wrongs. He was prepared.

"No need to worry about bars. I know a girl who always has plenty of good stuff in the house. It's not a classy joint but a drink will surely go down well. Boy, you surely put it over me tonight. You surely did."

Terence McKeon was not totally surprised to find himself in Hilda Slansky's room again. She looked frightened when they came in, and she scuttled off to bring them a bottle.

"The glasses aren't so fancy," she flustered. "They're all I have."

"As long as the drink's all right it'd taste as good out of a piss pot." Tashy poured, and McKeon had no difficulty this time in detecting his pass with one hand over the amber liquid, a pass that certainly included the dropping into the glass of a Mickey Finn.

One glass, McKeon's, was a tumbler. The other was a large wine glass. There could be no switching of the glasses. But switching would not be needed. In his hand Terence McKeon held the small green glass bottle he had taken from Moira Burke's room. *Chloral hydrate,* said the druggist's spidery writing.

Terence McKeon had planned for the diversion which would allow him to drug the other's glass. In the event, he needed to provide none. A fire engine clanged past in the street, and Hilda Slansky and the man rose.

Instantly McKeon tipped half the contents of the bottle into the other's drink.

Tashy noted that the glasses had not been touched. He raised his own in salutation.

"Slainte, as they say in the Old Country," he said.

"Slainte," McKeon agreed and filled his mouth with whiskey.

Dapper Tashy drained his own glass and then saw the whiskey pouring back from McKeon's mouth into the glass. His eyes began to widen in alarm, but as they did so they glazed. He swayed as choking sobs gurgled in his throat, then he fell on the threadbare, dust-laden carpet.

"You," he muttered. "Oh, you. . . ."

Terence McKeon drew from his pocket a small penknife and clicked the blade open.

"Mother of God!" the girl moaned. "Don't kill him. God, he's not that bad. I'll be jailed . . . The cops will—"

Terence McKeon ignored her as he knelt beside the unconscious man. With deliberate strokes he cut a large T on the skin of his forehead.

"I'd have written traitor," he said mildly, "but he has a rather small forehead. That will be sign enough to any Irishman. T for traitor. And I bid you good morning, Miss Slansky, and my thanks for your assistance."

When he looked back she was crouched over Dapper Tashy, weeping, mopping at the blood with her skirt.

There were a good many incomprehensible facets to the character of women, thought Terence McKeon as the fresh morning air greeted him in the street outside and the rattle of winches from the quays echoed nostalgically of home.

6. The Wild One

"Hey, hey! Declan's at it again. Down in Grogan's beyond there. Oh, there'll be sport tonight. . . ."

The word had passed swiftly around Kilcroom, shouted or whispered or called through an open door. There had been sly smiles and laughter and the tense, delighted feeling of school-boys about to see someone else write a rude word on the blackboard.

Declan was at it, and there would be sport in the village all right. The roaring boy was roaring again, and God save the hindmost.

In the barrack of the Royal Irish Constabulary at Kilcroom John Clancy heard the news with both relief and alarm.

Relief came from the fact that now he could with decency set aside the matter of this court order that lay before him. Constable Clancy was a blunt-faced, gray-haired man nearing his pension time. The quiet life was all he sought, was all he had ever sought. He had always preferred to turn a blind eye rather than the pages of his notebook.

"You'll need to come back tomorrow," he told Raymond McCarthy. "Can't you see we're busy?"

"I've a court order for possession," McCarthy insisted. "See there the date on it and the signature and all. It's due for enforcement this minute. . . ."

He spoke in a whine that combined an underlying arrogance with a superficial humility, harsh and oily at the same time. Constable Clancy gazed at him without favor, seeing the dark-toned face, the hooked nose, the restless eyes, the thin, ruthless, greedy mouth. His clothes had a curious drabness, never so worn as to be called rags, never ever new. And yet this was a man who could buy a new suit every day if he wished.

"Not tonight," said Clancy. "We're busy. Didn't you hear?"

"Ah, now, Mr. Clancy, sure a gentleman like yourself, you wouldn't want to see a poor man done out of what's his rightly and me able maybe to do you the favor some day when you'd need it. If it's not tonight I'll never be to Waterford for tomorrow's night where I have the small bit of business to keep my poor children with the food in their mouths and—"

Business! Some other poor widow woman to be evicted, robbed of her last possession to satisfy this man's greed for wealth. Someone else like the Widow O'Hara, who had borrowed a few shillings from the gombeen-man, signed a paper and condemned herself by her own name.

"I have my rights in law, Mr. Clancy," hinted McCarthy. "I'm a man who knows his rights."

There was a hint of a threat now. Constable Clancy drew himself from his chair, rose to his full height, scowled down at the gombeen-man who crouched in a crablike way as if his back was injured, though he could stand tall when he wished.

"I'm also a man who knows the law," said Clancy. "And—"

An excited voice shouted in through the barrack door: "O'Donovan's just broke a window. Is the peelers doing nothing to stop him?"

Glumly Clancy reached for his night helmet.

"You may come back tomorrow, *Mister* McCarthy. We have other work than putting a widow's few things in the street."

But his heart was heavy. Dealing with O'Donovan was a

chore he had contrived to evade since he was posted to Kilcroom. It was not one for which he felt himself physically fitted.

Then relief came. It came with chevrons on its sleeves. It loomed tall in the door from the charge room to the barrack living quarters. It bore the name of Sergeant McAllister.

"Did I hear the name of O'Donovan? Is that ruffian at it again?"

Clancy hesitated. Declan O'Donovan he knew. The sergeant was more of a newcomer. He had the reputation of a hard man. But it would take a very hard man to deal with O'Donovan. He tried to voice a warning: "Now I'll tell you what it is, Sergeant," he said uneasily. "This O'Donovan, he'll cause a bit of stir all right and talk wild and maybe there'll be some glass broke. But sure Grogan doesn't mind a bit of glass broke once in a while, for when Declan's at it there's trade going. He gets them all to drinking and singing, and there's more of a turnout in his pub than he'd see in a week. But no harm done, if you follow me, no harm done. Just in the way of sport."

But he could see it was no use. Sergeant McAllister was setting his spiked helmet firmly on his head, and his face—with its brown bush of sergeant major's mustache—was as implacable as destiny.

"Disturbing the peace is disturbing the peace," he announced in a flat Belfast accent. "And I'll not have it."

He was a big man and strong, meaty-faced, bony-handed. Confidence sat on his shoulder. Fifteen years of regular service in the army, of making soldiers out of gutter trash and peasants and jail scum, had given him his confidence. Because he expected to be obeyed, he was obeyed—most of the time. And when obedience lagged, he had his fists and his truncheon. They had never failed to be obeyed.

Though his face showed nothing of this, he was looking

forward to his brush with O'Donovan. Since he had taken over Kilcroom a few weeks before, it seemed to him he had heard of nothing but this Declan O'Donovan. The wild man. The roaring boy. The boul' Declan. The man who would be up to any rascality just for the cod of it.

The man was getting away with murder, in a manner of speaking. When even his own police were either afraid of him or admired him, it was time to take a hand. It was time to put him down a bit and show the town the sort he was.

If it was fighting the man wanted, he would give him fighting. He would give him it where it hurt.

And somewhere in the back of the sergeant's cold, regimental mind a raw nerve quivered. For it never really left him that he should be fighting too; that he should be out in Flanders with the Enniskillen Fusiliers or some such regiment, where the real fighting was being done. And this Declan, too, if he was such a wild, bloodthirsty class of a lad, why didn't he go where he could get a bit of bloodletting?

A barroom brawler, that was his sort, thought the sergeant, and a Fenian too, without a doubt. That was the sort of them. All shout and no action. Well, he would deal with him this night, and that would be the end of one source of trouble in this corner of County Cork. Afterward he might think about having Clancy transferred. The man was soft, an easygoing, make-no-trouble sort.

He was no use to Sergeant McAllister. You could not keep the peace with that sort—not as McAllister understood keeping the peace. Which is to say, a policeman with empty charge sheets was neglecting his duty.

And Sergeant McAllister had never been a man to neglect his duty.

"Ah, Sergeant, sure it's great to see yourself going out to deal with yon hellion," McCarthy fawned. "Oh, you're the boy can deal with him. Oh, you'll sort him out, sure enough you will. And the constable here, a fine decent man he is, he'll can come out and do this wee bittie of a court order now for me, can't he so?"

McAllister looked down on the gombeen-man from beneath pulled-together eyebrows.

"Get out of my barrack," he growled.

"Sergeant, I have me order there and 'twould take only a minute for the constable—"

"You want your dirty work done by dark when there's nane to see it? The constabulary are not for doing the dirty work of keelies like you."

"I have the court order." McCarthy bristled truculently.

McAllister said no more. He swiveled to address Clancy.

"This is very like the man wanted in connection for that sheep stealing in Wexford. You'd best hold him for questioning."

"Very good, Sergeant."

With some pleasure Clancy advanced to lead the gombeen-man to a cell. McAllister moved out like a procession into the night.

Declan O'Donovan's huge, handsome head was thrown back, and his long, curling hair, dark and glossy, hung in a careless bang over his left eye. He was singing, and he had a fine baritone voice, untrained but deeply vibrant and supplied by a massive, forty-nine-inch chest.

There was silence in Grogan's long, shadowed bar as he sang, silence because no one could hear himself talk while the great voice hurled itself at the ceiling and reverberated from the walls. With training it was a voice that could have filled an opera house, and indeed had had its chance to do so, for Monsignor Carroll had heard it and had brought an Italian teacher to hear it. He had thought that O'Donovan might go to Milan to have his voice trained.

And Declan had refused.

"There's more call for Irish money in Ireland," he had told the priest. "With the poverty and the sorrow that's here I wouldn't feel right to be going away there to spend it."

And this was an argument that the monsignor had to accept, of course. He sighed, thinking of the beauty that was being lost and squandered, but accepted Declan's reason since Ireland was, of course, more important than a singer.

But Declan, being Declan, had other reasons.

"Sure, what sort of a life would it be at all? The Tally teacher told me the way it would be. Scales and practice, practice and scales, day after bloody day and week after bloody week, and never a wet o' porter in case it would damage me precious vocal cords. Now, could you see me at the like o' that—week after week and year after year? Could you see me, Tomeen? Could you?"

"It wouldn't be your sort at all," Tomeen Brennan had agreed loyally and thankfully. "Oh, it wouldn't be you, Declan. It wouldn't be the sort of you at all."

Tomeen had dreaded Declan's going, for Declan was God to Tomeen, who was small, thin, ugly and had as well a game leg that he dragged behind him wherever he went.

Declan had been his guardian since their schooldays, fighting off the bullies, casting the mantle of his protection around him. If Declan had a shilling, half of it was Tomeen's. And if Tomeen had a shilling—which was more frequent, since he was by trade a cobbler and an industrious one—then it was all Declan's.

Oh, the Erne shall run red with redundance of blood;
The earth shall shake beneath thy tread,
And flame wrap hill and wood,
And gun peal and slogan cry
Wake many a glen serene

E'er you shall fade, e'er you shall die,
My dark Rosaleen . . .

The silence held in the long bar, for long moments after Declan's voice had died away in a last, long-held note. Then there was a burst of cheering and clapping and "Good man yourself, Declan, what're you taking?" and before the big man the bar sprouted drinks like a miraculous tulip bed. Black pints of porter and the glowing amber of John Jameson's and Paddy whiskey piled up before the singer as the listeners expressed their appreciation.

"Tomeen, you're not drinking, me little leprechaun. Get that down your gob—"

Roughly Declan thrust one of his whiskeys into the other's grasp. And as he sipped the one Declan gulped two and then placed a pint of porter to his lips. He had the art of keeping his throat muscles still and he could pour the pint straight down into his belly.

It was an impressive sight to see the black drink vanish so swiftly, and men had been known to pay for the privilege and to time the drinking on their watches. Five seconds was the record.

Declan sang again . . . and again. Mostly he sang rebel songs, for he knew how they irked the quiet ones, the men in the snugs and the shadows, the men who loved England and what she stood for, the non-Irishmen, as he thought of them.

His eye glinted challengingly around the long, shadowed bar as he broke abruptly into the anthem of the unborn Republic:

Soldiers are we whose lives are pledged to Ire-
land . . .

But not even that provoked a stir. There were men on

leave there from the British Army, men who had a week before been fighting in France or Flanders and who a week later
would be returning to the mud and the blood and the agony.

Declan sought to provoke them by taunts.

"Is there not a man at all in the whole King's army?" he
ranted. "Will none of you speak up for his English Majesty?"

And his face reddened, for in the eyes of the quiet ones he
saw a sort of contempt. His bright eyes flickered from face to
face, seeking the faintest excuse for a fight, to snatch a soldier
from his seat and batter his face with the great meaty fists that
had pulped so many a nose and so many an ear in Kilcroom.

But no one took him up. They knew him, these soldiers.
They knew Declan, and they knew he could beat any two of
them together. They knew also that their leave was dying with
every minute, and they had no wish to waste the precious
minutes of peace and cleanness away from the stench of death
and the seeming never-ending noise of artillery barrages by
brawling with Declan O'Donovan.

Then Declan's mood flickered off on a new slant, for beyond the bar, in the doorway that led into the house, he saw
for an instant the flicker of a fair, curly head.

"Watch me drinks, Tomeen," he ordered loudly. "See you
none of these English or the English-lovers be taking it."

"I'll watch, Declan," Tomeen Brennan agreed eagerly,
bristling up proudly like a bantam cock, daring anyone to
touch the drinks—and knowing in his heart that since they
were Declan's drinks no one would dare.

The lavatory in Grogan's was across the yard, and in fact
it was just a whitewashed wall with a drain at its foot that
emptied, if it was not choked, into a gully that ran into the
farm dungheap over the wall.

Beside it was a square, whitewashed building that held the
gas plant, a carbide generator in which water dripped slowly
onto a carbide and turned the white powder into acetylene

63

gas that was fed by pipes to the bar and the neighboring houses. The characteristic smell of garlic always hung heavily about the yard, drowning the smell of the lavatory.

Declan did not reach the lavatory though. Instead he strode swiftly along the side of the dwelling house and tapped gently on a window, three gentle taps. The window slid up silently, and a curly blond head peeped out.

"Nora, my heart's darling," Declan murmured. "The day and the night I've longed for this minute. . . ."

And his arms reached for the supple, warm body of Grogan's daughter. His lips sought hers and he started to pull her from the window, lifting her with an ease that showed his strength and a dexterity which showed his practice.

But this time it was to be different. For her lips responded only for an instant.

"Ah, no, Declan," she begged. "For God's sake, no—"

She pushed him a little away and yet clung to him at the same time.

"What ails you then, macushla? Sure there's time and enough before yer oul' Da looks for you."

Across the path and around the corner was a stable, and the hay in the stable loft was soft and warm. Also it was very close by. There had been times when the girl and Declan had gone there and Declan had been back in the bar before the bubbles in his porter had died.

"It's not me Da," she whispered. "It's not him. It's oul' Shannon."

"The grocer!"

"He's took a fancy to me. He's asked me Da. . . . He's in the room beyond. Declan, what am I to do? What am I to do?"

Declan felt a rush of laughter surge up in him. Donal Shannon! Fifty years if he was a day. Spindly legs and a wart on his nose. A fine man to come courting a hot young girl like Nora!

The Wild One

"Tell him where he can go," Declan scoffed. "He should have more wit at his age."

"It's a good shop he has," Nora answered. "Me Da's keen. He'd like it fine to see us married."

Declan's tongue lashed Grogan for some long seconds, and then something in Nora's still face silenced him.

"There's more," she said steadily. "It's like I'll have to marry him—or someone."

Declan's heart skipped a beat, and a little iron entered his soul.

"You're sure?"

"I'd hardly be mistaken. Declan?"

She did not put the question into words. But it was there. And Declan did not answer it.

"This is serious—" he began.

And then to his relief he heard Grogan's voice.

"Nora! Are you there, Nora?"

Declan pushed the girl back into the room.

"Don't worry, me dotie girl," he whispered. "I'll see it's all right. Now off you go and don't be giving him cause to come lookin' for you."

The window slid shut, and he headed back to the bar, a new rage in his heart.

For Declan O'Donovan had seen a lot of years of freedom ahead of him before he settled down.

"Fug the hell o't," he growled. "Up the spout." And he smashed his fist into the rough stone of the building.

The pain was satisfying and inflaming at the same time. He strode into the bar and gulped down his drinks.

"We'll move on," he told Tomeen. "There must be some life somewhere in the town."

"Ah, that's it, Declan. We'll find a bit of life."

Limping, Tomeen followed the big man from the bar and into the night.

*　　*　　*

The Men That God Made Mad

THE IRISHMEN IN THE TRENCHES ARE CALLING FOR YOU, said the big recruiting poster on the gable end of Donel Shannon's general store.

There was a street light just beyond it, and the poster stood out very brightly.

Declan stood hands on hips, glaring at the poster and the khaki-clad figure in its center.

"They have their nerve," he growled. "England recruiting in Ireland."

He fumbled in his pocket, then turned to Tomeen.

"Give's a pencil," he demanded.

The little lame cobbler had no pencil, but he produced a piece of heelball and Declan advanced on the poster.

"And that'll be enough of that," growled a voice from behind.

"It's the sergeant," moaned Tomeen in anguish.

"You'd best come along with me," said Sergeant McAllister, moving in slowly, one hand on the haft of his truncheon. "That's a serious offense: defacing government property and incitement to riot."

Declan O'Donovan said nothing, but in his eyes a light of pleasure flared. After all, then, he was going to have his fight.

"Come along," the constabulary sergeant growled, and his hand went out to O'Donovan's arm.

It touched it for just an instant, and then Declan had snatched at the arm, jerked the sergeant to him and slammed his other fist into his belly with all his strength.

It was a punch that should have ended the fight there and then. It usually did. But the sergeant's greatcoat absorbed some of the force—and the sergeant's belly muscles absorbed the rest.

He gave a long grunt of pain. But he did not go down. Instead the truncheon swung from its holster and hissed toward Declan's shoulder.

O'Donovan wriggled from the path of the blow, but it still caught the angle of his shoulder, stinging him.

"Come quiet now and it'll be best for you," snapped Sergeant McAllister, advancing still.

"Make me," was O'Donovan's answer. "Just try and make me, you omadhaun."

And as the sergeant lunged, O'Donovan dodged the truncheon again and slammed a fist to McAllister's nose. Blood gushed down onto the brown bush of his sergeant major's mustache and flowed out to the ends of it by capillary attraction.

"Doul'll pay for dat," he muttered thickly and leaped abruptly at O'Donovan, folding his long arms about him.

O'Donovan strained against the locking arms and sensed their strength. They closed on him, tighter and tighter, arms that were as strong as his and arms that had the advantage of the hold.

Tomeen watched in awe as the two giants reeled back and forth in the pools of light from the lamp above. This was a fight to see. This was something to talk about and remember.

The night that Declan beat the sergeant. . . .

He had no doubt at all that Declan would win. Declan always won.

Down the road toward them there came the slow chugging of a car's engine, and hearing it, the sergeant slightly eased his grip, thinking that here without doubt would be the military and assistance.

Declan seized his chance and with a frantic wriggle burst free of the sergeant's grip. His jacket ripped down the back and was left in McAllister's hands. His shirt went with the jacket.

Naked to the waist, poised on the balls of his feet, he awaited the next charge as the sergeant threw away the clothes and rushed in again.

This time he used the truncheon as a foil, and the rounded end stabbed forward suddenly into Declan's face.

Declan backed at the blow, staggered and tripped in the gutter.

For a long instant he saw the sergeant's dark shape loom above him, saw the threat of the heavy boot that swung—infinitely slowly it seemed to him—for his ribs. Behind the sergeant were the staring eyes of the car's head lamps, for the car was stopped now.

To Declan, too, the car meant reinforcements for the law. In another moment he would be a prisoner.

His hand dug into the mud of the gutter, and with a deft flick of the wrist he hurled mud upward as the sergeant's boot hit him.

And then Declan was on his feet and his fists were pounding into the blinded man.

One and two and three . . . great full-blooded swings, each with all the time in the world, slammed home on the sergeant's massive jaw.

No man alive could have stood those blows.

Like a great tree falling, the sergeant fell.

And now it was Declan's turn for the boot. He raised a foot and then saw that the sergeant did not stir. There would be no sport in hitting an unconscious man.

"Lie there," Declan taunted. "That's where you belong. You and all your English-loving kin."

Still naked to the waist, he swaggered off down the street with Tomeen Brennan glowing admiration at his side and a pair of girl's eyes following him from behind the lights of the car, eyes that had never seen violence before or a man's strong body stripped to the waist.

7. Proclamation

"Not so much a rising—more a raree-show."

About the streets of Dublin a baffled populace watched the first blows of the Rising. The shawlies poured out from their tenements to cheer or jeer according to their mood. There was at the start more jeering than cheering, especially when the soldiers of the Republic had to drag out the possessions of the mean houses of the back streets to build barricades.

Red-faced with embarrassment, pouring out a multitude of apologies, most of the Irish troops wished themselves a thousand miles away at that moment. It was a queer sort of rising, they thought, when your first victims were your own people.

But there were soon to be changes.

At the South Dublin Union, Commandant Edmund Kent gazed across the fifty-two acres of his post and thought occasionally of the sheer impossibility of his command. His plans had been based on a full turnout of the Fourth Battalion, which would have given him a total strength of more than seven hundred men. In point of fact, only just over a hundred of his men had mustered in Emerald Square, under the cheering shadows of Guinness' vast brewery. The confusion of orders had kept the rest at home.

Taking the Union, the workhouse for the area, had been simple enough, though the porter at the gate had refused to hand over the keys. Holding it was going to be another matter. Now the main gate was barricaded and the offices which flanked it and crossed it above had been occupied.

Under the Yorkshire-born vice-commandant, Cathal Brugha, men were tunneling through the party walls to give them a completely covered defensive position overlooking James Street.

But there were altogether too many gaps in the huge area for the tiny force to cover properly and to perform their tactical function of stopping any advance of British troops into the city center from the southwest.

Kent scattered his men in groups on the perimeter and made his headquarters in the stoutly built night nurses' home.

In the distance a few faint, scattered shots could be heard, but from closer by, from Richmond barracks, the peaceful strains of a military band could be heard. Still, it seemed, the British did not know that the time of judgment had come.

Then, in midtune, the sound of the band was cut off. There was no need to wonder why.

Commandant Kent could hear the tramp of marching feet.

Section Commander John Joyce crouched behind a wall and endured the taunts of a little cluster of "separation women"—the wives of Irish soldiers of the British Army receiving separation allowances while their husbands were in France.

Joyce had four men under him, and their faces had been growing steadily redder under the taunts of the women, jeers which started with the merely rude and went on to the specific and detailed vulgarity which should be and never is beyond the range of the gentler sex.

It was not the kind of war they had been trained for or expected—a war of words and contempt from women of their own race. It was more daunting than any bullets.

70

But the bullets were coming too.

For with a fresh, raucous outburst of bawdry the women began to withdraw.

"Run for it, ye boys, ye! Here's the military."

Two hundred yards away from the cover where Joyce lay, a company of the Third Royal Irish Regiment had come to a halt. Lieutenant George Malone, the senior subaltern, was ordered to take a party of twenty men and march to Dublin Castle. Before leaving the barracks his men had been issued with ball ammunition—but they had not been told about the Rising, perhaps because no one knew definitely that it had happened.

Now the platoon came marching toward the ambush, marching in parade style, at the slope and with no rifle loaded. In a style befitting a regular regiment, they were in perfect step, buttons and equipment polished smoothly enough to please even Company Sergeant Major Banks, who marched beside Lieutenant Malone.

And if some of the men who had soldiered on the western front felt a reasonable unease at this unorthodox manner of approaching the obvious hostility of the Sinn Feiners visible behind the wall ahead, their murmuring did not rise above the sergeant major's "Quiet in the ranks there!"

The gap between Joyce and Malone at the head of his command was little more than five yards when Joyce's men could restrain their impatience no longer.

The cranky rifles of the rebels spat out a sudden irregular fusillade.

And suddenly this was war.

Three or four of the British soldiers fell, and the others scattered into cover at the other side of the road. For a few moments there was a spatter of return fire and then, almost inexplicably, a long lull.

But already the inexorable processes of battle were in motion. The main body had seen their advance guard fired on. And at last they knew where they stood.

Almost with the first shot the commanding officer of the Third Royal Irish had begun to plan his assault on the South Dublin Union.

And with appalling speed a curtain of fire began to fall on Joyce and his little group, fire that was directed by men whose trade it was, fire that filled the air, that killed and wounded.

The Rising was no matter any longer of parades and speeches and fine sentiments.

The killing time had come. And the killing ground was the streets of Dublin.

In St. Stephen's Green the usual collection of babies in their prams with watchful nannies to tend them and eager soldiers on leave to ogle the nannies could have been seen a little earlier. But not now.

Now there were only Volunteers under Commandant Mallin digging hasty trenches and the flamboyant figure of the Countess Constance Markievicz striding about in her own bizarre uniform of green woolen blouse and green tweed knee breeches. On a cartridge belt at her waist she wore a small automatic pistol at one side and a vast Peter the Painter Mauser on the other.

She might have looked like a figure from a Ruritanian musical comedy, but she meant business and the weapons were not for show. A member of the Anglo-Irish aristocracy and yet a leader of the Rising, she now led a column made up mainly of Boy Scouts and women. But she was to play a vital part in the events to come.

With the curious air of the garden parties among which they had been reared, two of the Countess' ladies—Miss Margaret Ffrench-Mullen and Miss Cathleen Clery—set up a first aid post and a running buffet with sandwiches and cakes.

The countess busied herself with more military matters, and when Constable Michael Lahiff tried to force his way into the green, her Mauser was one of three weapons which fired. As he fell, hers was the voice that claimed the kill.

John Pritchard, as usual, was walking back to his big Grafton Street shop after luncheon at home. Unless it was very wet he always walked to work, conscious of the increasing portliness of his stocky figure, conscious of the need for exercise.

Occasionally a passerby would raise a hat and he would bow stiffly, smile inflexibly (he was shy and his smile had thus an uncertain stiffness which gave him the reputation of being a hard man) and pace on.

With him was Clorinda, his youngest daughter, a slim, dark beauty whose prospects in the marriage market were rated highly. Her dowry would be in the ten-thousand-pound range, and there was no shortage of suitors already, though she had left finishing school only a few months before.

Pritchard doubted his wisdom in taking Clorinda with him, for rumors of the Rising had been about the city even before he left the shop for luncheon. On the other hand there were always rumors of risings. And Clorinda wanted to choose some new clothes from a consignment which had just arrived.

"I've no doubt it will be no more than another demonstration by the Volunteers," he said. "The people are in no mood for rebellion now. Why should they be? What's to be gained from rebellion? The Home Rule Bill will come into force as soon as we've won the war. Ireland will have all her proper rights. Meanwhile we've got the Germans to beat."

"Yes, Papa," Clorinda agreed dutifully. She was playing her

own part in the war by going to dances and soirees with officers. Secretly she hoped the Germans would not be beaten too
quickly.

"Not, of course, that I am opposed to a proper realization of
Ireland's aspirations," Pritchard went on thoughtfully. "Our
family, indeed the whole Presbyterian history, has been on the
side of liberty. As you know, your great-great-great-grand-
father fought with Wolfe Tone. And on your mother's side
we are descended from that great Belfast patriot Henry Joy
McCracken."

The streets were unusually quiet, and he assumed that this
was because so many of the people had gone to Sackville
Street to watch the Volunteers march.

Pritchard was not at all sure where he stood these days. He
had never been a Fenian, for this would not be good for
business. But he had decided that on balance Ireland was due
for a change, and he was thankful that the English Liberals
had passed their Home Rule Bill. That done, he thought, there
was no further need for patriotic action.

"At any rate, whether we're under the English or not, I'm
quite sure we'll be better off than we would be under the
Germans. How that fellow Casement could go running to
Berlin knowing what the Germans have done in Africa I can't
imagine. I—"

He became conscious that he had lost his daughter's attention.

Clorinda was staring fixedly across the street at a young
woman hurrying down the far sidewalk. Suddenly she began
to wave excitedly.

"Maggy!" she called. "Maggy! Yoo-hoo, Maggy—"

But the other did not pause or even turn her head.

"Surely they didn't teach you to shout in the streets at
your school," said Pritchard severely.

"That was a girl from the school, Papa," Clorinda answered.

74

"Margaret Kingston. At least I think it was. Oh, it must have been! You've heard of the Kingstons of Kilcroom. They own half of County Cork."

"She didn't look like a lady," Pritchard answered sharply. "And she was practically running. You must have been wrong."

"I knew her . . . very well. At least, she was in her last year when I went there and—"

John Pritchard had no time to note a sudden confusion in his daughter's manner.

From nearby came the sound of firing, and it grew plain that rumor had not lied after all. Someone screamed wildly, and there was a rush of feet, a confused shouting and further shots.

John Pritchard drew his daughter into the shelter of a doorway and considered how to return safely home.

And on the steps of the G.P.O. Patrick Pearse was reading the Proclamation of the Republic.

"Irishmen and Irishwomen: In the name of God and of the dead generations from which she receives her old tradition of nationhood, Ireland, through us, summons her children to her flag and strikes for her freedom."

James Connolly, at his side, looked down at the polish of his leggings and could see only a shining blur through the tears that were in his eyes. This day had come then, he thought, this day at last.

"Having organized and trained her manhood through her secret revolutionary organization, the Irish Republican Brotherhood, and through her open military organizations, the Irish Volunteers and the Irish Citizen Army, having patiently perfected her discipline, having resolutely waited for the right moment to reveal itself, she now seizes that moment and, supported by her exiled children in America and by gallant allies in Europe, but relying in the first on her own strength, she strikes in full confidence of victory."

Volunteers and Citizen Army men backed their leaders under the G.P.O. portico, and a medium-sized crowd listened on the sidewalk, some of them comprehending what was afoot but as many of them in a blank hubbub of plain curiosity. "What did he say, then? What's it about? What's he at on the steps? Who's yon?"

"We declare the right of the people of Ireland to the ownership of Ireland and to the unfettered control of Irish destinies to be sovereign and indefeasible. The long usurpation of that right by a foreign people and government has not extinguished the right, nor can it ever be extinguished except by the destruction of the Irish people. In every generation the Irish people have asserted their right to national freedom and sovereignty; six times during the past three hundred years they have asserted it in arms. Standing on that fundamental right and again asserting it in arms in the face of the world, we hereby proclaim the Irish Republic as a sovereign independent state and we pledge our lives and the lives of our comrades-in-arms to the cause of its freedom, of its welfare and of its exaltation among the nations."

Now two flags flew above the post office: the green flag and the tricolor which was to become the flag of a later Republic. They waved so gently in the breeze that only one who already knew their meaning could have distinguished their colors.

"Would you watch yourself, boy," a sharp-faced fish hawker hissed. "Be ready to run. When he stops talking he'll be taking up a collection."

Pearse's face was lighted by an inner exaltation as his voice threw out the challenge to the power of England.

"The Irish Republic is entitled to, and hereby claims, the allegiance of every Irishman and Irishwoman. The Republic

76

guarantees religious and civil liberty, equal rights and equal opportunities to all its citizens, and declares its resolve to pursue the happiness and prosperity of the whole nation and of all its parts, cherishing all the children of the nation equally, and oblivious of the differences carefully fostered by an alien government, which have divided a minority from the majority in the past."

Some of the Citizen Army stiffened a little at this.

"Does that mean," a private demanded from the corner of his mouth, "that we don't get a lick back at the Protestants? God, I thought that was what we were out for."

An elbow thrust fiercely into his ribs. "The Republic's not a minute old and you're throwing away its ideals!"

Pearse heard nothing of what went on behind him—or before. He was on another plane from them all, in a world of his own as his sonorous voice drifted across Sackville Street.

From a window of the Imperial Hotel, almost across the road, Major Thomas Greyson, formerly of the Eighth Royal Irish Hussars and later of a number of regiments, now awaiting court-martial, plucked at his hard-bristled mustache and shrugged with a pleasant cynicism.

Of this he had warned the authorities, he was thinking. The bloody damned fools chose to ignore him. Well, they would know now. They would know all right.

"Sweet ducks," cooed the voice from the bed. "Little Lettie's getting so cold without her big, strong soldier man."

Major Greyson's nostrils were pinched in as he swept the curtains together and turned toward the bed. The pleasurable stirrings in his loins died completely, and there was a withdrawn coldness to him that the woman in the bed could not thaw.

For he had seen a face in the crowd beneath that he had incredulously recognized, a face that should have been more than a hundred miles away, that had no right to be in this city at this time.

What had brought Raymond McCarthy, the gombeen-man, to Dublin? As the girl tried to rouse him, Greyson knew the answer. McCarthy had followed him; McCarthy would always follow him. Where there was money, McCarthy would never lift his hooked nose from the trail.

"Until our arms have brought the opportune moment for the establishment of a permanent national government representative of the whole people of Ireland and elected by the suffrages of all her men and women, the Provisional Government, hereby constituted, will administer the civil and military affairs of the Republic in trust for the people.

"We place the cause of the Irish Republic under the protection of the Most High God, whose blessing we invoke upon our arms, and we pray that no one who serves that cause will dishonor it by cowardice, inhumanity or rapine. In this supreme hour the Irish nation must, by its valor and discipline and by the readiness of its children to sacrifice themselves for the common good, prove itself worthy of the august destiny to which it is called. Signed on behalf of the Provisional Government: Thomas J. Clark, Sean Mac Diarmada, Thomas Mac-Donagh, P. H. Pearse, Eamonn Ceannt, James Connolly, Joseph Plunkett."

Pearse's voice drifted into silence, and James Connolly reached for his hand and wrung it warmly.

"Thanks be to God, Pearse, that we've lived to see this day!"

From the Citizen Army and the Volunteers both inside and out there were rousing cheers. But from the crowd on the sidewalk the response was less heartening. There were cheers. But there were jeers, too, and snickers. Perhaps the Irish people had heard too much of fine speeches. Perhaps they did not understand that this time there would be action.

8. Connolly for Ireland

In their post at the rear of the building the Kilcroom detachment had heard only faintly the reading of the proclamation. Terence McKeon had kept them hard at work, saying: "It would be a grand thing, wouldn't it, if we were out front listening and the English were coming in through the back door."

But when a scurrying Boy Scout brought a copy of the proclamation he halted the work and himself read it aloud in his precise, unemotional, schoolteacher's voice, the voice of reason.

There was a long silence when he had finished, and the heads of the men were bowed as if in prayer. And perhaps indeed they did pray, for this was what they had sought so long.

Then Declan broke the solemnity of the moment with his usual joke: "God, and not a word at all about free porter for the masses. Now what about that, Peadar?"

Peadar Casey said nothing, but his dark, withdrawn face hardened a little more and he jerked a shoulder to the shovel on which the big Declan was leaning. From McKeon he took the proclamation and read it through, trying desperately to draw comfort from its lines somewhere. There was disbelief in his heart, disbelief that James Connolly should ever have put his name to these words.

Only the Irish working class remains as the incorruptible inheritors of the fight for freedom in Ireland. Those had been

Connolly's own words. But where was there a mention at all in all this rigmarole of the proclamation of the working class? Where was the social justice? The equality that could come only from true socialism?

While his eyes smoldered over the copy of the proclamation, Casey had one hope only—that James Connolly had gone along with the others on this first proclamation, gone with them for unity against the joint foe. But afterward, surely afterward, James Connolly would take control and bring the true freedom. That had to be the answer. He was biding his time.

The picks and crowbars and shovels, whose need McKeon had foreseen, were eating their way into the wall that separated the post office building from the next one in Henry Street.

Big Declan O'Donovan was at the crowbar, levering away great masses of plasterwork with contemptuous heaves of his vast shoulders.

Suddenly there was a gap in the wall, and he peered through. Finger to his lips, he spun around with an exaggerated air of caution.

"A sentry!" he hissed.

And all work stopped abruptly, the men leaning on their tools or grabbing in alarm for their rifles. The mortar dust clung to their sweating skins and powdered all their uniforms.

"I'll get him," Declan whispered, and his two hands edged out through the gap he had made.

No one in the room thought to wonder what kind of sentry this was who had not heard the crumble of the wall behind him. Declan, as usual, had them in his thrall. Gulping, licking the dusty saltiness from their lips, they waited.

And suddenly Declan lunged forward, head into the hole.

"Got him!" they heard his muffled shout. "Got the dirty English tyrant!"

He thrust back into the room.

And their appalled eyes saw that now his hands held a head —a severed head with a uniform cap still on it.

Two men retched uncontrollably, and Tomeen Brennan slumped in a faint on the floor.

And it was only after Declan's boisterous laughter that they saw that it was no human head he held but one of wax, the effigy of Lord Kitchener.

For beyond the wall lay the Henry Street Waxworks.

"God almighty, boys," Declan whooped. "If you'd seen your faces! If you could've seen them. . . . Oh, your faces! I'll never forget them."

He took off the cap and set it on his own head, tossing the effigy lightly aside. Dramatically he posed in the posture of the famous recruiting poster.

"Kitchener wants you," he announced theatrically. "Boys, I'll just bet he does. If he could lay hands on us now, eh?"

Terence McKeon had not interfered during the little scene, thinking that it would make a good foil to the solemnity of the proclamation, that Declan's clowning would keep the men in good heart.

But enough time had been wasted.

"Right, let's get the wall down," he ordered brusquely.

And with fresh energy the men fell on the wall and forced an entry through into the waxworks and its tawdry images.

In Sackville Street, by the Parnell monument, a troop of the Sixth Cavalry had come to a halt, horses champing, bits jangling, the glitter of lances bright in the air. It was a sight to stir the heart of any Irishman.

It was also the most useless body of troops that could conceivably have been used for city fighting. It was an echo from the past, from the days when the horsemen dominated the battlefield. There were still generals who believed that some day on the western front the great breakthrough would come, a day when the cavalry divisions would burst from the stranglehold of the mud, the wire and the trenches and sweep like a blaze of fire across the enemy rear.

It was a dream that was dying in France, but in Ireland it had seemed natural that there should still be a cavalry unit. And in its curious, twisted way it was appropriate that one of the last cavalry charges should be made down Sackville Street, where so many cavalry officers had bitten the dust after a night in the Gresham Hotel.

Colonel Hammond, commanding the regiment, was with the troop, and cautiously he surveyed the scene ahead, liking it less with every moment. He could not have liked what he saw.

He was about to attack an entrenched enemy behind solid walls, an enemy whose strength and armament he did not know and which was, very largely, unreachable by the arms of his men. Conceivably he could have fought a dismounted action, his men using their carbines.

To add to the final confusion the street was still packed with the jumbled, gaping, eager mass of the civilian public. And to clash with the public, perhaps cause injuries to some unfortunate but litigious civilian, is the ultimate dread of every officer serving in any army anywhere.

The crowds were enjoying it, of course. This should be better than Fairhouse Races.

"Are ye scared, Colonel?" an urchin shouted from the gutter. "The boys in green has ye scared right enough."

Colonel Hammond did not hear the taunt or heed it. His mind was already made up. To retreat before the jeering mob was unthinkable.

He could only order the charge—and hope for a miracle.

Hooves drummed on the square setts of thoroughfares. The steel of the hooves struck sparks from the stones. With their lances at the same impeccable angle, pennants flying and line

82

as even as on parade, the lancers broke into a trot, a canter and a hand gallop.

The charge was on.

Even at the rear of the G.P.O. there was no mistaking the distant clatter of the hooves. From within the building came the shouts of officers as they barked at the defenders to hold their fire.

And Peadar Casey left his post.

"The cavalry!" He heard the shouts as he ran down the long corridor, away from the men of Kilcroom. "The cavalry's charging—"

He shouldered his way to the nearest window and thrust his Martini out through the jumble of smashed furniture that was the barricade.

The troop of lancers were about thirty yards short of Nelson's Pillar when he saw them coming, saw the swift, keen beauty of them, the power and the glory of the charge.

"Will ye stop yer shouldering?" the man beside him grumbled. "Sure I can't see a thing—"

Peadar Casey could see all he wanted. He could see the line of horses in their swift approach, the massive strength of the great beasts, the controlled majesty of their movement.

And his face hardened into a wolfish snarl as his sights swiveled slowly across the front.

"Hold your fire, men, hold your fire!" someone was shouting behind him. "Let them get to close range. Hold your fire!"

His aim steadied, and the blade of the foresight was exactly in the center of the U of the backsight as he had been taught so carefully. The tip of the foresight hovered just ahead of the heart—

The heart of the horse, not its rider.

Very slowly, smoothly, he pulled the trigger and felt the gun buck in his grasp. And his shot was the trigger for a whole ragged volley from the others, a volley that brought four riders down to their deaths and scattered the even discipline of the charge into a ragged headlong run.

But Peadar Casey was not interested in the charge or its dissolution or the panicked retreat of the British cavalry.

He was still watching the horse he had hit, seeing its head dip and its legs sprawl suddenly and splay. The rider flew wildly across its neck to land in a still huddle on the roadway. Casey did not look at him.

He watched the horse go down, half on its side. There was a moment when the stricken beast seemed about to rise, but the strength went suddenly from its back legs and it fell to its side with back legs kicking wildly and the life fountaining out from the wound his bullet had torn in it.

Eyes hot, heart cold, he watched the horse die.

"We've turned them!" someone was shouting. "We turned the cavalry!" Incredulity rang in his voice.

"They'll be back," a sour voice rejoined. "They've plenty more."

Peadar Casey drew in the long barrel of the Martini and jerked the lever to eject the empty cartridge.

"Aye," he said, to no one in particular. "They've plenty more."

And he began to shoulder his way back to his post at the rear of the building.

9. Horses and People

"Sure they've plenty more, your honor."

Peadar Casey was twelve years old when he heard these words: twelve, thin, half-starved . . . and standing by the side of the body of his youngest brother, Liam.

The man who spoke the words was Henry Turkson, land agent to Colonel Kingston and real master of the thousand acres or so that made up the Kingston demesne which included most of Kilcroom within its boundary.

Turkson was a thin, active man of Welsh descent with a blunt, honest-looking face and eyes that could read the cards in anybody's hands. It was Turkson who really decided what rents people would pay, what repairs would be made to their dwellings and who would be "for the road."

The words were heard by Lieutenant Colonel Kingston, then on leave from Hobson's Horse of the Indian Army, his coachman, Patrick Coughlin, his wife, Margaret, and his daughter, who was also Margaret and then six years old.

The daughter was leaning out over the side of the carriage, peering at the still, childish figure on the ground, her big eyes wide with interest.

"Why has he got jam on his head, Daddy? Is he dead, Daddy?"

The colonel had turned indignantly from his seat on the box and glared biliously at his wife. "Good heavens, Margaret, don't just sit there letting the girl *look*!"

"What . . . what shall I do, dear?" the wife moaned.

"Make some sort of blasted bundobust. Good heavens, that's no sight for a child!"

Peadar had seen the mother drag the daughter away, despite her protest, swing her around to the other side of the carriage and herself sit very stiff and looking straight ahead.

Nobody thought to remark that the dead child was an unsuitable sight for Peadar. So he stood there helplessly, looking sometimes down at Liam and sometimes at the horse that had killed him.

It had, of course, been an accident. Liam had run down the bank of the narrow road as the carriage approached and waved his arms and piped a tiny cheer for the lord of Kingston Castle. He had darted from Peadar's grasp, run down close to the horse and waved and shouted.

It was not the sort of treatment any spirited horse would stand, and Colonel Kingston had always prided himself on his horseflesh. It was very natural that the startled animal should lash out.

And that its hoof should smash in the skull of a three-year-old child.

"You. What's your name, son?"

Turkson's finger beckoned, and Peadar Casey edged forward humbly, still shocked, still numbed by the disaster.

"Peadar Casey, sor."

"Who's the child?"

"It's Liam, sor."

He spoke to the agent, knowing him as the master of his life and destiny, not knowing that the agent was only the colonel's servant. The colonel was such a rare visitor to his home that he was scarcely known.

"Liam who? Come on, boy, speak up! Liam who—and why did you let him run down like that?"

Turkson waited for no answer but turned to Colonel Kingston: "This will be the youngest of the Widow Casey's brood, your honor. She has the cottage by the old mill. A good woman and a reliable tenant."

Colonel Kingston dismounted slowly and looked down at the crumpled form of the child. He plucked at his lower lip.

"Poor woman," he said absently. "Poor woman."

"A mouth less to feed, sir," Turkson pointed out.

The colonel glanced toward Peadar, who still stood numbly and unbelievingly, looking down at Liam and up at the carriage alternately.

"Terrible," said the colonel. "Terrible for the lad. To see a thing like that."

He shrugged his shoulders helplessly.

"My dear," wailed his wife, her cloak across Margaret's head. "It's not very . . . *suitable*, standing here. Can't—"

Suitable, the colonel thought, that was all that was ever in her hen brain of a mind, what was suitable.

"Go on home," he said gruffly. "Coughlin, take the carriage home. I'll walk."

And so the carriage had rumbled off and left the strange trio standing awkwardly by the body.

"Awkward," the colonel grumbled. "This is going to be awkward. Police. Court case. Inquest. All that damned nonsense."

"It *was* an accident, sir," Turkson said smoothly and soothingly. "Not a court in the world would say anything different. If this boy had looked after his brother properly it would never have happened."

It was in this instant that hate probably was born in Peadar's mind. Now, with Liam dead on the verge of the road and the carriage rumbling off into the distance, all the unfairness of the world crystallized into a little icy block of hate that would never leave him. For they were blaming him. They had killed Liam and he was to be blamed.

And the blame would stick. Their word would be taken

87

and his mother's sorrow would be on his head. And because, in fact, he was in some degree to blame he hated them the more. These men and their horses and their high, haughty ways.

"Turkson, I think I'll walk into Kilcroom and inform the police. Perhaps you'll see the mother, break it to her gently. And—er—attend to the . . ."

He nodded down at the body.

Neither of them paid any attention to Peadar, whose face was working now with the understanding immensity of the disaster sinking in at last to his consciousness.

Of the talk of courts and police and inquests he understood little enough. He understood only that Liam was dead and that on his head would fall the blame for the death. The bitter bias of the world was suddenly more than he could bear.

A long, retching sob burst from his lips, and then he turned and ran abruptly up the bank and across the fields.

"Poor lad," the colonel commented. "A shock for him. Frightful shock. . . . Hmm. Well, see to it, Turkson, see to it. Oh, and see the widow is looked after. Don't forget that."

He started off down the road toward the village. It was too bad, he thought, too bad.

Turkson stooped to lift the body of the child and then thought better of it. He took off his jacket and wrapped it around the body before he raised it.

Then, lighting his small-bowled pipe, he started toward the old mill and the Widow Casey. The inconvenience of the matter did not worry him much. Dealing with inconvenience was what he was paid for.

Nor should there be much trouble. The coroner, old Dr. Groves, would certainly bring in a verdict of accidental death. When the evidence was given there would not even be any real need for compensation. But then again, a little show of

88

generosity at this stage might be a good thing. There was some restiveness among the tenants.

The gesture to the widow would cost little enough: a few shillings a week, and it would be a sort of weapon to use against those whose rents were due shortly to go up. Not that all the rent increase would be shown in the estate books. Not by any means. A due proportion would go toward the agent's own nest egg.

As he walked on with the child's body in his arms, Turkson was entirely unaware of the hot-eyed scrutiny of Peadar Casey from behind the trees. Nor could he know the mental processes that were already at work in the boy's mind, processes that edited the facts to suit his wishes, processes that exculpated himself from blame and put it all on the castle people—and the horses.

The horses and the horse people. Those who had killed Liam and would put the blame on him.

It was the horses Peadar always hated after that, the horses more than the people. Even when he was a grown man and thinking hard about the way things were, it was the horses he hated and what they did to people.

A horse set people aside. Literally, it put them on a different level. A man on horseback was always looking down on the man on foot, never meeting him eye to eye. It was horses that set the rich aside from the poor, horses more than anything, more even than their money. Of course, without their money they would have no horse. But without the horse they would be on a level with the common people and would have to meet them eye to eye, on the one level.

He wondered sometimes why James Connolly had never seen this great truth or mentioned it in his writings. Nor was it in any of the other labor or socialist or Marxist literature that by now he was often reading. Or if the truth was in them, he was missing it.

Horses and their riders. And the horse was the one he hated more.

And yet when Margaret Kingston rode to a gate he would hurry to open it before her and salute as humbly as the next one. Which of course was natural, for anyone working in the Kingston estate as he was then. For Turkson had been as good as his word. He had looked after the Caseys in his way, seen all the family settled in jobs, let the old woman keep her cottage. The fact that they had a reputation as good workers would have helped, of course, not being like the O'Donovan rowdy and others of his ilk.

For Margaret Kingston he had opened the gate often enough, pulling back the bolt and swinging the gate wide so she could ride through without the bother of dismounting.

He would give a humble sort of bob as she rode through, and she would pay him no attention at all, though she would have paid enough heed maybe if she had not been on the horse, seated daintily with her right knee cocked high and the long skirts of her habit trailing down to the length of her stirrup iron. Probably she did not see him at all save as a sort of a living machine for opening gates.

First she had ridden with a groom attending her, and the groom would be as haughty as herself, though he was only Paddy O'Shea that was reared as poor as dirt down at the Tannery Fennel. But Paddy was on a horse too, and that made him a big fellow.

Then it had been the gentry attending her, one or another of the sprigs from the big houses about, lively, hearty fellows that were beef-fed from the cradle and loved nothing better than to give a man a cut across the back with their crop if he dallied a bit at the gate. Or at any rate, one of them had once given him a cut from his crop, and that could have been an accident, in all fairness—though he thought not.

That one had been Captain Greyson, the cavalry man, the one from the Eighth Hussars, the one who had sniffed around Miss Kingston for leave after leave. An older one this, and not like the young sprigs who, when all was said, had a bit of life to them.

But Greyson, he was a cold man and hard with watchful eyes that ranged every road before he reached it. Also he was the laugh of the countryside, though he did not know it. For the young gentry it was a sweet and natural thing to be chasing a young lady, and maybe there would be a quiet happening in a wood when they would stop to breathe their horses.

But the captain, he was different. The captain was a cold man and hungry for more than flesh. The captain had his eye on the aging Colonel Kingston and the broad acres of the Kingston demesne.

He had no money himself or else was more than ordinarily mean, and this was plain from the way he would treat his soldier servant when he came to stay at the castle. For whatever poor fellow was his batman never had a shilling in his pocket to pleasure himself in the village, and barring his uniform, he wouldn't have a backside to his breeches often enough.

When he thought of horsemen and hated them, it was of Captain Greyson that Peadar Casey thought most often: of the proud, arrogant set of his back and the way his hand always tightened on his crop going through a gate.

And even the horses the captain rode seemed to share his arrogance.

Peadar never forgot the day when he was doing a turn in the stables and had just polished up the captain's saddlery and laid it out on a bench at the rear of the stall. Gleaming with that deep, living glow that comes only from hours of earnest hand labor, beautiful in its way—and suddenly fouled when the horse, a big, hammerheaded bay, lifted its tail.

On purpose, Peadar always believed. The brute had done it on purpose. It had heard the captain coming and it had fouled the harness on purpose. It had shown its contempt for Peadar Casey, the horse's contempt for the human race that was not of the horse people.

And the captain had trembled with rage yet had said coldly: "Clean it then, clean it quickly."

"Me rags, sir, me polish. The coachman's just after taking them."

"You've got hands, haven't you?"

That was horses for you, and horse people, and he hated them all.

10. Opportunities

Captain Thomas Greyson, in his room at Kingston Castle, gazed sourly at his wardrobe. There was no denying that his mess dress was almost past wearing. The glossy high boots were paper-thin at the ankles, and the tight overall trousers were so shiny at the knees now and also on the seat that the next violent strain could very easily cause some disastrous exposure. The lancers would not be for him at the ball that night.

He rubbed the short bristles of his mustache and wondered if there was any possible way of extending his credit with his Dublin bookmaker. And knew the answer before he formed the thought. There had been an increasing asperity in the last few notes from the same bookmaker.

From: *No doubt the enclosed account has escaped your notice,* it had become: *Prompt settlement will oblige* and *Little as we would like to take any other steps* . . .

Only one thing would improve his credit in that quarter— or any other. A sudden accretion of actual cash was the only hope.

There was one way a penniless cavalry captain could acquire sudden real money, and that was by marriage. Not for the first time he regretted his decision not to join the Indian cavalry. The pay itself was far better in India, and there were, as he put it euphemistically, "opportunities."

A gently blind eye to certain deficiencies in feeding stuffs or troop rations would always be handsomely rewarded by the contractors. There was even the imprest account itself, which was not at all hard to pad with the names of nonexistent troopers whose wages could be diverted with ease into the pockets of the account holder—or so he had been told by a certain school friend who had opted for the East.

He regretted his folly in choosing the Eighth Royal Irish Hussars, where alone among the officers he had no private income, where he lived on his pay plus what he made in a little genteel horse dealing and an occasional run of luck on the races.

And there was no doubt, he mused often, he had been unlucky even in the Hussars. While they were writing their names into history with the charge at Omdurman he had been lying in a base hospital with an ankle smashed at polo. That squeaky-voiced little upstart Winston Churchill had been in the charge and made a good deal of capital out of it afterward. He had done very nicely for himself, had Churchill, writing for the newspapers, easing his way into politics.

The Boer War, which had brought promotion for so many brother officers (and newspaper money to Churchill), had done nothing for Thomas Greyson. Secunded to a mounted rifles unit, he seemed to pass the war riding convoy escort across endless shimmering plains. Occasionally he was ambushed by Boers but never in a position where he could gain any hint of glory. Even the looting from Boer farmhouses was not worthwhile in that mean and miserable land which brought riches to others.

In occasional moments of self-appraisal, Greyson was aware that his lack of advancement was not totally due to bad luck. He lacked patience. He was unwilling to work in the present for the sake of future reward. He wanted it now. In cold reason he knew that almost no one could become rich by gambling. And those who did were the ones with the patient self-control he never had. He knew horses. He knew the theories of odds. If he had been willing to accept small profits over a longer period he could even have made money racing. But reason left him when a race was in the wind. If he won on the first race he would be sure that this was the day he would go down the card. Experience never convinced him to the contrary.

Captain Greyson cursed the army, his regiment, his luck.

And also he cursed his father's folly. If Canon Greyson had not been an unworldly visionary, he might have been a bishop now with means aplenty to keep his son in the style to which he aspired. But the canon preferred the quietude of his cathedral close to the hurly-burly of church politics.

There was left only matrimony—to an heiress.

And Margaret Kingston was proving uncommonly hard to catch.

She was attracted. He knew that. He knew there was about him a certain animal magnetism. He had proved its power often enough in the past. But so far it had failed to draw this particular bird to the catcher's net.

Perhaps after all, he mused, as he began to change reluctantly into his worn uniform, he had been using the wrong tactics. He had been perhaps too gentle with this particular little bird. She might be the kind who liked the rough approach. A little violence, a little show of strength—that might be the game.

But if it failed . . . the strong approach left no line of retreat. It was win or lose. And whatever else his faults the captain was enough of a soldier to like a line of retreat in all circumstances.

Angrily he looked at his chain mail epaulettes, last vestige of the cavalry armor of old. Trooper Jones had forgotten to burnish them again, and the tiny links were dull.

For a moment he thought of ringing for his batman but remembered he had sent the man out to place a bet with the village bookmaker, a cash bet since the bookmaker was too small to operate on credit—or too wise to offer it to Captain Greyson. And the bet being both small and in cash, Captain Greyson regarded it as beneath his dignity to place it himself.

He shrugged and began to pull on the tight tunic. The tiny badges of rank on his sleeve—small because in the cavalry there was the ostentation of no ostentation in matters of rank —glittered in the gaslight that came from the castle's own carbide plant.

He gazed at himself in the mirror as he buttoned up his high-necked tunic. *A fine figure a man now, isn't he so?* He smiled as he remembered the tribute he had heard from one of the village women as he rode through Kilcroom.

And a good soldier, he thought, a first-class soldier. Now if only they would get on with this war in Europe they were talking about . . .

Promotion, a regiment, a brigade even. Promotion came quickly in war. And there were "opportunities." It was a poor soldier who could not bring home his share of loot. And the cavalry had the best chances there. Ranging ahead of the infantry, they reached the great houses before the artillery had time to destroy everything worth taking. And a cavalryman had his horse to help carry his gains.

He thought longingly of the taking of Peking, where his great-uncle Joseph had laid the foundation of that side of the family's fortune. A fortune which had stayed very much on that side of the family.

But it was no good dreaming. The Kaiser or the Czar would have too much sense to go to war, worst luck. It was marry a fortune for Captain Thomas Greyson, marry a fortune or have a dirty Jew of a Dublin bookmaker put him in Queer Street.

One way or the other, he would have to have Margaret Kingston and her reputed ten thousand a year.

It was, in fact, only a bedroom, but Margaret Kingston in the privacy of her mind always referred to it as her "boudoir."

Even to use a French word gave her a delicious feeling of sin, and to sit at her dressing table, making up her eyes and lips, with her dressing gown ("peignoir" in her mind) open so that her breasts peeped shyly out for only her own eyes to see, made her feel beautifully, utterly depraved, one with the women in the books in the locked compartment of her cupboard.

The makeup was pretense only, of course. It would all have to be wiped off before she went to kiss Mama and be inspected before she left for the ball.

Once, just once, maybe she would go into Mama's room with all the makeup still left on. How Mama would jerk upright in her bed! How the dried-up, melancholy face would set in rigid lines! How the eyes would widen! For a moment Mama would really come to life.

Margaret Kingston giggled to herself as she thought of the scene.

And then she grew serious as she pondered the fact that she could very easily insure for herself complete freedom from Mama forever, bring herself at one great stroke among the company of those who did as they pleased.

Just a tiny moment's extra encouragement to Captain Greyson, and she knew with a sure inner instinct that he would propose.

She thrilled and shuddered in the same instant at the

97

thought. The bristly mustache would press on her lips, that undeniably hard male body would fold her close. . . .

There had for Margaret Kingston been certain moments of furtive pleasure with those of her kith who were her own age. There had been clumsy kisses in the shrubbery, squeezing of hands, languorous looks.

Teddy Ffrench-Blake from Clanmire had even written her a poem and made an assignation which she failed to keep. There had been the night she held hands with young Billy Travers at the Palace Theatre in Cork. There had been no follow-up to that, either. And there had been Percy McGrath at the grammar school speech day.

But when all was said, they were young, like puppies. They were fun, gay, do-anything comrades. But she could not think of them as men. Not the boys she had first known at nursery teas. They were like brothers, all of them. She knew them too well.

Captain Greyson—for thus she thought of him, though she called him Tommy—though, was a different matter. What went on inside him she did not know. There would be dangerous, explosive depths to plumb.

With cold cream she began to remove the makeup and then rang for Maire, her maid, to help her dress.

Margaret's deep blue eyes watched carefully as the hands of her maid worked through the long, pale-gold texture of her hair.

"Not so tight. I've told you before, not so tight."

Maire blushed as she always did when rebuked and let her mistress' hair fall in softer loops about her forehead. In her mind she thought that Margaret was a fool, for the tighter curls showed off the line of her forehead far better. But Maire Casey knew her place better than to argue. The best way of dealing with these ones was to say nothing except when they wanted admiration—and then pour it on by the bucketful.

As when at last Margaret Kingston pirouetted lightly before her mirror and demanded: "How do I look?"

"Like a princess, miss. Like a living princess out of the silver towers of fairyland. Oh, it's the joy and the pleasure to the eye you are, miss, and that's no lie."

Nor indeed was it, and Captain Greyson would have confirmed her words had he been present.

11. The Ball

It is better to travel hopefully than to arrive. This is not exactly how Margaret phrased to herself her feelings about the ball, but it was pretty much how she felt. It was pretty much how she felt about every ball she had attended.

Beforehand the pleasures of anticipation, of choosing a new gown, of indulging herself with exotic private viewings of outrageous hair styles and grotesque makeup mingled with daydreams of the glitter and life there would be, of the elegant dancers, the gorgeous music, the flavor of life in the high world.

But the reality of Leonie Byrne-Fairfax's coming-out ball at Ballyfastin Castle was no different from the reality of every other ball she had ever attended. The band was Mr. Antoine Pierpoint's ballroom assembly which seemed to play at every large occasion in County Cork and consisted mainly of four emaciated violinists in blue uniforms with gold piping—or rather of yellow piping, as could be seen close at hand.

The castle ballroom floor was no better than the floor of any other of the big houses, which is to say it contained here and there irregular planks which could catch the heel of an unwary dancer. The buffet was cold salmon, cold grouse, cold pheasant, cold ham and the sherry-fortified trifle which was standard fare at every house in the land.

The supply of drink was more liberal than in some houses, which was something in favor of old Byrne-Fairfax and was accounted for no doubt by his naval background, for he was a retired commodore.

The partners were, of course, the same as they were at every dance—the same young men she had known from her childhood. There was no prospect here of an unexpected Prince Charming. Margaret felt almost glad of the presence of Captain Grayson, though she still did not know her father had invited him to the house. They had met, she gathered, in India. Some sort of vague invitation had been extended. And Greyson had appeared with his batman, prepared, it seemed, for quite a long stay.

On the whole, yes, Margaret thought; she was glad of the captain's presence. At least he was not one of your callow young bloods still fresh from their public schools.

The two circled a nearly empty ballroom to a new waltz tune. They were watched by an almost hostile ring of ladies, for the men—as was their custom—were still taking full advantage of the commodore's hospitality. Generally the men clung together for mutual support and encouragement until they had drunk their self-consciousness away and could cavort without inhibitions.

"They do this sort of thing rather better in London," Greyson murmured and realized from a momentary stiffening of the girl's body that he had blundered. He went on quickly: "I mean, of course, that staff are better trained, musicians . . . the company, of course, is not so good."

"You are very gallant. Have you any theory why the gentlemen should always be so tardy coming onto the floor?"

"Fear. Pure fear. Irishmen, of whatever class, are terrified of their ladies. Therefore they fortify themselves as if dancing was a penance instead of a pleasure. And I blame the Irish teachers of dancing. They seem unable to make their pupils differentiate between the ballroom and the hunting field."

Margaret allowed herself a small laugh. The remark was apposite enough, for a red-faced man in too-tight evening dress was circling the room with his partner as if approaching a double oxer on the gallop.

Greyson felt that he had gained some advantage.

"You can bet that in the bar they'll be talking of hunting—not dancing."

And indeed hunting was being discussed in the room which had been converted to a temporary bar.

One of the Welleslys, a distant kinsman of the Duke of Wellington, was declaiming: "I know what I'd do with these damned Fenians—hunt the devils down. Hunt 'em down, rout 'em out and hunt 'em down. Damned rascals. Hang a few priests, burn a few houses over their heads. I'd like to set my wolfhounds on them."

"Your *Irish* wolfhounds, of course, my dear Wellesly," said someone to a barely concealed snicker.

Wellesly's wolfhounds were famous as a triumph of gullibility over experience. His pack had been gathered up from every reputed specimen of the old breed which had come to Ireland with the Gaels two or three thousand years before, vast gaunt hounds which were taller than any other dog in the world.

Wellesly had obvious Great Danes among his pack, and others whose origin was equally obviously Russian or German. It was odd that a man so besottedly against anything else of an Irish slant should accept the word of almost any tinker when it came to the pedigree of wolfhounds.

But certainly his pack was large and probably savage.

In a corner Commodore Byrne-Fairfax, a tall man with shaggy silver hair, was engaged in more or less serious conversation with others of his own generation.

"That man Wellesly is an utter fool," said the commodore.

"I trust that when it comes to burning houses his own is the first to go."

"Will it come to that?" asked a landowner from Meath.

"In Ireland it always comes to that," said the commodore savagely. "Some day we may learn some sense, but—"

"You speak like quite a Liberal. You can't really want the Home Rule Bill to go through?"

"It would be the best thing that ever happened to Ireland," the commodore insisted. "You all know what's happening in this country. There's a ferment abroad. And if I were a poor young lad living in a filthy cottage and being overcharged for the rent of it I'd be fermenting too."

"I'm surprised, Commodore. I'm really surprised. A naval man like yourself. Discipline must be maintained. You know that—"

"Or the appearance of discipline, eh, Brewster?"

His interrogator blushed deeply, and only the commodore knew the cause.

Brewster was a neighboring landowner, apparently as crusted a Tory as any of them. He made a show of getting eviction orders against any tenants behind with their rents, and he was fond of declaring: "They always pay up. It shows that if you put the screws on them they can always find the money."

Byrne-Fairfax had learned, however, that it was Brewster himself who secretly supplied the money with which his tenants then repaid him. It was a delicious irony, and though the commodore had kept the secret he delighted in hinting at it in public.

"As to the navy, I know discipline. You've got to give men a chance to blow off steam. A quiet ship means there's trouble brewing. I like to hear men chewing the rag, moaning about their food, trying to scive on their duties. When they can blow off steam there's no danger. Ferment! You mention ferment! And what happens when a brew ferments in the bottle? Unless it's controlled the bottle bursts. The Irish Parliament will be like a loose cork. It'll let the gas blow off and maybe save the bottle."

"I'm glad you mentioned Cork," drawled a crooked-nosed judge of the high court, a cousin of the commodore. "What about Ulster under home rule? The Protestants won't stand for it, you know."

"I don't quite see the connection with Cork and the North," the commodore bristled.

"Carson, my dear fellow. Edward Carson. He's a barrister from Cork, and if there's anyone behind the Ulstermen it's Ned Carson. A brilliant orator—and a devilish dangerous man. You know he's getting thousands of signatures to his Solemn League and Covenant. Getting the Presbyterians in, you see; they couldn't resist the 'Covenant' tag. The North won't have home rule, you may be sure, and I find it hard to blame them."

"If the government says home rule, the North will have to have it," growled the commodore. "I don't care if there are a hundred of your Carsons."

But he did not feel the confidence of his words. On his last tour of duty he had been in Belfast. And it was true that he had felt there as strong and even more hostility to home rule as there was support for it in the South.

Could it come to civil war yet? To the North versus the South? That Carson had won over the Presbyterians from their traditional hostility to the pale was a pointer. In former risings the leadership had come from the Dissenters. Wolfe Tone, Henry Joy McCracken, Emmet, other names ran through his mind. Most of them had been hanged.

The peculiar perversity of Irish history afflicted him again, especially with the irony of this Cork man, this Carson leading the North. It was the final twist, and it augured badly. Cork men usually chose the winning side.

The commodore signaled for a drink and got it.

"This is supposed to be a festive occasion," he declared. "I never heard that politics were festive. Shall we see if anyone's dancing yet?"

"Ah, now, Mr. McGrath, sure I only want to see the dancing, sir. Sure where's the harm in that? Isn't there a wee gallery high up where I could look down and never a soul know I was up there admiring the ladies and the gentlemen in all their finery?"

The commodore's butler should have been attending his master's guests, but the gombeen-man's importunities, transmitted by a harassed footman, had brought him out to the castle yard where Raymond McCarthy had a cart already loaded with empty bottles.

It was for the bottles he had come to the castle, for he had a steady market in Cork and Dublin for good-quality wine bottles with unstained labels. There were plenty of merchants glad to fill a vintage bottle with common wines for sale to those of less discriminating palate—and indeed, McCarthy suspected, to many a connoisseur too. Many a bottle returned to the same house whence it had come and none noticed the difference in the contents.

McGrath feared that McCarthy wanted to drive a harder than usual bargain this time. He was relieved to find the request so simple—or at least, not to cost anything. Money from the empties was never shown in the household accounts. On the contrary, McGrath always showed a figure "for disposing empty bottles." The bottles were his main insurance for his old age, his principal hope of becoming some day the owner of a little hotel.

Now he thought quickly.

"The back stairs," he murmured. "You go up them. You

come to the small minstrel gallery. It's unlit, so take care. And if you're found. . . . You're a burglar, understand?"

"Ah, you're the decent man, Mr. McGrath. I'll not forget it. I'll not be seen. I'll not be seen."

He skipped through the doorway to the back stairs, and the butler watched him go with a frown puckering his forehead.

What was the gombeen-man really after? He was so devious that it was impossible to believe he only wanted to watch the ball like some dazzled second parlormaid.

What was he really up to? The butler was still wondering as he returned like a bishop to officiate over the service of the drinks.

For perhaps the first time in his life, Raymond McCarthy had been done an injustice. For indeed all he wanted was to watch the ball, to gape at the glittering scene, to take in the gorgeous dresses, the brilliant uniforms, the sheer richness of it all. Just to see was all he wanted, and to dream.

There was scarcely any other softness in the nature of the gombeen-man. But the word "ball" acted on him like some strange elixir, like an oil drill tapping an unsuspected gusher. It was magic to him, pure magic, letting his one weakness suddenly suffuse him.

Looking down from the gallery at the stately figures circling slowly beneath, at the color and the uniforms, and hearing the music drift upward, savoring the scents and the cigar smoke, Raymond McCarthy was no longer thinking of money.

". . . and then Cinderella went to the ball in her coach drew by them four white horses. . . . Them that was mice before, d'ye see? And the coach was the pumpkin. The coach was the pumpkin . . ."

In the straw in the loft young Raymond listened to the story Grania told. He had heard it a hundred times. He could never hear it too often.

He would have been three or four then. His age he never knew any more than he knew his mother or his father. Grania was his sister, he thought afterward, but maybe she was his aunt or maybe just another waif like himself living in the loft behind the warehouse down by the timber dock.

She was older than he was. She brought him food, and sometimes they went begging together in Patrick Street, when he would pretend to be ill, which he probably was.

He had been eight or nine when she died. Or he supposed she had died. He had been gathering rags then for a dealer called Leahey, and when he came back to the loft it was burned to the ground. He had run away in case he would be blamed.

What happened to Grania he never knew, but he never forgot her either, or the story of the poor girl and the prince and the wonderful magic of a ball.

Logically he knew that those people down below were just the same arrogant rich who would drive him from their doors. But the magic of the very word "ball" had transmuted them into that dream of Grania's which had comforted them in the straw.

No one knowing him in business would have recognized the gombeen-man in the simpering face at the gallery rail.

It was some time before he recognized Margaret Kingston. Then he began to notice how often she danced with Captain Greyson, and the magic of the ball faded slowly.

He began to think again of business.

12. *Where Is Reason?*

Terence McKeon always took the Wild King's Loaning when he was thinking hard. And this was a night for thought. For at long length the arguments for him to join the Brotherhood had been made so convincing that he could gainsay them no longer.

There had to be reason in insurrection, he had always held. Without reason a rising was bound to fail. It was no manner of good to cry "Up Ireland!" and have a few poor devils hanged at the market cross, as the past had shown. Reason and purpose —these had been the missing links in the past. But now he believed there was reason at last coming into the fire of freedom.

Lost in his thoughts, he did not consciously notice the halted carriage until he was almost abreast of it.

Even then he might have walked on past but for the sounds that came from within, the cries of struggle.

"No!" he heard a girl cry. "Stop it! No—"

And there was a wild note of fear in her voice.

The Wild King's Loaning was a noted place for courting couples of one kind or another, and Terence McKeon was a broad-minded man for a small-town teacher. The voice of reason told him that often a girl said no when she meant yes.

The voice of reason told him: *Go on quietly about your business, McKeon abu. There is no good for you in this place.*

And the voice of reason did indeed impel his feet to turn himself about and back down the lane, beneath the weeping oak trees that shadowed it so well.

108

But then the girl cried out again, and reinforcing her cry was the sound of ripping cloth.

And the sweet voice of reason said: *Well, maybe* . . .

Thus Terence McKeon stepped back, reasonably noisily, toward the carriage from which he could now hear the sounds of thrashing bodies, of panting, and of low, masculine grunts.

"Would there be some trouble here?" he inquired politely, peeping delicately within the carriage as he did so.

Two pale legs were flailing in the air, and there was a soft foam of lingerie about them. There was also a dark, angry, masculine face turned toward him.

"Go to hell!" roared the voice of Captain Thomas Greyson, which was known to McKeon. The expression and the sentiment were reasonable, and even then McKeon might have withdrawn, for in the circumstances a man might not be inclined to be overpolite. But to these words Greyson had the folly to add: "You dirty Irish bastard, you!"

And the voice of reason was forgotten.

For strangely, though to insult a man with a multitude of epithets may be forgivable, to couple these epithets with his race, religion or color is the ultimate insult.

Thus "You filthy, moneygrubbing swine" may eventually be forgiven. But "You filthy, moneygrubbing Jewish (or Scottish or Levantine or Muslim or black) swine" means blood.

Why this should be so delves perhaps into the realms of ancient tribal security. But it is so. There should be a smile when such remarks are passed.

And there was no smile on Captain Greyson's face. There was only a hot irritation and contempt.

"You are no gentleman," Terence McKeon observed.

And the blackthorn stick which had been an aid to his meditations swung sharply in his hand.

He had never in his life hit a man before, and he was surprised at the vast tumult of inner exultation that exploded in him when the stick made contact.

Captain Greyson subsided instantly into a slumped heap among the petticoats, and reason reasserted its dominion in Terence McKeon's mind.

A King's officer, said reason; *you have struck a King's officer. Probably you have killed him. So run like hell. Otherwise you will surely be hanged.*

But unreason had him firmly in its grip for a little longer.

"Are you all right, miss?" he inquired gently.

There was a sob from within and a further flutter of garments. A pale face was hidden instantly and a coif of pale blond hair. Nor did it matter that more was left exposed than hidden. For what was hidden was identity, the face. It was any girl who hid behind that raised skirt, any girl who brusquely said: "Please go away."

Which instruction Terence McKeon obeyed, recognizing instantly that here the laws of reason were not applicable. Also there was the point that if he could not see her face she could not see his . . . or give evidence about who had struck the captain down.

But as he hurried homeward to his mother's house McKeon was pondering the curious interaction of reason and unreason.

There was a lot of the latter in women, he thought . . . and Ireland too. It was little wonder they called this land of his Kathleen ni Houlihan.

"It is, of course, a very fine and splendid thing to die for Kathleen ni Houlihan. But it may very well be—and I suggest it with due deference—that Kathleen herself might prefer her menfolk alive."

Thus his mother, thus the tall, slender and still beautiful Eileen d'Silva Mackenzie McKeon. Thus "the widow lady, God save her, that was Ranty McKeon's wife." Thus the dry, appraising humor of her voice. Thus again, the voice of reason.

"Mother, I wasn't proposing to be killed. The last thing I wish is to be killed. *'Dulce et decorum est pro patria mori'* is one thing. And no doubt it is very suitable to be killed for the motherland. But I agree. It is unreasonable. It is better to live for one's country."

"And yet, my dear, sweet, reasonable son, you had to take your blackthorn stick to the head of an English officer, didn't you? Was there any sweet reason in that? Especially before witnesses. If you had to break the man's head you should have broken the woman's, too. Then there would have been no witnesses."

As ever, Terence McKeon was a little blinded by the sense his mother always talked. He looked at her and wondered however that gay, brilliant sea captain who had been his father could have found it in himself to leave her. Even now, he thought, at this time and long past her alleged prime, she was the most beautiful woman in all Kilcroom. And certainly the cleverest.

"She didn't see me," he pointed out. "My head would have been against the moon, and in any case she pulled up her own skirts to hide her face so I wouldn't recognize *her!*"

He chuckled softly at the memory, and his mother shot him a swift glance and then smiled before she lit the long, thin black cigar which had been unlighted in her mouth since Terence returned.

"You don't get much fun with the girls now, and that's a fact," she observed. "Did you feel a sudden rush of blood to the head, or maybe to other parts of you, at seeing the legs of a girl?"

"I was disturbed," he conceded after a moment's thought. "I believe I had what Father Roche would call sinful thoughts. Indeed, Mother, thinking back, I believe I have them yet."

Eileen McKeon gazed at her son across the long, thin cigar

that she would certainly not have smoked in public and said nothing at all. She was, or so she considered herself, a woman of knowledge and wisdom. She had tried to impart the wisdom at least to her son. She had tried to impart the rationality of her Lowland Scots ancestors and the intuition of her Latin ancestors to this son who had also the unreason of the Ireland of his father in him. She wondered if she had succeeded. Or if even the sight of a woman's bare legs had sent unreason into reason.

Three days later the engagement of Captain Thomas Greyson of the Eighth Royal Irish Hussars to Miss Margaret Kingston of Kingston Castle was announced.

And that in itself was proof enough of all the unreason in the world.

Captain Greyson was as bewildered as anyone else, maybe more so. His head ached furiously when he came around in the carriage, and with that and the vagueness of the after-effects of the drink he had taken at the ball—in itself the prime cause of his lapse—he was in no condition to reason clearly.

Margaret was dabbling at his head with a scrap of cambric moistened with eau de Cologne, and when he stirred she sat up swiftly.

"Do you feel well enough to drive now, Captain Greyson?" she asked coldly.

He had muttered something and clambered to his feet. He took the reins in his hands and clicked the amiable gray, which had not stirred throughout the fracas, into well-bred motion. The only good thing about it, he thought sourly, was that there was no coachman to observe his humiliation. Patrick Coughlin had fallen in the stable that day and broken a wrist, and that was why he had driven and why they had been in the Wild King's Loaning at all.

It was Coughlin's fault, all Coughlin's fault. If the damn fool of a coachman had kept his feet the captain would have kept his head.

When he drew up at last at the castle door and leaped down to hand Margaret to the ground he tried to mutter a hoarse apology.

"My head . . . the brandy . . . I regret—"

"Please take the coach to the yard, Captain Greyson," Margaret answered coolly. "If you ring the bell on the stable door one of the lads will put the horse away."

And she had swept distantly up into the house.

Going to his room, Greyson had wondered gloomily if he should call his batman, pack and leave there and then. But his head still throbbed, and the thought of a night ride with the throb pounding within him was too much. He would wait until the morning and the stiff note that would surely be brought with his tea: *A carriage has been reserved on the 8:15 to Dublin. No doubt Captain Greyson will wish to take it.*

He threw himself on the bed with a groan. Why had he been such a bloody, bloody fool? And yet for an instant she had seemed so willing. Her lips had yielded to his, and she had not stirred at the first tentative move of his hand toward her breast. Only when he had pulled at her skirt had she begun to struggle.

"Hasty!" he groaned. "Too bloody hasty. I had it in my hand and I threw it away like some floss-bottomed young subaltern with a week's service in."

For a long time he cursed himself vainly and thought of the ogre of his bookmaker and the waste of days to come. Then he turned to the bottle of whiskey that reposed beside every male bedside in the castle and drank himself quietly to sleep.

The morning brought tea all right—but not his dismissal.

Dumbfounded, he examined the silver tray again and again. There was no square envelope. No curt indication that his *persona* was no longer *grata*.

He was still sipping his tea, still in the mess dress of the night before, when Atkin the butler, a middle-aged Londoner, rapped discreetly and entered.

"Miss Kingston—" he began, and Greyson's heart sank. "Miss Kingston wishes you to know that the meet this morning is at nine o'clock. The first draw will be at the Traitor's Tree—that's beyond the Wild King's Loaning, sir. Shall I have your man come up now?"

Captain Greyson scratched his head and numbly began to change. So it was not the bullet. But why not? Forgiveness? Heaping coals of fire on the sinner's head? He poured some whiskey into the tea and gulped it down. The inner warmth helped his body—but not his comprehension. He would never understand women, he thought, never.

And as they rode out after breakfast that morning, Margaret on a lively bay and Greyson on a rangy black, both from the colonel's stables, with two grooms on spare mounts behind them, Margaret herself was wondering about her attitude and intentions.

A *nice* young lady, she was thinking, would certainly have run sobbing to her mother when she returned from the ball. A nice young lady would have seen to it that Captain Greyson was drummed from the castle with the utmost expedition, never to be allowed within its gray portals again.

Could it possibly be, she wondered with an inner excitement, that she was not altogether a nice young lady? It was an amazing thought, a wonderful thought.

And as they cantered across a field of pasture with the dew still caught in rainbows across the cobwebs on the grass, she allowed herself to smile—just a little distantly—at the cavalryman.

"Scent should be good this morning, don't you think, Tommy?" she asked.

He agreed fervently, though knowing quite well that there was too much wind for the scent to lie. They would be lucky to see a fox, let alone kill one.

As the hunt jostled into the yard of Grogan's inn and the temporary waiters rushed out with trays of drinks, he kept close to the girl, studying her, wondering, hoping.

And when they moved off he continued to keep close, despite the pressing attentions of some others of the young sprigs. The usual crowd was in the street of Kilcroom to see the hunt go by, for this was color, this was life, this was the Gentry. Out along the country roads there would be laborers and message boys and farmers neglecting their duties to head a fox, halloo—or simply watch the hurrying pageant pass. Not many of them would be hoping for an Englishman to fall and break his neck.

Even without looking, Margaret could sense Greyson's presence. When she swerved, he swerved; when she slowed, he too slowed. It gave her a wonderful feeling of power. Not a boy, not a young sprig, not an almost-brother, but a man . . . a man who desired her with an almost insane passion. This was better than any of her novels.

And in the coach—that had been proof of the passion. In the novels there were men like that. Now there was a real man.

But she hoped Terence McKeon, the schoolmaster, had not recognized her. He would know the carriage—but many people rode in Kingston carriages. Surely he could not have seen her face?

As the hounds suddenly bugled the message of the find, she wondered about McKeon. Maybe it would be better to have him transferred where he could not gossip. A word perhaps to His Majesty's deputy lieutenant of the County of Cork that Mr. McKeon was a Sinn Feiner should have him shifted all right. Not that she knew or even suspected he was a Sinn Feiner. Nevertheless, it might be better to have him removed. She would think about it . . . later.

Meanwhile there was the swift thrill of the hunt, the hoarse cry of the master's horn—and the perturbed shadow of Captain Thomas Greyson always about her.

For his part, Captain Greyson was enjoying a feeling of tremendous relief. There was still hope. . . . And yet, before breakfast, all had been despair.

Now, with a hot breakfast inside him, a few generous stirrup cups warming his bloodstream and Margaret Kingston's strange acceptance of the events of the night before, the future looked less bleak.

13. *Trade and the Flag*

"Fine feathers do not invariably make fine birds, my dear," John Pritchard told his wife somewhat sourly. "The birds at any rate owe no one for their plumage."

Mrs. Pritchard had been perusing the photographs of recent balls and hunts, exclaiming over the hats and gowns, admiring even some of the men's clothes.

"Oh, fie, John, never tell me that these gentlefolk do not pay for their finery!"

She spoke in a railing tone, but she knew, for Pritchard confided in her his business problems, how long he had to wait for payment from some of his wealthiest customers. She suspected also that the same accounts would be well padded in compensation.

"Don't pay! Some of them have never even heard of the custom," he grumbled. "I can tell you, if some of those ladies there in their finery were reduced to what they had paid for there would be little enough chance of the photographs ever being printed."

Mrs. Pritchard was not quite sure whether or not to laugh. Propriety said no. But the idea of a host of naked lords and ladies had delicious possibilities. It was a day for being broadminded.

She laughed and was rewarded by a faintly impish grin from her husband.

"They would be rather chilly, wouldn't they?" she asked.

"Above and below," he assented. "And there might be

some very curious shapes among them when deprived of their corsetry!"

"John!" she cried in delighted protest, for the mores of Victoria still clung to the city. Corsets might be sold, might be advertised to the public even, but they were not mentioned.

She looked at the portraits with a fresh eye, seeing the elderly women without their fashionable accouterments, the older ones sagging, the younger ones skinny. She laughed again. But behind her laughter she wondered just how business matters were with John. Recently he had been not actually stingy but certainly careful. Really they needed another girl in the house, and it would be no more than the neighbors had. But John did not see the necessity. How many of these aristocratic families owed him money?

"I see that cousin of yours has been making a fool of himself again," he said suddenly from the pages of the *Irish Times*.

"Basil?" she asked, knowing that he could only mean Basil Crookshank, the Belfast solicitor. "What—what has—"

"Politics this time," Pritchard grunted. "Inflammatory speeches—'Home Rule Is Rome Rule' . . . 'Ulster Must Be Free of Popery.' What sort of fools does he think we are down here? He's aping that Carson fellow."

"But in the North they do see it a little differently," she pointed out diffidently. "They're nearly all Protestants there, and in the South it's the other way round."

"What of it? There's no reason why an Irish parliament should have any clerical domination of any hue. The Church is not interested in politics. Why, the Roman Catholic hierarchy is solidly behind the British Crown and always has been. Do you know they excommunicate these Fenian fellows, the violent ones at any rate?"

He glowered at his paper.

"If the Liberals get their Home Rule Bill through, which they will, you can expect to see some changes for the better

here. Some of our fancy friends who fail to pay their bills
might find life not quite so easy in the future. And an Irish
parliament will know how to deal with the rabble-rousers
and all the private armies too."

He gave a sudden outraged snort.

"Really, you'd think a Northerner would have more sense!
This fellow Connolly and his socialism! How does he suppose
the trade of the country would be carried on? Who'd run
things if Jack and Paddy and Mick and Sean were all as good
as their masters?"

He huffed and puffed a little more before he finished his
luncheon and returned to the shop.

As he reached its broad, elegant frontage he contrasted it
with another establishment he owned, a mean, ramshackle
warehouse which stank of ancient rags. It looked like nothing,
but in terms of clear profit it was of a good deal more use to
him than the store—or at any rate than the store was with so
many thousands of pounds' worth of what were virtually bad
debts.

Rags and scrap, he thought, the unwanted detritus of a
wealthy society. Yet there could be more profit in them than
in this store with its assistants aping the rich even to their
clothes.

There was still more space available in two further sheds
beside his own, and he decided to take a lease on them.

His own office in the store was on the top floor, beside the
linens and household furnishings. As he settled into his seat
behind a broad, untidy mahogany desk, another memory of
the magazine his wife had been reading returned.

One of the guests at the ball at Ballyfastin had been a girl
called Kingston, Margaret Kingston. He remembered the
name—which was more than his wife had done, he thought—
from Clorinda's letters. Margaret Kingston of Kilcroom. Clorinda's friend. In a year or two without a doubt Clorinda her-

self would be featuring in those photographs on the glossy pages. The swell of pride he felt was not diminished at all by his opinions of those nonpaying aristocrats. Clorinda would outshine them all.

14. The After-Breakfast Time

Revolutions should always start after breakfast. This was the theory of Ivor Churchill Guest, the Baron Wimborne and viceroy of Ireland. Exactly how he had formed this theory was not known—perhaps it came from the idea that troops fought best when their bellies were full or that an early start would mean having more of the day to fight in.

At any rate, when 10:30 A.M. had passed on Easter Monday he was satisfied that there was going to be no revolt—and this despite the warning rushed to him by the district inspector of the Royal Irish Constabulary at Tralee, where Sergeant Daniel Bailey, of Casement's Irish Brigade, was freely talking of what was afoot.

Dan Bailey was one of the unlucky trio who had been landed from a German submarine. Like Sir Roger Casement, he walked more or less straight into captivity, and his warning could easily have stultified the whole Rising . . . if it had been heeded.

But the fateful hour, as Wimborne thought, had passed. His earlier urgent demands on Sir Matthew Nathan, the under-secretary, to reinforce the Dublin Castle and Vice-Regal Lodge guards were not pressed. Nothing was done, even when reports began to come in of damage to railways and telephone lines far out in the country.

Nor were the military any more alert. The officer commanding troops in Dublin was absent from his office when the Rising began, and his deputy was convinced that if anything was going to happen it would have come on Saturday, when the captured Casement was taken swiftly through the city.

No special precautions were taken, and the normal pickets of a hundred men from each of the Dublin units—four in all—were not augmented.

There were then in Dublin some two thousand British troops—eight hundred of the Sixth Cavalry, three hundred of the Third Royal Irish Regiment, six hundred of the Third Royal Irish Rifles and four hundred of the Tenth Royal Dublin Fusiliers. As well, there were about a hundred and twenty officers. They were scattered over four barracks, and a high proportion of officers and men were on short leave—for Fairyhouse Races.

The rebel forces on the morning of the Rising numbered somewhere between seven hundred and fourteen hundred, an accurate figure being impossible to reach since paper work and nominal rolls were not favorite rebel occupations.

Certainly the rebels were vastly outnumbered, even at the start of the operation, and had the intelligence and police reports been accepted at their true value the Rising could have lasted for hours only instead of days. Perhaps if the arrest of the leaders sought on Good Friday had been carried out as Wimborne wished, the Rising might never have taken place.

But as too often elsewhere and in other times, vacillation at the top was to bring chaos and disaster. The men in green were to have this confusion in their favor in their brief bid for freedom.

In Hanlon's snug the poet McMahon was declaiming as usual.

"Now I said to Willy Yeats, listen. It's not suitable, it's not apt, it's not poetic to associate with such scions of the aristocracy as your ladyship of the Gregory persuasion. Ask yourself, I told him, what contribution the Anglo-Irish have ever made to the true heritage of Irish culture, to the vital cause of Irish freedom . . . give's another ball o' malt there, man at the bar. Now, what was I saying . . ."

"What's the real truth about Oscar Wilde?" someone diverted him. "You knew him, didn't you? Before he went to England."

"Wilde! Oscar!"

McMahon was a tall man with very long hair and deeply sunk eyes. His eyeteeth were long and yellow and showed each time he spoke, though his incisors were hidden by the center of his lips. He seemed to have but these two eyeteeth in his head.

"Of course I knew Oscar. Oscar Fingall O'Flahertie Wills Wilde. Sure I knew him well—though not as well as your Marquis of Queensbury's son, eh? Nothing like that about McMahon. Nothing. McMahon is an Irish poet and uncorrupted by your dirty English habits. Where's me ball o' malt, man of the bar? Where's me drink?"

There was no response from the barman, for McMahon's slate had already passed the point of no return.

"Wilde, Shaw, Synge, Yeats—sure I know them all."

"Swift and Goldsmith too," someone muttered. The aside went unheard.

"Anyway, as I was saying, I told Willy Yeats he should be like me, writing for Ireland's glory. You heard my new anthem, didn't you? 'March of the Men of Ireland.' Here's a line or two—"

A bookmaker in the corner who liked to be associated with culture signaled to the barman, and a glass of whiskey was placed by the poet's hand.

"You took your time," he growled ungraciously and then began to declaim:

The Men That God Made Mad

Where shall the Saxon hide his head,
Where will the English run?
When the streets of Dublin all run red
And the march to freedom is begun?

What will we care for London's power?
Or why the cannon's muzzle dread?
Oh, see how the fronts of battle lour—

The door of the snug burst open violently.

"It's started!" a voice cried. "They've started the Rising. They've took the G.P.O. already and we've men in the castle as well and—"

The poet McMahon was not a man to miss opportunity. As his companions gathered about the news bringer he reached out a skeletal arm to as many drinks as he could seize and began to pour them back.

"Freedom's hour," he hiccuped to himself. It was a good rhyme for "power" and "lour."

At Trinity College a motley collection of Fellows, university servants and undergraduates were arming themselves from the magazine and taking up positions on the roof or in the upper rooms to defend the university against the rebels.

In the magnificent room over the front gate an elderly Fellow snoozed in a deep leather armchair with his finger on the trigger of a Lee-Enfield rifle. His presence was less lethal than it seemed. No one had explained to him the necessity for ammunition in a firearm.

On the roof a divinity student crouched behind a rifle and greeted his relief with heartfelt thanks.

"I didn't think I could last out."

"What's wrong then? Where are the rebels?"

"It's not the rebels. I'm bursting for the lavatory—"

*   *   *

Philomena Doherty was plying her trade at her usual place, a two-roomed flat two streets away from the Union. A pert little twenty-year-old, she had been on the streets since she was fifteen. She would have been astounded to know that anyone felt concern, pity or any other emotion for her. She considered she was lucky. Her mother worked a twelve-hour day six days a week, picking rags for a shilling a day. Philomena often made three pounds a day.

Mostly her clients were British soldiers. She preferred sergeants, they having more money, but would settle for corporals. She never aspired to officers and was too expensive for privates.

There was a Staffordshire corporal in the overfurnished waiting room and a sergeant in her bed.

She was urging him on to greater speed.

"It's not I don't like you. It's just it's coming near the busy time. . . . Ah, come on, me fine boul' man . . ."

The sergeant was reaching for his trousers when the outer door was thrust open and three Irish Volunteers darted in, rifles at the ready. One ran to the window and the others covered the bemused corporal.

"Any more of yiz in here?"

The answer came from Philomena Doherty as the window shattered. A little tornado of rage, she whirled from the bedroom as the Volunteer at the window thumped out the last of the glass from the frame with his rifle butt.

She wore only an unfastened dressing gown, which flapped open as she glared at the intruders.

"What the bloody hell are yiz at? Jazuzchrisalmighty, yiz've broke me window. The landlord'll put me out. It's always been a quiet house, this. Get the hell 'n' blazes outa here."

All this poured from her in one furious breath while the oldest Volunteer tried to stem her speech.

"Be quiet. Be quiet, woman! Think shame to yourself parading there. Don't you know the Republic's been declared?"

"Republic, me ancient Irish arse. Get out of here, the lot of yiz, and let a girl get on with her work."

"We can't do that. The commandant said we was to take up positions here, and we're obeying orders."

He glared at the English corporal.

"Furthermore, he's our prisoner, and if you've any more English about you may as well hand them over. Jasus, woman, do you not know there's a Rising on?"

Philomena smiled suddenly and pushed closer to him.

"There's only one kind of rising interests me, me fine strong man. Would you come through a minute to the room?"

She shrieked with laughter as he blushed deeply, being a quiet country boy who had never seen a naked woman before. The other two tittered.

"Have you another man through there? I'm taking a look."

"I thought you'd come to me room."

She giggled as they went into the now empty bedroom—for the sergeant had gone through the second door and into the corridor at the first sounds from the waiting room.

She barred the way as he came out.

"Aisy now. Am I doing no trade with you at all?"

The Volunteer struggled past her, eyes terrified. She laughed longer than before.

"Jasus, but you'll make a quare hand of it with the English if you can't manage a bit of a girl—"

Her gaze went to the English corporal. "What about him?"

"He's our prisoner."

"And he's my client. I've took his money. Are you going to have him say he was cheated by an Irish girl?"

The two younger Volunteers were almost helpless with laughter as they urged the other to let the corporal go through.

And at last they had their way. But fear of instant death

had taken from the English soldier any possibility of exercising the desire that had been so strong in him a little while before.

Philomena's lip twitched in a smile as she showed him the other door and he slipped out quietly.

"I doubt I'd be no more good to you than you would to me," she whispered as he went.

She threw herself onto the bed and lay there waiting, a malicious smile on her chubby lips, until the knocks on the inner door, the cries of "Isn't he finished yet?" reached a crescendo. She was a girl who had always felt a sort of loyalty to her clients. And both the English soldiers were regulars.

At last the door burst open and the shocked Volunteers gazed at the girl on the broad, soft bed with her legs suggestively apart.

"Where is he?" they demanded, hot-faced.

"I always knew it would happen one day," she answered dreamily. "One of them would go too far and lose himself entirely."

Her screaming laughter drove them from the room, and they were greatly relieved when the first column of British khaki came in sight and they could open fire at last.

The priest was an elderly man, and his clothes were shabby and stained even before he came through the gap in the wall into the waxworks.

"I am not allowed to say whether what you are doing is good or evil, my sons," he said mildly. "But it is certainly dangerous, and it may be that some of you will die soon. Therefore, if there are any who would have me hear their confessions . . ."

The Church was maintaining its usual policy of noninvolvement. At this stage, indeed, the weight of the Catholic hierarchy had been thrown against the rebels, for in every country the Church pursued its policy of rendering unto Caesar that which is Caesar's, of maintaining the status quo.

On the other hand, among the rebels were souls in need, and ministering to those souls was not a task from which the Church could draw back.

A little line of Kilcroom men formed, and in the strange confessional of a replica of an Eastern palanquin, the priest heard their confessions.

All save one.

Peadar Casey stood at his post at the barricaded window, glowering sometimes at his comrades, scowling at the priest.

He was remembering little Liam's death, remembering that the same priest who had buried the child so swiftly had gone on then to dinner at the castle, where the Protestant Kingstons had always allowed him to hold a service for their Catholic servants.

He was remembering too that the Church had still sought its petty contributions from his widowed mother; the rich were always more popular in that church than the poor.

It was a long, long time since he had bowed his knee to a priest, and he was not going to start now.

"And you, my son?" the priest asked.

"I've no call for priests!" Casey snapped. "And never will have."

He could sense the shock in the others as he turned back to the window. But he did not heed it. In the new Ireland there would be no need for priests and churches. When they were free from poverty they would be free too from the superstition of religion.

Declan O'Donovan turned a shocked face in his direction. At a time like this, Declan was thinking, it profited a man to show respect for the Church. Though in the past, he admitted ruefully, there had been times when he had shown scant respect himself.

15. The Legend

If women had been a mystery to Captain Greyson, they had been an open book to Declan O'Donovan—physically, at any rate. He could not remember the time when he had not known all there was to be known about girls, physically at least. So far as their minds and their emotions went, he did not care.

The Tannery Fennel was no place for the physically reticent. It was no place at all for any human being that had the wit to get elsewhere.

At one end was the tannery itself, a ramshackle building in whose vats and pits the hides soaked and stank. From it a stream ran down the middle of the Fennel, a ditch which carried off the effluent from the tannery and also the seepage from the privies at the head of the winding lane which was the Fennel.

They were dry privies, of course, and they were emptied once or twice a year when they grew so full that a buttock could not sit on them without being fouled. Then some of the men of the Fennel, nagged to it by their women, would borrow a handcart and dig out the offending area and cart off the spoil to Go-Go Gogarty, who ran a market garden which supplied vegetables to the gentry and to the city of Cork.

It was only the adults who used the privies. The young, girls and boys alike, used the stream. Each morning the little row of shining bottoms was a familiar sight by the side of the stream as they relieved themselves in their various ways and commented on one anothers' feces.

It was a sight that always distressed Father Roche when his duties brought him that way. The Fennel was as low as anyone could sink in Kilcroom and not be a tinker or a tramp. Six shillings a week was a man's wages in the tannery, and the food they ate was stirabout and potatoes with sometimes a pint of milk and, rarely, some butter. For a treat there were "scrapings," and these were exactly what they sounded—the scrapings of meat that still adhered to the fresh hides that came into the tannery.

A penny a pound the scrapings cost, and the penny was the perks of Mike Mulcahy, charge hand at the tannery. If the hides were coming from a careless butcher, he might make as much as five shillings in the week from the scrapings. And when the hides came fresh enough and had not been gathered up over the week the scrapings made a wholesome enough addition to the diet. In any case, it was about the only meat a Fennel person was liable to taste except for a poached rabbit or a hare.

The tiny tumbledown cottages lined the Fennel on each side, rubble-built, sometimes lime-washed and with thatched roofs from which the grass was often growing.

Visitors would pass along Kilcroom's upper streets and look down on the Fennel and exclaim, "How charming!" or, "How picturesque!" But if they ever got close enough to smell the stink of the place they would hurry off with their hankies to their noses.

It was, in brief, a disgrace to humanity, and there were many places like it—not only in Ireland.

Only one good thing could be said for the Fennel. At the lower end, beyond the Croom River that its ditch polluted, were open fields and all the green and pleasant countryside.

Yet perhaps also it was to its credit that here all the mysteries of life were laid bare, pathetically bare. No child who had, morning after morning, seen the bare posteriors of sister, brother, cousin and unrelated children of either sex would have any morbid interest in the actual details of the sexual apparatus.

Nor the purpose either.

When Declan O'Donovan was about eight, his mother having then gone to her work at Murphy's farm, Stacia Connolly from next door came to beg shelter from the rain.

"Me Ma told me to get out," she said.

"Why was that?"

"Me Da's up her," she said. "They didn't want me watching."

Declan was an only son, unique in that terrible place, and his mother was also a widow. Therefore this was something new to him.

"What do you mean?"

"Ach, you know. . . . Making babbies."

Of this he had heard, but being a wholly natural function it was not much discussed in the Fennel. He felt a sudden urge to watch. And it was not difficult.

The cottages had a common, irregular roof, and the dividing walls did not quite reach the thatch. It was simple enough to climb up the wooden dresser and hoist himself to the undressed wood of the rafters.

He hesitated for a moment and looked down at the girl, who was seated before the fire.

"Are you coming too?" he asked.

Stacia shook her head in disdain. "I've seen them," she answered curtly and stretched her hands to the tiny glow from the smored turf fire.

Declan clambered up onto the dividing wall and peered down, watching with the detached curiosity of a bird in a branch. In the shadows he was unseen.

Thoughtfully he clambered to the floor again.

"I wondered," he said. "I often wondered. That's the way? I wondered."

He felt for the first time a stirring that was to become over-familiar in later life.

"Could we make babbies, Stacia?" he asked, with the bluntness that was also to be familiar later.

Her little mouth twisted in disdain.

"You don't know much, right enough. Sure, you can't make babbies till there's hair on it."

She lifted her skirt to show him. The children of the poor rarely wore underclothes until puberty was reached and often enough not then, for such things cost money and a bare bottom was better than an empty belly.

"All the same, we could try," he suggested.

They had just begun to experiment when Stacia's mother called for the girl to go to MacSwiney's shebeen for twopence-worth of porter and the experiment was discontinued.

Declan was, in fact, eleven before he took these particular experiments any further. Fishing was more interesting to him, or snaring rabbits in a field or throwing stones at passing coaches on the main Cork Road, or listening to the speeches of the Sinn Fein at the market cross or singing in Father Roche's choir—the only boy from the Fennel to have this honor. At that he had to go to the parochial house an hour before Mass and be washed clean of the pervading Fennel stink and equipped with a clean, fresh suit—relative to his ordinary clothes at least—for to appear *au naturel* would have meant a choir of one.

Before Declan O'Donovan turned to the serious business of sex he had left the Fennel and was living with his mother at the timberyard manager's house, for the manager, a Mr. Mc-Gregor from Inverness, was single and needed a housekeeper.

Now Declan was at school and had been for two years, racing through four standards in that time, for he had a facile brain that mopped up knowledge and he was only two standards behind Terence McKeon, the acknowledged genius, who was due to start at the North Monastery in Cork next term.

At eleven he was prowling the lane behind Murphy's farm, for he had seen a hen in the hedge there a day before and from its behavior he had known it was laying. He knew where he would get fourpence a dozen for the eggs and no questions asked—or tales told to his mother, either. It was not Declan's way to bring home any little gains he made.

He had just marked down the nest from the cover of a hazel clump when faint footsteps approached him through the trees.

"Stacia!" he exclaimed.

There was a bundle of sticks in the girl's arms, and she dropped them as she heard his voice, startled and turning toward him.

"Sacred heart! It's yourself, Declan. You had me scared. Oul' Murphy said he'd tan the arse off me if he caught me next his trees again."

Stacia Connolly was about two years older than Declan, though not so tall—for already he had begun to sprout upward—and her breasts bulged against the thin cloth of her faded dress that was ragged and patched and reached not much below her knees. Like most of the Fennel ones she was barefooted, and it was to the boots on Declan's feet that her eyes went first. Slowly her gaze rose up the coarse tweed of his suit and the rough flannel shirt.

"Bejasus, now it's yourself is the grand one become. They'd never know you in the Fennel."

Declan smiled and felt an instant's shyness at being so grand while she stayed so ragged. Then he jerked a shoulder casually and said: "This oul' thing? Sure I've three more better suits than this at home."

Stacia had pale, slightly watery eyes and mousy hair, and the eyes widened at this revelation of wealth.

Then for a little while they talked of the past and who was dead and who was in the barracks and who had gone to the soldiers. Her mouth was still small and well shaped, though her skin had that grayness that once Declan had thought the natural color of skin but now knew to be merely dirt.

The girl stooped to gather her sticks, and as she picked them up a twig caught her dress and pulled it high. She stood for a moment like that, exposed to his gaze, and he felt an uncontrollable excitement stir within him. His tongue grew thick in his mouth, and the girl began to flush as he stared on at her.

"There's hair on it now," he said hoarsely.

Afterward, when she had gone, he collected his nest of eggs and found that of the dozen four were rotten. He threw them against a tree trunk, enjoying the crunch of the shells and the stench of hydrogen sulfide that came from the mess.

That was how Stacia Connolly smelled, he thought suddenly. That was the smell of the Fennel. God, he wouldn't like to be back in that again.

His next girl did not come until he was thirteen, when a dark down had already begun to appear on his cheeks and upper lip and his voice without breaking had changed to the baritone that was to stay with him forever.

This girl was in his class at school—from which Terence McKeon had now gone, first to the North Monastery, then to college to become a teacher. Teresa O'Riordan was a chubby redhead with bad breath which came from her father's owning a sweetshop in which she had the run of her teeth.

Sometimes Teresa used to pass little notes to the dark, hand-

some giant in the front desk, and eventually the evening came
when she returned to the school for books she had left behind
—and whether she meant to or not only she could have told;
certainly she knew it was his duty as monitor to tidy up after
old Mr. Fitzgerald, the teacher, had gone.

They stood in the shadows for a moment, eyeing each other.
Then, without a word, Declan reached for her. He kissed her
fiercely, not minding especially that her breath was bad. Her
lips at least were sweet with the stickiness of Peggy's Leg
candy that she had been crunching.

Without premeditation he kissed her and pushed her back
against the nearest desk. Without further preliminaries or the
tenderness he was to learn later, he jerked at her skirt and
began at the elastic of the knee-length bloomers beneath.

"Stop it!" she gasped, trying to thrust him away. "Stop it,
Declan! I'll tell, I'll tell!"

But his hand searched onward and his mouth pressed down
on hers, and into his mind a lesson seeped as her struggles les-
sened.

They did not always mean no when they said no.

"I wonder what's to become of you, Declan. I just wonder."

There was no heat in his mother's voice as she gazed at him.
Literally, she did wonder.

"Going with girls at fourteen. Thrown out of the school
for hitting the teacher and being drunk . . . I doubt you'll
not have your troubles to seek. Or those that go with you."

"I'll manage," he said sulkily.

"I've no doubt you will." Mrs. O'Donovan sighed. "You'll
manage. It'll be all for Declan. That's how you'll manage. . . .
Well, tomorrow you can see how you manage carrying gro-
ceries for Donal Shannon. I got Mr. McGregor to speak him
a word and he's taking you on."

This was all that was ever said in their home about the

matter. In Kilcroom it was otherwise. This was the beginning of the Declan O'Donovan legend.

"Come in roaring drunk after putting half the girls in the school up the spout," they would say. "Roaring drunk and bate the b'jasus out the master, put him in hospital. Oh, he's a boy, Declan, a right boyo that one."

And of course the legend was based on some degree of fact. It was true that Teresa O'Riordan was pregnant. It was true also that others of the girls were less innocent than they had been.

But as far as Teresa was concerned, Declan was not necessarily the parent. Very soon he had sickened of her bad breath and with a casual generosity had mentioned her availability to some of his classmates. Teresa had taken a taste for the game as well, and as little Emily Blackwood mentioned in bated breath in the seclusion of the girls' lavatory: "Her drawers is more often off than on."

It was Emily, a narrow-eyed, tight-lipped damsel who came from a Protestant family that had "turned"—a rarity in Ireland—and was therefore full of all the enthusiasm of the convert, who revealed the truth in confession to Father Roche which was, about the same time, being revealed to Teresa O'Riordan's parents by their doctor.

Declan had known instinctively that morning when he saw the parish priest striding sternly toward the school that trouble had come to roost.

Mr. McGregor had always kept a well-stocked cupboard which Declan had sampled surreptitiously before. Now he put a whiskey bottle to his head and gulped a good quarter of it down before he hitched his school satchel defiantly to his back and strode off to meet what might befall.

His mother found the cupboard open and noted the drop in the level of a bottle that had been half full the night before.

Like his father, she thought. *Like that poor, daft, traveling fool.*

For Declan's father had, in fact, been a member of a traveling troupe of actors who had stayed a few nights in Kilcroom and had sired this wild child without the benefit of any marriage ceremony. It was after that that she had gone to the Fennel, disowned by her family in the best Victorian tradition, for the O'Donovans were a respected farming family from a town three miles farther west on the Cork road.

Like father like son, she thought, and added in fairness— *and like mother too.*

The Fennel had been a kind of purgatory in which she had purged her earlier state.

In Kilcroom at least she was now accepted as a respectable woman, though she had still not spoken again to her father or her mother. Sometimes she saw them on market day. Neither looked at the other or tried to speak. She felt no guilt about the past, for she had paid dearly for a few hours of pleasure and folly—and the pleasure had not been all that much, either.

Now Declan was drinking and in trouble, she thought, and what was to become of him?

"Is it true," Father Roche was asking, "what I hear about you, Declan O'Donovan?"

He had gray eyes in a tired, gray face. He had a bad heart and knew that at any moment he could be called to Judgment. Sometimes he hoped that moment would not be too long delayed. His labors in this particular vineyard were not easy.

"It would depend"—the boy smiled back easily and thought how brilliant he was—"what you hear about me."

Mr. Fitzgerald's thin cheeks flamed.

"Don't you dare speak to Father Roche like that! Have you no respect, boy?"

He was a thin, small man with a bald head, and his clothes

were permeated with chalk from the blackboard. Declan
looked at him with the contempt of the whiskey blazing
through his frame. Who was this scrawny old cockerel to
talk to him? He could take him up in one hand and set him on
his desk.

"You know perfectly well what I mean, Declan," said
Father Roche—wishing now that he had made this interview
a private one. "I have heard that you have misbehaved yourself with some of the girls."

"With some of the girls?" Declan echoed, and then thought
of another brilliant stroke of wit. "Oh, you're wrong there,
Father. I'm sorry, but with all respect you're wrong."

A little light of hope glowed for an instant in the priest's
heart. For he had wished much from this lad, with all his gifts
and unrealized brilliance. Could the girl perhaps have been
mistaken? He had heard lies before in the confessional.

"Then . . . it's not true?"

"Not with some of them, Father . . . with nearly *all* of
them."

A great gusty bellow of the laughter which was to ring
about Kilcroom burst from his throat as he looked at the
shocked face of the priest and the scandalized face of the
teacher. He turned and pointed to the awed, shocked, horrified
and delighted faces of the class.

"Her . . . and her . . . and her," he chortled, lying and
knowing he lied, and enjoying the depth of the shock on the
men's faces. "There's hardly a one in the school I haven't had
down."

Father Roche's eyes flickered for a moment to the beetroot
faces of the girls, and he knew a terrible sense of failure. He
had taught, cajoled, preached and prayed—and now this.

At his heart there came a sudden stab of pain. His hand went
to his breast and he rocked a little on his feet. The gesture

sank through even to Declan, and he reached out a hand to steady the parish priest.

Mr. Fitzgerald misinterpreted the gesture.

"God almighty! You'd strike a priest!"

He leaped forward, and Declan's drunken intention changed. He would put the wee cockalorum on his desk after all. He would sit him up on the high desk and let them all see the strength of Declan O'Donovan.

And again his hand stretched out swiftly. But instead of seizing the man's coat his fist crashed into his jaw.

The teacher slumped to the floor with his head sprawled back against the desk and his mouth gaping wide. A little trickle of blood ran down his chin.

With a desperate effort that reached out for calm and found it despite everything, Father Roche pointed to the door.

"I think you'd better go home, Declan. I'll see you later."

Then he stooped to attend the teacher.

Declan hesitated only a moment, then turned for the door. He swaggered to it and paused there an instant, winking broadly at the class.

"Then," as he would say when telling of it later, "I walked out into freedom. You could say that it was the end of me first rebellion. . . . Hey there, Pat, is that yourself? Bring us the same again and keep the lousy froth out of it this time."

16. Glory, Glory, Hellelujah!

While chaos and consternation reigned in Dublin Castle and contradictory orders snapped and crackled over such of the telephone lines as had not been cut, the fighting was beginning to spread out and intensify.

At the Rialto Gate of the South Dublin Union, a British assault was led by a veteran of Gallipoli, Lieutenant Ramsay of the Third Royal Irish Regiment.

Rebels who had established themselves in corrugated iron sheds intended to house male lunatics found themselves under a crossfire from Lieutenant Ramsay's men and from the other side of the canal, where another British force had established itself.

The thin metal of the sheeting was no protection at all, and in no time the shed was as perforated as a piece of zinc ventilation sheeting. The rebels' morale was not helped by the presence of the patients, many of them screaming at the noise and the unexpected break in their normal routine.

"Jasus, we're in the right place all right," a sour-faced Kerry Volunteer observed. "In among the loonies. Glory, glory, hellelujah—and I mean *hellelujah*."

Irish patriot blood began to stain the rough floor.

And at the Rialto Gate, Lieutenant Ramsay led a charge through a small side door. Fire from the sheds brought him down with a wound in the head from which he was soon to die.

"Let them get their wounded," Commandant Kent called,

and there was a brief lull in which the British troops took back the bodies of those who had fallen.

Lieutenant Ramsay's company commander, Captain Warrington, led the next charge through the narrow entrance. But the concentrated fire in the narrow passage was too much for the regular soldiers. Warrington, too, fell, and again the khaki-clad figures took back their wounded.

The Republic was holding its ground in this sector at least.

But not for long. Pressure on the main gate was increasing, and though the Irishmen picked off some of the British as they scaled the ten-foot wall, the gate itself gave way at last under the pounding assault of the troops outside. They swept in and fanned out into the open.

At the Rialto Gate the little detachment which had held on so determinedly was doomed to be cut off between two bodies. Soon they were forced into surrender.

Yet they had served their purpose. They had delayed the British advance. There would be no advance to the center of the city from that direction this day.

Down on Sackville Street the part of the Rising that brought more pleasure to more people had begun. The looting had started.

Dublin had perhaps the finest main street in Europe, perhaps in the world. But behind the glorious Georgian façades festered slums that could have marched shoulder to shoulder in degradation with anything anywhere on earth. Within good spitting distance of the broad and glorious highway rotted a primal decay, and out of this decay there flew suddenly the bluebottles from the maggots of the past.

In Sackville Street the great plate glass windows shattered and an endless tide of shawlie women and their children and, to a smaller extent, their men clawed at the rich goods of an age that had already ceased to exist.

It was fantasy then, pure fantasy. Paris of the barricades all over again.

Aged, moldered hags clawed their way into great windows and caparisoned themselves in the fashions of the day, hoisting silken knickers up their swollen, varicose legs, trying on broad floral Ascot hats, wolfing handfuls of Carlsbad plums or crystallized fruits or whatever chocolate or other delicacy might be on view, grabbing and stealing and destroying all within their sight.

Girls ran out of Dunn's, the hatters, wearing two and three silk toppers on their heads for the few moments it took for other girls to knock them off.

From the Saxone shop great squads of women emerged with armfuls of shoes or boots. And it made no matter that all these boots or all these shoes might be for one foot only. On the pavement a swift bourse was set up where a left could become a right and a size five be a seven and a half in three instants.

Pubs and bars were the first targets. Crates of Moët et Chandon, Mumm and Veuve Clicquot mounted on the pavement to be broken and demolished by the next wave of the women and children who surged out from the darkness of a life that was less than life.

Now they would live, now for one gorgeous, drunken, incredible hour before the police took over again and it was back to bare feet and torn seats of trousers. This was the time.

There was no talk of the Rising among the women in the street, no talk of a war, only a dazed and incredulous realization that for a few moments they had their pick of the world's bounty.

Steal and eat and drink—and as quick as you like before the miracle ends and the old, sad, grim reality returns.

Frenetic crones with brandy bottles to their mouths; young wives who had never felt silk between their fingers before, now handling it and wearing it; the shocked faces of the respectable who still thronged the street, disapproving, frightened, helpless.

Sackville Street, Easter, 1916.

And in the G.P.O. the weary helplessness of men who knew events were overtaking them.

"Fire a volley over their heads," Connolly ordered.

Looting was wrong, wrong for Ireland, wrong for the newborn Republic, wrong even for the poor besotted looters themselves.

James Connolly's heart was twisted in two. This had to be stopped for the Republic's sake. Yet these were the very people for whom the Republic was formed.

The volley was fired and the looters dispersed—and the looters returned. They knew. The Republic was for them. And the Republic was not going to kill them.

Noblett's and Clery's, all the great shops, were swiftly, wastefully, unsystematically gutted.

It was a strange, sad saturnalia of the slums.

"It's disgusting," said Tomeen Brennan, gazing out into Henry Street, where the looters surged back and forward in an orgy of ownership.

"Away to hell," chuckled Declan O'Donovan. "Sure them oul' dolls is having the time of their lives. They've never seen anything like it. Look at that one there! Sure I'll bet she never had knickers over it at all in her life, let alone silk ones. Isn't it doing them good, giving them a bit of a treat?"

"Yes, I suppose you're right. Yes." Tomeen could never really argue with his hero, however he might be scandalized within. He laughed in a forced way: "Look at her with the hat. Isn't she a scream, doing the Duchess down Henry Street!"

The next best thing to joining in a riot is watching one.

The Kilcroom detachment observed the scene outside with amusement, sympathy—and that just subdued unease.

"My God, but they'll be for it when the peelers come," someone said. "The Bridewell will be full this night."

"Peelers," Declan roared. "Have a titter of wit, man! The peelers will have more sense than show their nobs this day."

He broke into song:

> *Oh, Mary, this Dublin's a wonderful sight,*
> *The place is in ruins, the peelers took fright.*
> *There's sights in this city that never were seen*
> *Since the boys from Kilcroom set up the boul' green.*
> *Oh, there's dancing and dolling and looting the shops*
> *And sure who gives a shite for the law or the cops?*

Almost as he ended his impromptu song, Declan's voice harshened and Tomeen beside him saw the massive frame tauten and the muscles cord abruptly on Declan O'Donovan's neck.

"The bastard!" he roared aloud. "I might have knew that bastard would be here. When the sewers clog, the rats come out."

A flat cart drawn by a donkey had swung around the far corner of the street and halted. A shabby figure led the already laden wagon, and another, taller man strode at its side.

"I'll buy it!" cried a voice. "I'll buy it! Bring it here. I'll buy it."

"The gombeen-man," O'Donovan growled, his hair seeming to rise bristling on his neck. "The bastard McCarthy. We might have known he'd be here—"

He reached for his rifle and was starting to take aim when Terence McKeon's fingers gripped his arms and forced the barrel upward.

"We're not fighting civilians," McKeon said. "Not even gombeen-men."

"Men! It would take a dozen of that one to make one man." Declan lowered his rifle, and the congestion gradually left his cheeks. But a lingering ire still lighted his eyes as he glowered toward the huckster in the street haggling with the women for their finery, for the shoes and cakes and bottles of scent and everything else they were willing to sell.

On the flat cart the mound of goods grew steadily, and beside it stood on guard the craggy, battered, infinitely threatening figure of Big Teague, who may have had a Christian name but had never revealed it. Big Teague had always minded for McCarthy as long as Declan could remember. Big Teague was McCarthy's creature, and with the help of God Declan would kill him very soon. After, of course, dealing with the gombeen-man itself. But for Terence McKeon the moment would be now. It could not be long deferred.

Of all his mother's family, only one still maintained any contact with her after her disgrace, after she had gone to the Fennel.

Auntie Nancy was in fact his mother's aunt though Declan called her aunt also. She was a plump, shortsighted, half-deaf woman with a little farm of land of her own which she let in conacre—that is to say, annually for an auctioned rental. She kept chickens and geese also and a breeding sow.

She lived comfortably in a cottage with a slated roof up a lane off the Cork-Bandon road. She had never married, and perhaps because of this was less censorious than the rest of the family over her niece's lapse.

At any rate, she often came to visit the O'Donovans in the Fennel, bringing food with her and leaving money behind. When Declan was old enough to visit her by himself he always found a welcome, a hot cake and a glass of milk, a penny or even twopence to put in his pocket when he went home, a hug and a kiss and a regretful glance when he was not looking.

He often thought Auntie Nancy would have liked to have him stay there all the time. He thought that if she was not afraid of her brothers and sisters, or at any rate a little in awe of them, she would have done that. But she never did.

What hold the gombeen-man had on his aunt he never knew. Somehow she was in his debt, and no one once in Raymond McCarthy's debt ever left it.

Declan fancied it had something to do with the big chiming clock in the front room. Maybe the gombeen-man had sold it to her. Or she might have borrowed the money to buy it.

Sometimes McCarthy was there when Declan called, and when he was, there was never a penny for the boy as he left.

Declan was fourteen when he came to the cottage and found his aunt in tears and Raymond McCarthy shouting threats and abuse at her.

"You're like all the rest—you want to cut a dash and be big and grand, but when it comes to your lawful debts—"

"Leave my Auntie alone!" Declan rushed forward very impulsively, touched by the tears streaming down the helpless, usually happy face of his aunt.

"Get out of it, you brat—"

Declan, proud and strong in his youth, was grabbing at the gombeen-man when he was himself seized from behind.

He was lifted from his feet and turned slowly, helpless for all his frantic struggles, in the huge, implacable hands of Big Teague, a witless man-mountain of infinite strength, slow-witted but totally obedient to the creature who kept him, the gombeen-man who had recently hired him.

"Leave me down!" Declan roared. "Leave me down or I'll kick the shit out of you."

146

"Leave the boy alone," pleaded Auntie Nancy weakly. "Please, leave him alone. . . ."

The gombeen-man came close, peering at Declan as if he were shortsighted. He had something of the inhuman curiosity of a bird about him, a carrion-eater.

"Here's a brash young sprig, Teague," he said. "Here's a pretty cockerel crowing on his dunghill."

Teague was silent. Declan was spluttering with fury, almost in tears at his own helplessness in the grip of the man. Impulsively he spat, and for a frightened instant afterward saw a slow line of spittle run down the gombeen-man's cheek. Terrifyingly McCarthy did not show anger. He backed off a foot or two and stared implacably at Declan O'Donovan.

"You're a cheeky brat too . . . and there's only one thing for a cheeky brat. Smack his bottom, Teague. He acts like a cheeky kid, so give him the cheeky kid's medicine. Give his arse a good tanning."

This memory Declan almost expunged, but part of it remained with him forever. It was not the stinging pain of the huge flat hand that he remembered, but the humiliation, the sense of utter helplessness as Big Teague bent him across his knee, pulled down his trousers and began to beat.

He would have killed then had he been able. He would have killed the gombeen-man and he would have killed Big Teague. Maybe he would even have killed his aunt for being a witness to his humiliation. If it had been a stand-up fight he would not have cared even when Big Teague pounded him into bruised insensibility.

But this—to be made a child again, to have his vaunting strength useless to him. To be helpless. . . .

Long after the others had gone into the cottage he lay where the big man had thrown him. No doubt his aunt managed somehow to satisfy the gombeen-man. Declan O'Donovan never knew. He never returned to the cottage, never saw his aunt again. To see her was to remember.

Thenceforth, also, he avoided the gombeen-man and his aide. Even when he was the mighty Declan who could beat anyone in the county, anyone in Munster, he avoided those two.

Even when he had no more reason to fear Big Teague's strength, he still feared, somewhere deep within him, the tongue and the memory of the gombeen-man. That is, Declan did not consciously avoid the gombeen-man and yet the underlying directives of his character always saw to it that his and McCarthy's paths never crossed, just as a dog will always walk another way rather than encounter one which has drubbed it.

It was that part of his mind which obeyed Terence McKeon and was grateful to him for his interdiction.

Margaret Kingston had heard Clorinda Pritchard's call and had recognized the voice. Indeed no one else had ever called her Maggy. At school she had tried to break the younger girl of using the nickname, but there was a teasing, mischievous streak in Clorinda Pritchard. Without being actually sadistic she enjoyed vexing.

Margaret could imagine her at home, teasing her father, indulged by him, adored by him for her elfin beauty, for the unexpectedness of her birth long after her sisters.

Margaret knew the voice and felt an instant's pang of memory as she almost ran along the half-empty street toward the G.P.O. A part of her wanted to turn, go back to Clorinda, back into the safe comfort of the past, evade the conflict and the bloodshed lying ahead. Yet she ran on. She had to change still, get into her volunteer nurse's uniform. At last she would put to some use the nursing training which had been no more than a hobby so far.

Yet the past called violently to her.

It had been natural for Clorinda to cling to Margaret. They were aliens in a strange land.

In the English school they still called Margaret "Paddy." There were girls who thought it the height of wit to call her "Irish Stew," to ask how the pig was, to make all the time-honored jokes which rasped the more since few of the other girls could boast a comparable home or background. They were middle-class city girls, stockbrokers' daughters, bankers' daughters, merchants' daughters. They had no land, no lineage. At home, Margaret consoled herself often, they would simply not have been received.

Just the same, they constituted the majority in the school, and if she had not revealed talents for hockey, netball, riding —and writing maliciously witty little verses about the teachers —she would have had some very lean years.

When Clorinda came to the school it was natural for her to turn to her fellow Anglo-Irish girl.

It was as natural for Margaret to assume a protective pose. A younger sister (or brother) was something that Margaret had longed for consciously at home, for there was no denying that life in Kilcroom was lonely. She had her pony, her dogs, her occasional random pets from the wild—a badger, a hedgehog, a fox cub. She wanted people though, a companion. And of course in Kilcroom there were no suitable children. In Kilcroom even Clorinda Pritchard would not have been suitable. Here it was different. Here at the school they were linked by nationality, by something at least of a common background.

And by Anne Scott-Baxter.

Anne was a particularly acrid Irish-baiter, a florid, fat girl with buckteeth who emitted a faint spray of spittle with every sibilant and despite this exerted a great influence in the fifth and sixth forms. She possessed a forceful character, was one of nature's chairmen.

"Look," Margaret heard the voices from the dormitory. "Green knickers. I ask you, green knickers! Imagine anyone having the effrontery to come here wearing green knickers. Does Miss Pincheon know you're wearing green knickers? Search her case and see if she's got her pig with her."

A moment later there was a titter of laughter.

"Leave it!" wailed the youngster's voice. "It's mine."

"And it looks as if it had come out of a coal mine. Pfui! What filth! Burn it. Someone light a fire and burn it. It's bound to be full of germs."

There was a wail of despair as Margaret entered to see the young girl clutching desperately for the golliwog doll held high out of her reach by Anne Scott-Baxter.

Plainly the golliwog was Clorinda's dearest possession, a legacy from early childhood, a comforter for the dark and the loneliness of a foreign land, a foreign way of life.

"Leave her alone," Margaret called. "Give her back her doll."

Anne Scott-Baxter turned and saw Margaret at the door.

"This place gets more and more like a peat bog every day," she sizzled like a soda siphon. "I'm sure if my Pater knew the sort of girls—"

She turned as she spoke and with a glint of glee in her protuberant eyes threw the golliwog into the grate where some papers were already burning.

Margaret jumped forward and grabbed at the girl's wrist.

"Get it out!" she ordered.

A moment later they were struggling on the dusty floor of the dormitory, face to face, bodies writhing, pressing, thrumming against each other in an atavistic explosion.

Margaret's fingers twined deep into the English girl's hair,

150

tugged viciously. Anne Scott-Baxter responded with a raking slash of fingernails that just missed the eyes.

And all the others gathered in an excited, frightened mob about the pair, shrilling encouragement, stirred beyond measure by this explosion of violence.

The English girl had brothers, and wrestling was not unknown to her. But she was fat and slow. Margaret had only the advantage of a supple athlete's body.

The struggle thrashed back and forward across the floor, and twice Anne seemed about to pin Margaret down. Each time the Irish girl contrived a wriggle that set her free. Her own anger was mounting all the time, heightened by a loathing of the English girl's sour body odor, by the spray of spittle that greeted her each time they were face to face.

They rolled apart for an instant, and then as Anne lunged forward Margaret struck most scientifically yet instinctively with a balled-up fist which took the other girl full in the pit of the stomach. Breathless, mouth opening and shutting like a goldfish in a bowl, Anne Scott-Baxter crouched on the floor, helpless.

For an instant Margaret was about to strike again. But someone shouted a warning: "Here comes Baggy!"

And along the corridor sounded the heavy tread of Miss Bagshott, the two-hundred-pound house mistress.

With miraculous speed the floor was cleared. Someone dragged the still-wheezing Anne off to the lavatory.

Clorinda was cuddling her golliwog, pulled from the fire by herself. Wide-eyed, she stared at the other Irish girl.

"Someone's been lighting a fire," Miss Bagshott said disapprovingly. Her round nose sniffed the smoky evidence, but her myopic eyes failed to see anything unusual.

"Just some old papers, Miss Bagshott," Margaret explained.

"Just so, just so."

The heavy footsteps receded along the corridor.

"You mustn't let them worry you," Margaret advised the new girl. "Now, where are you from?"

She did not notice the adoration shining from Clorinda's eyes.

But later, asleep in her own study, she heard a faint sound which wakened her with memories of the fight and a suspicion of revenge on the part of Anne Scott-Baxter.

"I'm lonely," whimpered a soft voice.

Clorinda Pritchard crept into the study, and later as she lay in Margaret's arms, as she was to do often in the future, the girl from Kilcroom felt a strange conflict of tenderness and anger rise in her, a conflict in which other and less admissible emotions were gradually to blend.

It was recollection rather than the need for immediate haste which now prevented Margaret Kingston from pausing at Clorinda Pritchard's shouted greeting. Recollection from schooldays, recollection.

As she hurried onward on her mission, Margaret Kingston's mind was a confusion of memory.

"Ah, God bless ye, missus, you'll be to save our brave sons," the fat woman said to Margaret Kingston. "God bless the kindly heart of you. . . . Have a drink."

And Margaret Kingston, fresh and clean in her volunteer nurse's uniform with a tricolor brassard twisted on one arm, halted in a strange dismay. A vast, gray-haired virago with her shawl fallen back on her shoulders brandished a bottle of Veuve Clicquot at her, the champagne still foaming from its neck. Beyond her two others were struggling over the owner-ship of a set of pink silk petticoats. The delicate material ripped suddenly, and each was left gazing stupidly at a half of the garment.

"Never mind!" shouted one. "Sure there's plenty more. There's plenty more." And they plunged together into the rugby scrum of the shop behind them.

"Up the Republic!" hiccuped the virago. "Go on then, take a drink to our brave boys in green. Sure it cost me nothing anyway."

There was nothing Margaret Kingston felt like less than drinking. But argument would waste time—and probably be useless anyway. She took the bottle and with a quick "Slainte" put it to her lips.

"Thank you," she breathed. "Now I've got to hurry. There's work to be done."

Only after she had moved on did it occur to her that she had never drunk unchilled champagne before. If she had been asked she might have said no one *could* drink it uncooled. It was one of the multitude of things that just were not done.

Beside Nelson's Pillar a horse lay dead in the middle of the street, and Margaret felt a surge of pity, horror and indignation.

Killing horses, the savages! she thought. *The brutes.*

It was only as she hurried on that she remembered it was her adopted people who had killed the horse, that now she was on the other side, no longer of the horse riders but of the horse killers herself.

And for a terrifying instant of clarity she saw on what a crumbling foundation she stood. For what had she, of the Anglo-Irish Protestant ascendancy, in common with those ragged viragoes? Or the sweating peasantry fumbling with the unfamiliar mechanisms of their rifles? Or all the bumbling, inefficient host that was challenging so feebly the might of England's Crown?

Her place was back in the bar of the Gresham, or the Shelbourne, with the officers on leave, with the women of her own kind who would even now still be gazing down on the park as they had been when she left, pointing and laughing at the untrained, unskilled efforts of Commandant Mallin and his men to place themselves in defensive readiness.

"Bloody fools," an infantry major had commented at the

window. "They're wide open to enfilade from above here. They should have taken the hotel before they went near the park."

Without more interest he had turned away from another drink, to retire again to the corner where he had sat since coming in. He had seen more men killed in France than were in action in the whole of this city, and an apathy had held him in its grip from the moment his leave began. If he thought again about the rising outside it was to dismiss it as the bungling work of amateurs. Yet his own father had died in an earlier rising.

That was where she belonged, Margaret thought as rifle fire stuttered from somewhere to the south and the first smoke rose from the City Hall—in a gay, charming, civilized bar with all the rough edges of uncomfortable reality polished away and the conversation about the things she knew, about horses, hunting, balls, about the viceroy's latest whims and who had lost how much at the races.

The races! At this very moment they should be leading the winner of the last race at Fairyhouse, and all her friends would be bustling to collect their winnings or wryly tearing up their tickets with well-worn jokes about "visits to Uncle's" and "walking home."

And yet here she was in Sackville Street with a rebel brassard on her arm and the determination somehow to make her way into the G.P.O.

From the rear of the great, elegant building came a brief burst of machine gun fire, and her heart jumped painfully.

For she had been told the dispositions they would probably have. The Kilcroom detachment would defend part of the rear.

Kilcroom. . . . Declan. . . . Maybe he was dead already.

There were more old scores than those against the British to be paid off now.

Jack Hagan, chafing at inactivity in a position covering Mallin's men in the College of Surgeons, saw his wife going toward Sackville Street. She was not alone, and the man with her was as young as she was, which was a good deal younger than Jack.

He was a tight-faced, mean man, Hagan, and somewhere in his heart he knew that this meanness of his was probably driving his wife away. Consciously, though, he had only one feeling when he saw the two together, and that feeling was hate.

When a British machine gun opened up from the Shelbourne, he pressed his own trigger, saw the man fall, and as his wife stooped, fired again.

The Rising was long over when his wife was discharged at last from hospital, and he learned that the man he had killed was his cousin Sean from Mayo and the two had been off to church to pray for him.

The looting had worried Commandant General Connolly from the start. Several parties had gone out and fired shots over the heads of the crazed crowd as they surged out from the smashed windows with their booty.

At first the volleys had dispersed the looters. But like crows on a cornfield they soon learned that the noise hurt no one.

There would have to be sterner measures.

"Shoot our own people!" Peadar Casey cried when McKeon passed on the orders. "My God, McKeon, you're not serious! Sure that's no way to free a people, by killing them."

"The sooner it's put down, the better," McKeon answered. "If the people get out of hand the whole city will be destroyed."

"Isn't that what we're here for?" Casey cried. "Aren't we here to cast off the chains of oppression and throw aside the subjugation of the working classes?"

"Working classes, Peadar? Your head's astray," Declan put

in then. "Sure most of those ones out there looting never did a day's work in their lives—or wanted to. Take a look at them—"

"I'll not turn my gun against the poor," Casey insisted stubbornly. "Let them enjoy themselves for once. Isn't it English property they're taking?"

McKeon's face was troubled. Just how he should deal with this crisis was beyond him. He could understand Casey and even sympathize with him. But on the other hand the orders were plain. The street had to be cleared. The looting had to stop.

And as usual it was Declan who resolved the situation.

"Suppose, Captain, I was to take a stroll out there meself with maybe one or two of the boys? I have a notion there wouldn't be too much call for shooting."

Casey glowered at him.

"Oh, you'd be the one all right," he scowled. "You and your fancy friends. You don't want their stuff destroyed."

"Have some bloody sense, you eejit! Sure I know no more English than you do. And those I know don't have any property in Sackville Street."

He walked over and scowled down on Casey.

"Furthermore, you omadhaun, if it's Miss Kingston you're putting the evil word on, just say so, bad cess to you, and I'll have the tongue from your throat."

"That's enough!" McKeon broke in sharply. "We've got fighting enough ahead of us with the English. . . . All right, Declan. Take three men and see what you can do."

Tomeen Brennan was one of the three, and afterward it was he who told the others what had happened.

"They were at Clery's when we went out, a whole horde of them, shawlie women and ragpickers, and all the hooks and crooks you'd ever want to see.

"There was two oul' biddies fighting over a pair of drawers, and Declan, he walked betwixt them and he grabbed the drawers out their hands and he just tore them down the middle.

" 'There y'are,' he toul' them. 'There's fair. A half each. You'll can have half your bum warm anyway.' Then he gives them both a kiss . . . which is more than I'd have done, I can tell you.

"Then there comes along a young fellah drawin' a handcart piled high with enough to start a shop.

" 'Oh, you're the greedy one,' Declan tells him. 'The rest are content with what they can carry, but you have to do it the big way.'

"Then he tips up the cart and there's a great oul' scramble for what fell, and the boul' Declan is roaring and laughing at them.

" 'You're as greedy as pigs at a trough,' he tells them. 'And with just about as much wit. Don't you know the police will be searching every house in the city this night?'

"Then up come a couple of big fellahs. 'Who're you calling pigs?' they say. 'Anyone that acts like one,' says he.

"So they went for him, went for him hard, the two of them. Well, I need hardly tell a Kilcroom man what happened then. Oh, it was a joy to see the way he dusted the street with them.

"It was a wonder right enough. In no time at all he had the whole damn crowd eating out his hand. I tell you, he stopped the whole damn riot in less time than a hungry man would eat a length of drisheen. And then he starts to sing to them and damned if he hasn't them all with him this minute, meek and mild the lot of them, as if they were all on the way to Mass."

But Declan's intervention lasted only as long as his presence.

By the time he returned to his post the looting had begun again.

157

17. A Sudden Sweetness

Long engagements were, of course, the custom, even when the clouds of war were growing darker.

When Captain Greyson returned to the Hussars no date had even been fixed for the wedding. Mrs. Kingston was not the kind of woman to make decisions on her own account, and though Margaret could certainly have driven her into one —for she had some skill now in the manipulation of people— she did not try.

She was enjoying life very well as it was. As an engaged girl she had a greater degree of freedom than before—though in truth she had led a very reasonably free life to that time—and she had a host of experiences to go through before she finally went to the altar at St. Finn Barre's Cathedral. Perhaps even then she had some reservations about marriage to Greyson. Certainly on his leaves she contrived to keep him at a baffling distance.

Occasionally she might grant him a kiss, a discreet, unpassionate kiss. But there was no repetition of the night in the carriage in the Wild King's Loaning.

Nor could Captain Greyson afford to press the pace. His credit had been restored by the announcement of his engagement. But to break off the engagement or have it broken would mean an instant flood of writs from every quarter. He could only fume uneasily and hope nothing would happen— and enjoy himself in other quarters.

The real answer, he thought coldly, would have been to get the girl in the family way. That would have solved all his problems. But whenever he did try to arouse her he failed with a miserable completeness that nagged at his own self-assurance and sent him out to restore it elsewhere.

Margaret herself marveled at her own skilled assurance in dealing with him. She sensed his uncertainty, and though she did not know how much he was depending on her fortune she realized her power over him. And, maliciously, enjoyed it.

She could not of course know what went on in his mind when she flouted him, thwarted him, mocked him in a school-girlish way, sent him on petty errands or kept him waiting endlessly for her. Nor could she know what sweet revenges he promised himself when the marriage was consummated, or the humiliation that he, in turn, planned for her. She only knew that it was rather fun.

And when he pressed for a marriage date she would only answer: "But we couldn't possibly get married until Papa comes home."

When Papa came home he was strangely changed. No word of what had happened in India was ever brought back to Kilcroom. All that was known was that the colonel had resigned his commission—and had professed the Buddhist faith.

Mrs. Kingston had kept the normal life of the castle going in the colonel's absence, which is to say that from time to time she gave languid orders for a ball or rout which would be organized entirely by Atkin the butler, and which she rarely attended in person.

When the colonel returned, all that ended. For one thing Mrs. Kingston did not wish anyone to see her husband now, shaven-headed, saffron-robed, pattering around the house in sandals or bare feet and spending most of his time in the library, which was also a Buddhist temple, dominated by a life-size statue of the Gautama set where the light of dawn could strike on its calm bronze features.

The scent of incense would drift out from the library and down the long corridors, and sometimes the chanting of the colonel's voice could be heard as he recited the endless prayers of his new faith.

It was, of course, an impossible situation, and Mrs. Kingston did the only thing possible for a woman of her breeding. She died.

In the countryside there was a delicious, scandalous hope that the funeral might perhaps be conducted according to the Buddhist rites, which, they rather thought, included a funeral pyre. In a confusion of the Hindu custom of suttee with Buddhism, there was even the rumor that the widower would cast himself into the flames.

In fact, it was a quiet, normal Church of Ireland funeral, which the colonel attended in uniform instead of his robes, only his shaven head marking him out from the other mourners.

Margaret had found herself sorrowing with a surprising vehemence, for before her mother died she had ceased to think of her as a person at all. Now she mourned genuinely—and found ample excuse in her mourning for a further postponement of the nuptials.

And then, of course, there was the war.

In the North the Protestant Ulster Volunteers had been arming, training themselves for a war to stay within the British realm. In the South the Irish Volunteers had been training and arming themselves for a war to remove themselves from the British realm.

When Germany marched into Belgium and Britain declared war, the Northern leader, Sir Edward Carson—who was naturally a Southerner, since this was Ireland—grandly declared that the Ulster Volunteers would join the forces of the Crown.

The Ulster Division was formed and splendidly massacred in France.

No less generous, John Redmond, leader of the Nationalists, avowed full support for the British cause against the common enemy.

The Southern Volunteers, however, were less acceptable to Kitchener—who was of course Anglo-Irish—and were not formed into a division but scattered among other formations.

And there were many in the South who did not at all relish the thought of assisting one tyranny to defeat another. They had nothing against the Germans. But they had plenty against the English.

ENGLAND'S DIFFICULTY IS IRELAND'S OPPORTUNITY was the slogan that began to be whitewashed on the walls.

And a new crop of Volunteers began to drill and train, watched with a certain anxiety by the powers in Dublin Castle, who yet did not strike to crush the budding force since they hoped that their own liberalized policy would meet with a generous response.

And indeed this was so. The new middle class of Ireland, English in manners, customs and outlook, was more sympathetic to England than any previous section of Southern Ireland had ever been. Their sons officered the new British Army, their daughters married British officers. And wasn't home rule on the statute book anyway?

But the new poor of the South were the old poor of the South, and they had no more love for the English than they had ever had. There were Tannery Fennels all over the country, and the slums of Dublin were the worst in Europe. They might send their young men to fight for the English— but it was mainly for the separation money, for the family allowances that kept food in their children's mouths. An unofficial recruiting slogan proclaimed: THE TRENCHES ARE SAFER THAN THE DUBLIN SLUMS.

Thus the Irish Volunteers paraded, the Brotherhood plotted, and all with the covert knowledge of Dublin Castle and its network of spies and informers.

And Sir Roger Casement hastened off to Germany, sure that England's enemy would be glad to have an ally behind England's back.

At first Casement was received well, for he was a man of international stature, a man whose almost single-handed endeavors had stamped out the excesses of King Leopold's Belgian Congo slave state and the massacre of the South American *indios* by the rubber barons.

Vague promises were given. But gradually he became less and less *persona grata* in high places. The earlier suggestions of a landing by German troops in Ireland diminished to promises of arms. And the arms diminished from artillery and machine guns to, eventually, one small shipload of antique rifles.

As usual, Ireland was being betrayed.

But the Irish Volunteers continued to drill. The Citizen Army of James Connolly marched the streets of Dublin with the plough and stars banner flaunted under the unseeing eyes of the Royal Irish Constabulary.

And in quiet places the Brotherhood made their plans.

Margaret Kingston heard the sound of shots and frowned a little, for there was something different about the sound. The soft bark of a shotgun was, of course, familiar to her from childhood. But there was a sharper crack to these shots.

She reined in her horse in the shadow of the oak trees and listened intently. In the distance she could hear shouting.

To her right and before the trees was a bank with the gaping mouth of a badger burrow black in its face. It was the badger set which had halted her, for her skittish pale bay mare had winded the creatures and begun to pantomime a great and terrible fear, rearing, prancing, passaging sideways as if she did not know that badgers were the most harmless of animals.

Margaret had reined the beast in, her intention to make it sniff at the set mouth, to familiarize itself with the scent so that in the future its strangeness would not upset the delicately strung nerves of the thoroughbred. And indeed the mare had settled—until the shots started.

And now she began to prance again. Margaret swayed easily in the saddle, the sense of control springing like a living force down her arms and through her wrists and hands to the reins and the single snaffle bit in the horse's mouth.

The mare, Kathleen she had been named, would take more schooling yet before she was fit for the hunting field. And while by instinct rather than conscious effort Margaret controlled her steed, she was able to see down into the hollow beyond the ridge where she had halted.

From the hedge beyond the hollow, two or three hundred yards away, a little line of khaki-clad figures had appeared. Some were running, and others had rifles to their shoulders. The soldiers were shooting at something she could not see, something that must be in the cover of the wood or running up its edge.

She felt a spurt of indignation.

My land! she thought. *What right have they to shoot on my land?*

And indeed with her father even more of a recluse than before, it *was* her land. Since she had sacked the land agent she had taken over the running of the demesne. It had become more her home now than it had ever been before.

And now the troops were running wild on it, shooting her game.

Her lips closed to a tight, hard line. She would phone their commanding officer in Cork just as soon as she could get back to the castle. She would tell him—

Her anger was not with the troops but with her fiancé, Captain Thomas Greyson—and perhaps with herself. Her engagement was crumbling to an end, and though in honesty she might have thought this a relief, the manner of its crumbling offended her.

For Maire Casey had come to her in tears and confessed to "being in trouble." And the trouble had originated in the loins of Captain Thomas Greyson.

She had not as yet taxed him with his infidelity. For now her mind worked in cool, trained grooves and she was waiting for the moment of utmost advantage. She would dismiss him when the moment suited. But thus far the moment had not suited. And she held him like a restive colt on a lunging rein.

But the khaki figures advancing into the hollow and up the slope were identified in her mind with Captain Greyson. And they had the full benefit of her resentment.

With Maire, she thought. *With my maid*.

And it seemed inexpressibly disgusting.

Her left foot was about to nudge a spur into the mare's silken belly to send her racing down toward the troops when there came a crashing through the oaks and the sound of hoarse, panting breathing.

She swung that way, still mounted, and saw that a man was running through the trees.

A Sinn Feiner! was her first thought.

And her second thought was that she knew this man, that she had seen him before.

For a moment he halted, looking back and then forward to where the distant grind of gears and the chug of an engine indicated other troops. The light shafted down through the trees onto his face, and memory was instantly complete.

Kilcroom. Outside Grogan's pub. A fight with the Royal Irish Constabulary sergeant. A tall, pale figure that was stripped to the waist, standing in a splendid, blood-smeared triumph.

The light from the sun now struck through the trees in the same way the light from the acetylene head lamps of the castle Rolls had then.

The same man.

And afterward Margaret Kingston never knew whether it was for the sake of a memory or to spite by proxy Captain Thomas Greyson that she acted as she did. For as the man halted, drawing great breaths, his eyes searching for an escape route ahead, she called to him.

"Over here—"

For the first time he saw her in the shadows. For an instant he looked as if he would run on. Then he loped toward her, his breath already recovered and something of a smile on a face that was smeared with black boot polish.

"Into the badger's hole!" she ordered swiftly. "Quickly, man, they'll be up the hill in a minute!"

He looked at the hole and then at her.

"I'd sooner die in the open, if your ladyship doesn't mind. I've no liking to die like a rat in a trap—or a fox in its earth."

"Don't be a bloody fool," she ordered. "Get in there!"

"They'll see me for sure," he insisted, yet moving to the dark cavity of the set nonetheless.

"They'll not, I promise you."

She kept her promise. For as soon as the fugitive had backed himself into the dank recess—only just wide enough for his massive body—she seated herself on top of it, spreading her skirts wide across the bank and putting herself into the posture she thought appropriate.

She was seated when a panting, fresh-faced subaltern led a breathless file of soldiers up the field.

"Did you see him, ma'am?" the youth demanded. "Did you see the croppy?"

"What are you doing on my land?" Margaret retorted steelily. "I heard shooting. Don't you know this is private property?"

"It's one of the Sinn Feiners," the British officer insisted. "The blackguards raided our munitions wagon. And one of them was seen coming this way. Now, ma'am, how long have you been here? What are you doing?"

A middle-aged sergeant muttered something in the officer's ear, and he flushed an ever deepening red.

"Oh, I say. I'm sorry. Er . . . about turn, you men."

They marched off in confusion, and Margaret Kingston felt a sudden wild desire to laugh. As Miss Bagshott, of her old school, would have said, she had been acting a lie. And acting a lie was as bad as telling one.

Beneath her, in the shadows of the badger set, Declan O'Donovan shook with silent, appreciative laughter. She was a cool one and no mistake. She'd made the English think she was caught short out there in the country and she had put them to flight with their faces red at the thought that they had offended a lady in the worst possible way.

She was a right one. But why? Why had she done it? Why should the rich, proud, wealthy Miss Kingston, who had every reason to see a poor Sinn Feiner hanged or shot, save one of them, especially one she had never seen before?

The slim, silk-clad legs still screened him from the world, and there was in the set a scent he did not know. With it mingled the old, familiar female odor he knew so well. But there was a richness of strange places in this scent, the richness of money, heady, fascinating and strange.

A temptation came on him to reach out his hand and stroke

166

up along the slim legs, up above the silk of the stockings to where there might be real skin under his hand, to try whether it was as they said, that between a rich woman and a poor one the only difference was wealth.

And yet he held his hand, afraid. Not, that is, afraid of the English soldiers who must now be beyond sight and sound, but afraid of the girl. There were too many years between them, too many years of domination by her kind and subservience by his. He held his hand—and still breathed in hungrily the scents of the woman until he knew that ever afterward he would know her in whatever darkness by her scent alone.

"You can come out now," she said quite calmly as she rose from her equivocal seat and arranged her habit. "They've gone. You're quite safe."

Yet though her voice was calm she felt a wild inner excitement. All the time she had sat above the man she had been conscious of his presence beneath her, something warm and vitally alive that seemed even to cast a glow onto her.

As he wriggled from the set like a creature of the earth he could sense now the excitement in her and knew with a sudden wonder that he could have this woman.

But it was not the time. It was not the time or the place or the occasion. He would not meet her as the poor rebel on the run that she had saved as she might have saved a trapped rabbit or a wounded bird. He would have her when she knew him for what he was, greatly and magnificently he would have her then.

"Thank you, your ladyship," he said with an insolent smile. "May I have the chance to do the same for your ladyship one day."

And though the words were very proper, his way of speaking them brought a new flush to her cheeks.

"I doubt that's very likely. What's your name?" she asked haughtily.

"No names, no hanging parties," he retorted and started off into the trees.

As he went he could feel her gaze on his back, and he strode lightly for all the four miles he had just run across country with the bullets buzzing around his backside like flies at a horse.

Sometimes he skipped and danced as he ran, and the heady knowledge of the woman ran hotly in his veins.

"There'll be an O'Donovan in the big house yet," he promised himself.

Nor did he think then that from the Fennel the big house had always been in sight.

18. Gilligan's Corner

The ambush had, in fact, been Declan's idea.

The meeting had snarled up on the lack of arms and the near-impossibility of getting them.

Certainly Casement was in Germany trying to obtain guns. Certainly large sums had been raised in America—and had not Terence McKeon risked life and limb there in the cause. Certainly there was talk of the arms coming. But the talk had gone on a long time, and there were still only the arms they had begun with, the few old Mausers and Martinis, the shotguns and even the flintlock muskets.

"Anyway," said Sean Daly morosely, "when the arms do come, you don't suppose they'll send us any? It'll be the same as ever. The arms will go to Dublin and the big fellahs. We'll not sniff a bullet down here in Kilcroom."

They were having one of their periodical gloomy meetings in the room above Hanlon's livery stable, a loft really but very suitable in that it had three possible exits, not counting the window which led onto the shallow slope of the roof.

Terence McKeon had picked this room for their headquarters, though previously the section had met in a back room at Grogan's. The loft was, to his mind, more suitable on a host of counts.

For a start, it was far from any source of drink, which meant that the Brothers were liable to conduct their meetings with greater decorum. Also, the champing of the horses below would make it difficult for an eavesdropper to pick up anything that was said. The shadowed lighting, similarly, would make later identification more difficult if any spy did chance to gain a peephole into the place.

The variety of entrances was the most important feature of the loft. The sight of any group of men meeting regularly in any one place would create a pattern. And it was patterns that were detected, not individuals.

They could come singly, from different directions, and no one should be noticed, even by the informers. And in the final event of a raid they had plenty of ways of escape.

Terence McKeon had drifted into the leadership of this group just as he had been elected captain of the Kilcroom detachment of the Volunteers. Perhaps it was due to the glory he had won with his successful fund-raising trip to the United States. Perhaps it was no more than the fact that Terence McKeon alone of them all had had any contact whatsoever with "them others" who planned the rebellion's overall strategy. Whatever the reason, Terence McKeon was the person, plainly, most suited to leadership.

"He works with the head, does Terence," was their view of him. "He works with the head."

He was reason in the midst of unreason, the sobering influence, the planner.

Declan O'Donovan might have seemed, to some, a more suitable leader, with his gift for random oratory, his good-humored, easy command of men's spirits, his admitted daring, his flouting of authority in all its shapes. But Declan himself had refused to lead.

"You've got to work with the head for this job, boys," he had told them. "It's the steady man you want for your officer, and the man who can figure and do the paper work. Sure the only paper I ever use is on me backside."

So with an appreciative gust of laughter from the others he had abdicated from any pretension to power.

And in his heart McKeon knew he himself was best fitted for the job. He knew the facts. He could consider them coldly, decide in the light of facts and not of emotions what was the best course of action to take.

Yet there were times when he wished he was a little more emotional, wished he could pour forth the long, stirring speeches of the politician, the words that would put heart into discouraged men, that would fire them to action.

But he stuck to facts, stuck to what he knew. And told himself this was the better way.

And now he was a worried man. The Volunteers were content enough. For the majority of them it was sufficient to drill, flaunt their flag and occasionally fire off a strictly rationed few practice rounds from their rifles. The majority of the Volunteers had no real wish for actual conflict. It was sufficient for them to act out their weekly charades, to boast and make speeches. For them the Volunteers was another sort of club, another way of niggling at the English, like the Gaelic League or pulling down recruiting posters.

They were being patriotic and enjoying themselves at the same time. And while they professed eagerness to be at the throats of the British Army it did not altogether displease them to find the moment of conflict postponed. This applied especially to the tradespeople among them, those whose shops and businesses were prosperous, who sold expensive goods to the gentry and the British troops. They were willing enough to be heroes and die for Ireland—but not just yet, please.

Terence McKeon knew this, knew his men for what they were. And knowing, he did not despise them for their nature. His reading had indicated that it was always thus, that every band of willing heroes is backed by a multitude who, when the crunch comes, follow in the others' paths.

The French Revolution had, of course, been a particular study of his, and he knew how much it and every other successful rising depended on the hard core of eager fanatics, the extremists who had no rationality, only a blazing belief in their cause. He had that blazing belief himself. But he also had a brain to use.

And this was what disturbed him now. For there had come an edginess into their meetings recently, an air that approached defeatism.

He knew the cause. They needed action. They needed violent and successful action if they were not to lose their greatest asset, their fire.

Carefully he eyed them. Donal Geary, who had fought his way up from the Fennel to be a flesher's assistant, in whom perhaps too much of the blood of animals had nurtured the desire for the blood of people, who had no resources to sustain an inactive spell like this.

Then there was Declan O'Donovan, of course, the boul' Declan who could charm the birds off the trees and get away with murder. Probably he had. But Declan, for all his fiery strength, was as ebullient and reliable as a butterfly.

Then there was Tomeen Brennan, who was there because Declan was there and for no other reason. Yet he was a useful man, too, skilled in his craft, able to make things, able too to slip unnoticed among people, to listen and report. No one suspected a cripple. No one ill-treated a cripple. "Sure to God, hasn't he troubles enough of his own as it is?"

Also McKeon had detected in Tomeen a cold and quiet determination like his own. And the cobbler had perhaps more reason than any of them to hate the English, his game leg being the result of a frolic between two drunken soldiers. An accident . . . but the leg was as bad as if it had been intended.

Then there was Peadar Casey. Old Man Silence, they called him. Casey had the bitterest heart of all of them. And tongue, when he unleashed it.

It was not only the matter of his sister Maire dishonored by the English captain. That could happen between any man and any woman, though his race made it worse. Nor was there cause for him to love the English in his being dismissed from his work at the castle for speaking too freely of his rights. But there was some deeper pulse there, a pulse that made McKeon regard Casey always as the most valuable of his men.

He did not know about little Liam Casey, killed by a horse, or about a mind that equated Englishmen with horsemen. If he had known he would still have thought Casey his best man.

Of the others, two were tenant farmers who had been dispossessed and evicted by Turkson, the former bailiff that Margaret Kingston had dismissed: one was Phelim O'Keefe, the pharmacist's assistant, and one was a red-faced Kerry man, Haggerty, who lived alone in a cottage outside the town and of whom nothing was known save that he was vouched for by the Kerry Brotherhood.

Yet at this moment, different though they all were, all shared the same discontent. All needed action.

And Declan O'Donovan provided the spark for that action.

"There are," he said, "plenty of arms in the country. The only trouble is—it's the wrong ones that have them."

"How do you mean now? How do you mean?" demanded O'Keefe, who had a habit of repeating himself. "Who's got arms? Where would we get arms? Who from?"

"The English, of course," laughed Declan. "Sure aren't their soldiers marching the streets with rifles enough to arm the Volunteers ten times over?"

In his mind was the thought only of waylaying a few troops and wresting their arms from them as had been done before. But Terence McKeon's keen mind saw instantly the possibilities and wondered how he could have neglected them before.

"You're right, of course, Declan," he said slowly. "An ambush . . . the munitions convoy."

The British Army had not yet moved into the mechanical age. There were a few lorries, a few ambulances, a few staff

173

cars chugging their way around the narrow Irish roads. But the vast bulk of the factories' output was going directly to France, where it was more needed. And Ireland was in any case the home of the horse.

Thus it was the sound of hooves that heralded the approach of the convoy to Gilligan's Corner—otherwise known as the Long Road Corner—where the ambush had been laid. One tree was already felled, and when the convoy came to a halt another tree would fall behind it, cutting off escape.

"I could do with a smoke," Declan muttered as he crouched in the ditch. Like the others, he had a handkerchief tied around his face as a mask—or if not a handkerchief in the case of some of them, a piece of rag. They wore their oldest clothes, stained coats and battered hats. Their best friends would not have recognized them.

"Whisht now, Declan," Terence McKeon ordered. "No talking at all till the tree's down."

His hand was on the butt of his pistol, a Peter the Painter Mauser. The Painter was to be a much-favored weapon in Ireland. Apart from its greater availability through the good offices of the Germans, it was a much more versatile weapon than most of the pistols available at that time.

Firing a heavy nine-millimeter bullet at a muzzle velocity of just under a thousand feet per second, it was a good stopper for closer work, and the length of its barrel made it more accurate for long-range shooting than the average revolver. Furthermore, its wooden holster could be clipped to the butt to make a rifle butt stock that gave it an effective aimed range of well over a hundred yards, more than enough for most ambush purposes.

McKeon had no expectation of having to use the pistol in real earnest. When the second tree fell behind the convoy, he expected that the resultant panic would be enough for the attackers to take the British escort without bloodshed.

The convoy was in sight at last, swinging slowly around the bend in the road but not yet in sight of the barrier in front. The escort was a half section of lancers before and behind the two rumbling wagons of the convoy. They were marching at ease, under the command of a bored corporal, smoking, and with their lances housed in the saddle buckets.

On one of the wagons the driver's mate was sleeping against the tilt of the wagon. On the other the driver himself was writing a jerky letter home while the reins lay slack on his knees. The pair of horses, two gleaming blacks with the government brand the only scar on their silken quarters, knew their way as well as he did. He wrote:

> *Dere Mum,*
> *Same as last week. Not nothing happening only when the dog bit the sarn't major going off parade. Talk about a laugh—*

The corporal reined in as he saw the fallen tree. He had been engaged in a long mental soliloquy about what he would say to the corporal major if he just got the chance one dark night behind the cookhouse, and it was some seconds before his mind transferred itself to the present, his hands reined in, and he started to swing to halt the convoy.

Even then he had no suspicion of an ambush. Life had been quiet in County Cork for the last few months, and though the ensign was always going on about keeping on the alert against ambush, no one really expected anything to happen. Besides, there had been a thunderstorm the week before, and the roads all the way to Cork were littered with fallen branches. Terence McKeon had picked his time well.

The wagons were still halting, their drivers reining in and winding on the brakes against the slope, when Peadar Casey and the two farmers threw their weight against the branch

—a long, straight pole of larch they had already lodged deep beneath the roots of the second tree, a tall beech with broad, shallow roots. The roots were cut, and only the leverage of the pole was needed to send the tree tottering.

"One more for luck!" Peadar Casey yelled.

And his voice as they strained was the first warning the convoy had.

The second tree fell so close to the rear guard that the branches stung the horses into a wildly rearing, prancing confusion. And as they neighed their panic, the blacks of the second wagon caught the fear in the air and charged forward. The unready driver, one hand on the brake and the other on the letter to his mother, could not halt them before one of the wagon's wheels was in the ditch at the far side of the road.

The convoy was in utter confusion when McKeon stepped from the ditch, fired one shot in the air and called loudly: "This is a raid. Surrender and no one will be hurt."

"The Sinn Feiners, by cracky!" swore the corporal. For an instant his hand strayed to the butt of his carbine in its saddle holster. Then he thought better of it, and his hands went up. He was, in any case, nearest to the threatening muzzle of the Mauser.

Only the farthest trooper of the advance guard had his wits about him. Even as McKeon appeared he spun his horse on its heels, headed it at the hedge on the far side of the road and went over and through the barrier in good hunting style.

Terence McKeon snapped one quick shot after him and did not know if he had hit or not. The man vanished from sight. And before McKeon could cross the road for another shot he was away through the trees and out of range.

McKeon swung around on the others.

"No one else try anything!" he barked. "We're only after the rifles. We don't want to harm you. Dismount and stand with your hands up."

Behind the rearmost wagon a horse began to scream its agony. The Kilcroom men gaped at Peadar Casey.

"Now what the hell did you do the like of that for?" one demanded.

Casey, eyes glazed a little, wiped the blade of the knife with which he had cut the horse's hamstring.

"One's run," he said. "It'd be better there'd be no more."

The horse's rider, a young trooper, looked indecisively at the Irishman and then at the horse, its leg drawn up and helpless.

"You bastard!" he hissed. "Oh, you Irish bastard!"

For like many of his fellow Englishmen he was fonder of animals than of people.

He brought his hands down and strode grimly to his saddle. He snatched out his carbine even while the farmer who was armed—he had a single-barreled hammer shotgun—cried out to him to stand where he was.

The trooper's only intention was to shoot the horse. The high screaming he could not endure or the blood that dribbled down the maimed leg to the dusty road surface. But to the farmer he was an enemy reaching for a rifle.

The shotgun blasted underneath the horse's belly, and with the surprise of death on his face the trooper fell, clutching at his chest.

And with that shot the ambush turned to battle. The other troopers, convinced they were about to be murdered, grabbed for their rifles and carbines.

The swift, peaceful coup Terence McKeon had planned had turned from the image of war to its reality. His Mauser banged out twice, and the corporal spun, hit in the shoulder. The mate of the leading wagon's driver had his rifle in his hand and fired blindly, bringing Tomeen Brennan down with the blood pouring from his head.

Declan plunged forward, unarmed, and snatched the driver

from his seat, hurling him clean across the road into the ditch. He did not rise again.

Two of the troopers and one of the drivers dived for the ditch at the far side of the road, rifles or carbines in their hands.

McKeon's men in their turn took cover in their own ditch, and a brisk, inaccurate fire began. Tomeen Brennan stirred where he lay on the roadway, and Declan O'Donovan's long arm stretched out to drag him to safety.

The regulars' shooting was a little better than the rebels', and soon three more of McKeon's men were nursing wounds. One of the troopers was dead, but the others were still shooting.

McKeon sized up the situation. Reason indicated that withdrawal, immediate withdrawal into the cover of the trees, was the most sensible course. They could get their wounded away all right—and he did not think the tiny British party would attempt to follow.

But reason told him also that retreat now would mean a probable end of the section. He knew his men. He knew their virtues and he knew their faults. History was against him, the long history of failure in rising after rising. Despite the oaths of the Brotherhood, the men could melt away if this setback became actual defeat.

For this action at least they had to have victory—or what looked like victory.

A charge then? A swift, bloody charge across the road surface, swamping the Englishmen by weight of numbers?

Then he had the answer—and acted on it.

Deep in the ditch he made his way past the root of the fallen tree and then clambered up onto the road. Now he was hidden from the soldiers. Now he could scurry across the road, almost flat on the ground, and from above and behind cover the whole English position.

They were enfiladed, and for an instant he gazed curiously at them as they worked their bolts, bobbed up, fired and bobbed down again. This was the face of the enemy, and he held them in the hollow of his hand.

At this range he could not possibly miss. . . .

And in the ditch behind him Declan O'Donovan was crouched low, gazing in mounting horror at Tomeen Brennan's bloody face.

His hands were quivering, and he glanced quickly up and down the ditch in case anyone should see them shake. Everyone was much too busy. Declan found himself flinching at each explosion, and there was a strange marvel within him. He could not believe that he was afraid and yet he knew that he was. Or he did not consciously know, but his body knew—that strong, vital body that could outfight any other in Kilcroom, that was indestructible, life-loving and life-giving, that did not want to be hurt or to be killed. . . .

One of the troopers had had exactly the same idea as Terence McKeon, but not quite so soon.

In the very instant before McKeon could call out to the troops that he was behind them, that they had to surrender, the trooper rose and for an instant his face was staring into McKeon's, incredulity filling his eyes in the second before reflex action pressed the trigger for McKeon.

There was no change in the expression as the gun slammed off its bullet, but the trooper's mouth opened a little wider and a blue hole was punched abruptly in the forehead. He turned as he fell, and McKeon saw there was scarcely any back left to the head. It was like a turnip that had rotted in the field, a turnip with brains the gray pulp of decay.

"I'm behind you. The rest of you surrender now—sharply!" McKeon ordered, voice calm but incisive.

This time the surrender was complete. The Englishmen,

those who were left, threw down their rifles and were swiftly tied with lengths cut from the horses' reins.

"Now let's get those rifles," McKeon ordered. "We've wasted enough time."

Tomeen Brennan, his own head still bleeding, was stooped over one of the troopers, bandaging his shoulder. The others were standing by the ditch, their faces a little blank, hardly appreciating that it was over.

Then Peadar Casey threw his hat in the air. "We've won, me boys!" he cried. "We've won! Now let's get them rifles and get using them again."

Then the final irony of the ambush hit them as they peered in through the tilts of the wagons.

For weeks this convoy had come regularly at this time, and all the information was that it carried cases of rifles being returned from the armory in Dublin after servicing for the troops in the Cork area.

But not this time.

This time the crates in the rear of the wagons held shells, hundreds of twelve-pound shells for the artillery. Their raid had gained them precisely nothing.

And it was as they made this discovery that in the distance they heard the sound of lorry engines being driven hard and remembered the single trooper who had escaped.

Reinforcements were arriving. They could be in the jaws of a trap.

"Gather up their rifles and carbines," McKeon ordered briskly. "Take the back out with them. I'm going to fire the wagons."

Then there was a frustrating delay while they sought for matches. No one had a match, for none of them now smoked, this being one of the pledges they had made—that the money from their cigarettes and tobacco would go into the unit funds.

It was from one of the trooper's pockets that they got matches at last and started the work of destruction. And by now the lorry sounds were ominously silent.

Declan should have matches, McKeon thought angrily as he touched off a scrap of paper to make a short, uncertain fuse beside an open shell case. Declan was still smoking secretly despite his pledge. He knew that. And come to that—where was Declan?

In the distance, and not a far distance, there was a spatter of shots. The lorries had halted.

"It's Declan!" someone shouted. "My God, would you look? He's gone leading them off on a false trail—"

"Isn't that Declan all over?" another answered. "Wouldn't you just know he'd do the like?"

The sounds of firing faded as the column moved out from the ambush, heading unseen back to their homes, back to their friends, back to safety.

In the wagons one shell case flared into white heat—but went out without communicating its fire to the rest. McKeon and his men still had a lot to learn about demolition work.

But even if they had failed here, McKeon thought, the raid had been a success. They had laid their ambush, they had killed the enemy. They had shot and been shot at. Though he had gained no rifles, and even the shells had not blown up, the raid had been a success.

"Did you ever know a man like Declan?" Tomeen Brennan enthused as they neared Kilcroom. "Going off like that on his own, off to draw the others away from us. There isn't a one like Declan anywhere."

McKeon nodded. But somewhere in his mind he was wondering about Declan O'Donovan, wondering about the way he had slipped off, wondering . . .

Part Two

The bells of Shandon,
They sound so grand on
The pleasant waters of the River Lee.

—Cork ballad

19. On the Town

T HE Victoria Hotel, in Patrick's Street, Cork, was well accustomed to the roistering of the gentry. There was a veteran staff of servants who knew at just what time they should start to put away the more fragile items of furniture, when the outer door should be shut to prevent any excessive reinforcements to the numbers and exactly how much each guest would consider sufficient cash to salve his conscience on the morning after.

There were nights, of course, when the bar was quiet, when there was no cry of: "Throw another peasant on the fire—I'm getting cold," when the accepted sport of shooting the passing waiter with a cork from a champagne bottle would not be indulged.

Indeed, since the war the nights had on the whole been quieter. A gloomily large proportion of the prewar guests were already dead. And many of those who returned from France on leave had a bitter introspection about them that not all the whiskey in Ireland could drown.

Too many of the wartime guests were gentlemen only by the grace of the King's commission, Englishmen or Scotsmen or Welshmen who lacked the money to behave with the careless, openhanded generosity of the old days. Many of them were middle-aged men, and many of them had memories that were not improved by the sudden pop of a champagne bottle.

It was too like many other pops they had been hearing, and for some of them reflex action would take over at the first cork and they would fling themselves flat, to rise sheepishly when they found carpeting instead of mud beneath them. Sheepishly and to laughter.

There were still people, plenty of people, in Cork then who thought fear funny—in other people, at any rate.

But despite all this, despite the alleged rationing and the occasional shortage of the better brands of champagne and spirits, there were still nights in the Victoria that brought back the eager, acquisitive glint to the eyes of the staff and spurred memories of older and still greater nights.

The colonel wanted only to be left alone to expiate whatever sin or experience it was that had brought him home so strangely from India. Occasionally an official letter would arrive which he would throw in the fire without reading. Margaret never asked what was in the letters or conjectured deeply what might be in them.

Perhaps they were summonses to her father to return to the colors. If so, there was never any more direct attempt to recall him to duty. Perhaps the Indian Army had no jurisdiction in Ireland. Perhaps, indeed, they did not want him back.

She was well enough content in her way. Despite the war, life was gay. She was "doing her bit" by attending volunteer nursing classes, though she had no intention at all of going out to some smelly hospital in France and attending soldiers' wounds. She had absolutely no bent toward this work and was honest enough with herself to know that she went to the classes only because there were others going from the big houses.

Occasionally she would complain wryly about the work involved in running the estate—for she had still made no great effort to find someone to replace Turkson—but in fact she thoroughly enjoyed the work, the minutiae of the books and the sense of creative power that came from making decisions and giving orders. Continually she was coming across examples of Turkson's past iniquities—tasks undone, illicit profits, bullying and sheer downright roguery.

Sometimes a party would be called off as a name of a neighbor cropped up in the endless casualty lists of the war, but for the most part Margaret and her friends were not directly affected by the conflict. It was an offstage diversion which could be talked about reasonably, coolly and without involvement.

Of much more interest was the local situation, the talk of imminent rising, the "incidents" in different parts of the country, occasional destruction of a familiar Protestant home by fire in the night, the ever more overt parading of the Volunteers and, in the cities, the Citizen Army.

The convoy ambush of Gilligan's Corner of course proved a fruitful source of discussion, especially as it was represented in the press as a murderous onslaught by a huge force on a tiny group of soldiers—from the reports an impartial reader might have gathered that the unarmed troops of the convoy had been tied up and then treacherously shot—with the craven assailants having been driven off finally by the miraculously timely arrival of the reinforcements in their lorries.

In the nationalist papers an opposite and equally unreal version prevailed, in which some Volunteers peacefully drilling in a field had been violently and viciously attacked by a body of drunken British troops. Defending themselves heroically, they had driven off the oppressors and destroyed their munitions.

To Margaret Kingston, reading the accounts of the ambush, came the uneasy thought that she herself was guilty of some degree of treason in aiding the escape of the man she had concealed in the badger's set. What would happen if he talked? If any of her friends knew she had been helping a rebel? In particular, what would Captain (acting Major) Greyson say?

The newly promoted Major Greyson, by some judicious

manipulation, had become assistant provost marshal of a Cork district. It was a move he had made reluctantly, for there was no credit to be gained in a job like this. He himself had always despised the provost branch—as did most soldiers. There would be no promotion now, no regiment or brigade.

Many of his contemporaries had surged past him on the promotion ladder and were now brigadiers and even major generals. It was galling to meet them on his brief visits to London, to see the red tabs and hatbands, to know that he had been left behind in this race.

He had hope of only one thing—there was plotting and scheming going on in this country, and soon, with luck, it would flare up into the open. If he were to be active enough in its repression, he might yet make some gain.

Meantime he was close to his investment, as he thought of Margaret Kingston, and based in Cork city he had no lack of diversion. Already he had set up a little ring of spies and informers who kept him primed with news of the Sinn Feiners —and anything else he wished to know.

It was a ring that in some ways duplicated the police intelligence network and sometimes ran counter to it. The county inspector of the Royal Irish Constabulary did not care to have this rival organization working in his territory, and the old animosity between civil authority and military authority resulted in several of Major Greyson's informers' being arrested on one charge or another. But his group kept working, nonetheless, and Major Greyson stayed in Cork.

The Ross-Nagle engagement party at Inniscarra had gone off well earlier in the day, and now at least half the guests had come on to the Victoria Hotel to continue with the celebration in a manner less inhibited than old Ross-Nagle would have approved. He was a stuffy old stick whose idea of unparalleled license was a second glass of champagne.

Now the short, comfortable bar was packed with the well-dressed guests bringing a breath of peacetime prosperity to the place. The waiters scurried happily around with well-filled trays, and in the lobby beyond—between the entrance door and the bar door—the porter made ready to reap his rich, rare harvest.

There would be tips for calling carriages, for beckoning cars and their chauffeurs. There would be further tips for sticking plaster and iodine. There would be muttered conferences on injured servants, and money would pass for the soothing of wounded pride.

With any luck at all it would be one hell of a night, and he would get enough out of it to take the five-acre field next to the fifty he already owned in the country beyond Glendale.

The curious ambivalence of the guests was well displayed within the bar as they drank and roistered and broke glass and reputations with equal enjoyment. Cigar butts smoldered on the carpets or in the ashtrays with equal indifference, and already the more delicate of the ladies had headed for home.

Margaret Kingston sat at the far end of the room with Major Greyson. Each exercised a sobering influence on the other. They had come together in the castle Rolls, battered now about the wings because the coachman, Patrick Coughlin, had been transformed to chauffeur and could not restrain his natural tendency to call a peremptory "Whoa there, girl!" before he slammed on the brakes.

The usual constraint was on them, the constraint of those who are bound to each other without any mutual interest whatever. Sipping champagne and watching Rollo Speke-Fitzroy doing his usual party trick of balancing three bottles, one above the other, on his nose, Margaret wondered within herself why she maintained the pretense of the engagement.

She knew in her heart that she was not going to marry this man beside her, who—she now suspected—wanted nothing of her but her money. On the other hand, he had no rivals. There was no one in the whole County Cork who had roused her interest. The young sprigs were too much of her own age, too empty of experience, too much of the same charming but negligible pattern, for her to be drawn to such of them as had not gone to war.

As for the officers on leave, they were too ephemeral for her to remember one from one day to the next. All had the same frenetic gaiety, the snatching at life while it was there, the flavor of death in their kisses. The shrewd core of her being told her that marriage with these, or even dalliance, would be a brief folly followed by a long sorrow.

Really, there was only Tommy. If only there could be something in him, something positive, something— What she sought she did not know. She knew only of its absence. Yet somewhere, surely, there was a man such as she sought? Somewhere . . .

"Oh, no, ye don't!"

The porter stood in Declan O'Donovan's way as he surged through the front doors and across the hall of the hotel.

"This isn't for the likes of you. Away down Old George's Street with you . . . or maybe the quays would be more your mark."

Declan O'Donovan was in fine form. He had, in fact, already been in some of the pubs on Old George's Street. They were middling good pubs at that, and nothing for any man to put his nose up at—which could not be said for the quays, where the pubs and the company were as rough as any man could expect to find in any port.

But into the Victoria Hotel he was determined to go, and he had two reasons. One reason was that Terence McKeon had sent him. Terence had flowered as a military commander in the last few weeks. And in particular he had come to realize the importance of accurate, firsthand information.

There was no place like a bar for garnering information, and he knew of no one better than Declan for holding his drink. Also, Declan was educated up to a point. He would be of more use than almost any of the others on a job like this.

In particular Declan was to watch the assistant provost marshal, search his coat if he got the slightest chance, overhear his conversations. McKeon knew all about Major Greyson's undercover service. One of the Cork Brotherhood was in it. Unfortunately he had not been able to uncover any of the others. Major Greyson kept them carefully apart and met them by appointment.

McKeon's man had even gone to the lengths of following one of Greyson's agents to St. Luke's Church for Holy Communion one Sunday morning. He had sat beside the agent and hoped for an opportunity to go through the man's overcoat pockets when he went up to the altar rails to take Communion. But the agent had not left his coat behind him in the pew, as expected, when he went forward for the Sacraments, so McKeon's man had to leave the church frustrated. Moreover, he had to undergo a severe dressing-down from his parish priest at confession: first, for entering a Protestant church at all, and second, for entering it with felonious intent. He had been rewarded with a whopping penance for his pains.

McKeon hoped for better results from Declan.

It was McKeon's view that if Major Greyson had a list of agents he would keep it on his person. He would not even trust his office staff. There could be a notebook somewhere on him. And Declan could, perhaps, get that notebook. It was a long chance but worth taking. It should cost only the price of Declan's drinking for a night. And the returns could be very high.

Declan, of course, was willing. Especially when he saw her ladyship from the castle go into the hotel with Major Greyson.

Margaret Kingston had been often in his mind since the day she had saved him from the military, or when, as he preferred to put it to himself: I ducked my head beneath her skirts.

The scent of her was still in his mind, alive there and niggling at him, the scent of perfume and woman and badger all mixed with the horse sweat from her skirt. Scent is the great evoker of memory, and when she passed him, not seeing him as he lounged at the hotel door, the scent brought the past to vivid, hungry life.

And now this grubby little gombeen-man of a porter thought he could keep Declan O'Donovan from the bar!

Declan smiled gently, and if he had known his man better, the porter would have blessed himself at that moment. For Declan O'Donovan always smiled before he fought.

"So you'll not be for letting me in, my good man?" he drawled pleasantly. "Is it that I'm not good enough to mingle with the officers and gentlemen—and their ladies?"

The porter smiled derisively, one comprehensive, insulting glance taking in Declan from his heavy-booted feet through his tight, roughly cut suit to his bare, untidily barbered head.

"Would you think so yourself?" he sneered. "Jasus, man, have you no shame or respect in yourself to be staggering in here? Go out that way before I call the police."

Hands in pockets, Declan continued to beam down on the porter, though the hotel servant was no small man either.

"They do tell me there's a law on the matter, that a common inn has no right to turn away a wayfarer, a traveling man. And there is a license on your walls signed by the magistrate, no less, declaring this establishment is an inn and bound thereby to succor the traveler, to give him refreshment when

192

he demands and this at the pain of losing the license. Is that not the law, me gentle little gombeen-man?"

The porter scowled, not at all sure that Declan was wrong. On the licensing laws he was no expert, for never in his time in the hotel had they ever been mentioned before. But he knew a troublemaker when he saw one. And he knew how to deal with him, he thought.

"You'll get refreshment," he growled, "but you'll take it out here. You'll go in no bar. You can have a sandwich and a glass of ale and then you can take yourself off with you and not be coming back."

He grunted an order, and a moment or two later a pert little page came out with a plate containing one sandwich and a thick glass of ale.

"A rich repast," Declan beamed. "Maybe too rich for my blood—and so you'd better have it yourself."

As he spoke he threw the beer in the porter's face and stooped to seize him effortlessly by the waist. In the same move he upended him and thrust him headfirst into a large empty laundry basket beside the reception desk.

For an instant the porter's legs kicked in the air. Then Declan yanked at the cuffs of the trousers and pulled them clean off.

"It's time you turned a new face to society," he observed as he strolled toward the bar door. "And buggered if that isn't a finer one you're showing now than the other."

The gibbering porter, mayhem in mind, had just pulled himself from the basket when a new surge of guests swirled through the door and, when they saw him, began to dance around him in a ring.

"Porter's lost his trousis!" someone sang. "Porter's lost his trousis. Tish-oo, tish-oo, they just fell down. . . ."

By the time the porter had recovered trousers and dignity,

Declan O'Donovan had insinuated himself into the same corner of the bar as Margaret Kingston and had been recognized by her. Now the porter could only withdraw, fuming quietly. He could not interfere now that the intruder had somehow made friends with Miss Kingston.

But he would remember Declan O'Donovan. He would most positively and definitely remember him.

20. Pub Crawl

There was in her father's library an edition of Dante's *Inferno* with illustrations by Gustave Doré, beautifully drawn, accurate and specific illustrations which left nothing to the imagination of prepuberty. Margaret Kingston had taken it down from its shelf often and pored over the illustrations—though ignoring the dreary waste of text.

There was no one to forbid her, not her absent father, or her mother, who was only too glad the girl was doing something quiet and harmless, or the servants, who never even opened the books in the library—though they dusted them quite often.

The book reminded Margaret a little of a cheap book of Catholic martyrs that one of the maids had shown her. In the abstract she had wondered why religion should be so concerned with the infliction on others of extreme pain. And why the depiction of torture should be wrong in a book of pleasure while all right in a religious volume—as she supposed the *Inferno* to be. But mainly she was concerned with the physical depictions, deriving a guilty—why she did not know—and slightly horrified pleasure from them.

Now in a pub near Merchant's Quay, the area known to seamen as Holy Ground, she felt the same sick pleasure as she looked across the smoke-filled room and into the alcoves where everything that should have been concealed was being flaunted openly. Truly, she had not known that places like

this existed. And yet she was glad she was here—with Declan
O'Donovan huge at her side.

The fearful reek of thick, black tobacco smoke, cheap ciga-
rettes, sweat, dirt, fish and raw spirits caught at her throat.
Yet she smiled secretly as she thought of Captain (acting
Major) Thomas Greyson.

There had been a raised eyebrow from Major Greyson
when he returned to her from the lavatory and found her in
conversation with an undoubted peasant. Greyson had no
actual prejudice against the Irish people—against, that is,
those of his own status. He accepted that they were only
slightly inferior, that they were quite good company, almost
witty.

But the roughs were different. Roughs in England were
different, too. Roughs anywhere were another race, people
to be kept in their place. They might make good soldiers
with sufficient training, but that was really all the use of
roughs. They certainly did not come into bars and hob and
nob with gentlefolk.

Gentlemen might, it was true, go slumming into the curious
places of the poor, and indeed this was one of his own secret
pleasures. But this was to be regarded as a mark of condescension. Return visits were not expected—or desired.

"One of my tenants, Tommy," Margaret introduced
Declan. "Major Greyson, Mr. O'Donovan."

Greyson had nodded distantly to Declan's broad smile and
he ignored the outstretched hand.

"Get Mr. O'Donovan a drink, Tommy."

Major Greyson obeyed. "What would you like, O'Donovan?" He was not going to "mister" any hairy-heeled country
oaf.

"Oh, a pint would do me well," Declan answered lightly.

Greyson was about to declare stiffly that in this bar draft
beer was not served when he had a better idea. A few mo-

ments later a foaming pint was in its familiar place at Declan's elbow. By what was almost a reflex action Declan's hand went out and lifted it to his lips.

"Your health, ma'am . . . sir . . ."

As he threw back his head he caught for an instant the glint of a smile in Major Greyson's dour eyes and scented danger.

Then the drink was bubbling and tingling in his mouth, and instead of the bland flatness of draft it was the sharp sting of champagne that met the palate and throat of the wild man of Kilcroom.

Now it is a known fact among drinking men that when the throat is prepared for one sort of drink and another meets it, the result is liable to be disastrous. This Declan had experienced in the past, when cronies had spiked his porter with whiskey or poteen. Without a doubt it was the hope and intention of Major Greyson that Declan O'Donovan would suddenly and violently throw up, disgrace himself, humiliate himself in the sight of Margaret Kingston.

And the knowledge, angry and bitter, brought a violent reaction. There was one precarious instant when he thought he had lost control, when the downward surge of the drink would be converted to a sudden windy eruption. Then the shock was mastered and the rest of the pint of champagne gurgled on downward unimpeded.

That in your eye, yeh Sassenach, he thought triumphantly as he slammed down the pot.

But aloud he said blandly: "Not a bad drop of stuff that, sir. Not bad at all, at all. A bit windy, though."

He belched unashamedly, and Margaret Kingston giggled briefly and then cut herself off. Belching was not yet for the gentry—in public at least.

She had herself only recognized the drink after Declan had started on it and when it was too late to halt him.

"We'll have another." Declan beamed at Major Greyson.

"But none of this windy stuff if you don't mind. . . . Oh, men of the bar there, with your long arm and your strong arm, will you be after pulling us a couple of pints of brandy? You'll take one too, ma'am?"

The last was added with a quick, impudent smile that knew already what the answer would be.

"Thank you, Mr. O'Donovan. No. Not just at the moment. But I'm sure Major Greyson is still thirsty."

Her eyes mocked her fiancé. He had provoked the encounter, her glance said. Now let him fight his own way out of it. And in the back of her mind she remembered the romantic novels of her youth in which strong men fought over beautiful women. She had never heard of them drinking over them. It was something completely new.

Greyson recognized the challenge instantly but did not at once respond. His mind, like a calculating machine, was working out the possibilities. This great ox of a peasant plainly had a vast capacity for drink. Equally plainly he had had a good deal before entering the bar. Already he was a pint of champagne ahead. Therefore the balance was certainly in his—Greyson's—favor. He could humiliate the peasant, drink him off his feet.

More important, he would show Margaret Kingston she could not shoot mocking glances at him.

All this had happened in a very few seconds. The gauntlet had been thrown down. Major Greyson picked it up by nodding brusquely.

"Thank you, O'Donovan. I prefer Remy Martin."

"Hennessey's good enough for me!" Declan roared. "A fine oul' Irish name. Come on then, man of the bar, be after setting up our drinks. Me and me friend here are dry as a baker's bum."

As the two pints with their golden gleam were set on the counter, an intuition of what was happening seemed to pass along the bar. The other guests began to press closer curiously, abandoning their various ploys in the hope of seeing something better.

"I remember a chap in the mess at Amiens drinking a bottle of Scotch straight down," an officer's voice fluted. "He dropped dead a minute or two later."

Declan raised his glass. "Your good health, Major."

He gulped hugely and left little more than half of the pint in the pot as he poured it down.

"Now that's not bad," he announced loudly. "You keep a drop of good stuff here."

The major had acknowledged the salutation with a frigid nod and was doing his best to match the other's speed. But less than a quarter of his drink had gone when he put the glass down.

The spirit was blazing its way down his throat and had lighted a fire in his unfed belly. Declan, on the other hand, had been eating steadily throughout the night, a sandwich here, a pie there. The absorption of the alcohol through his stomach wall was far slower than with the major's.

"You like brandy, Mr. O'Donovan?" Margaret smiled.

"I like everything in life," Declan answered. "I'm a man who's fond of pleasure—of every sort and kind."

She felt herself flushing faintly at the undisguised meaning of his smile. But she did not rebuke him.

The major's mouth hardened, and he forced back another swallow, cursing himself now for ever having embarked on this ludicrous duel. His glass was half empty when he put it down again.

"I'll give six to four the major," someone called raucously and found himself at once inundated with takers.

Declan took one more enjoyable swig from his glass and felt the brandy's fire begin to surge in his veins.

The first few notes of a rebel song burst uncontrollably from his deep chest before he realized that this would hardly be the most discreet place for such music. To his surprise several well-bred voices begged him to go on. Not for the first time the sheer perversity of the natures of the West British aristocracy was to bewilder him again. Only Major Greyson—thankful for the delay offered in his drink, which had by now brought him out in a rich sweat—offered any objection.

"As assistant provost marshal I can scarshly be expect—expected to approve," he muttered. "Really, Margaret!"

He was howled down instantly, especially by a red-faced young captain in trench-stained uniform.

"Provost!" he sneered. "Bloody Redcaps! Coppers! Why don't you join the army?"

Major Greyson seized the instant.

"You'd better give me your name, number and unit," he said coldly.

"Up you!" the young captain snapped inelegantly and started to square off for a punch.

This Declan would have liked to see, but he caught a quick-flashed appeal from Margaret and interposed his bulk between the two.

"Sure you're not drinking, Major," he beamed. "I'm way ahead."

Greyson's lips tightened, and he snatched up his glass and drained it. As the empty glass slammed down on the counter he scowled at the big Irishman, daring him to say more.

But Declan got no chance to say anything, for abruptly beneath the tan of the major's skin a sudden pallor appeared. Frantically he turned and headed for the door.

"Four to one he doesn't get there in time!" roared the betting man.

And this time there were no takers.

"A delicate stomach he'd have, the poor gentleman," Declan boomed, and the delighted laughter that greeted his sally followed the assistant provost marshal from the bar. It was a sound he would never forget and never forgive.

A multitude of pleasant revenges were in his mind as he helplessly retched with his forehead against the cool white sanitary porcelain.

And he would start right away. The man was a Sinn Feiner without a doubt, he thought. He could have him arrested, and when he got back to the bar he would start with a few crisp words to Margaret. It was time for the curb, he thought muzzily. He had ridden her too long on the snaffle. Fortune or no fortune, he was not going to be made a fool of, not by any damn woman.

But when, staggering because despite his vomiting a good deal of the brandy had entered his system, he got back to the bar Margaret Kingston was no longer there. Nor was Declan O'Donovan.

Mocking smiles met him when he asked where his fiancée had gone, mocking smiles and taunting glances. He knew the inner fury of a man who has never been popular when he trips up in public.

It was not an exaggeration to say that in those minutes Major Thomas Greyson actually ground his teeth.

Margaret and Declan were not, in fact, very far away. They were in the Oyster Tavern amid a noisy group of revelers, mostly solid Cork citizenry with a sprinkling of army. In a corner a group of prosperous-looking middle-aged men argued heatedly with two younger men over the fraught question of conscription. A red-faced elderly barman was adjudicating pontifically in the hope that the argument would not come to blows.

Over by the door three very young and perspiring English lieutenants were being engaged in conversation by a trio of painted ladies of the town. While Margaret watched, one of the lieutenants got to his feet and grinned at his companions with a bravura she felt sure he did not feel. He shrugged into his greatcoat, picked up his cap and swayed through the doorway and out into the alley beyond, arm in arm with one of the ladies.

"The North Main Street," she hiccuped loudly. "It's not far—"

Three drinks later Declan O'Donovan and Margaret Kingston moved on to a tour of the pubs of Old George's Street and its tributaries. In the Rob Roy, as he ordered porter for himself and sherry for Margaret, he paused suddenly and began to wheeze with laughter.

"I was just thinking," he declared gustily, "your gallant major will have another shock coming to him when he gets to the bar. I never paid for them two pints of brandy."

They laughed together, drank and moved on, each of them privately marveling at their sudden warm intimacy. Their ways of life were totally alien—he the Fennel boy who had not after all pulled himself so far from the Fennel and she the representative of a long line of landowners.

Perhaps, Margaret thought, as she drank in Clancy's, it was because they were extremes that they were close. For if life is a great circle, the extremes must in fact coincide. Certainly she did not feel for him the faint contempt that was always in her when she met Tommy.

Tommy Greyson was not at the extremes of anything. Fundamentally he was middle-class. And English, of course. That was curious too. She had never thought of the English as a separate entity before. Her own class in Ireland had always equated itself with the English. But when she considered the matter and recalled her own visits to England, the English gentry had always regarded their Anglo-Irish counterparts with a certain amused condescension. The same background they might indeed have—but they were still the "wild Irish."

The abrupt clarity that drink brings on occasions descended on her as she sipped her sherry.

"Do you know, Mr. O'Donovan," she said with a heavy formality, "it occurs to me suddenly that I, too, am Irish."

What she intended to imply was that she and her fellow Anglo-Irish were caught in a limbo between the native Irish whom they ruled and the English who ruled them—that she was realizing suddenly that this limbo was no longer the life she wanted or would maintain.

"What the hell else, ma'am?" Declan agreed, not understanding.

"Mr. O'Donovan," she stated with the heavy sincerity of the almost drunk, "I think I'll be a rebel also."

He stared at her, and for a moment his eyes narrowed suspiciously. Was she trying to trap him into some damaging admission?

"My whole way of life—" she began, and then faltered for words. She sipped at the sherry and put it from her in disgust.

"Get me an Irish drink," she announced with a hiccup. "An Irish drink for an Irish woman."

Declan laughed aloud and clapped her on the shoulder.

"That's my girl!" he cried. "Man of the bar, a pint of porter for the lady!"

For Margaret Kingston rebellion had begun, a rebellion that was to become as complete and a good deal more effective than the Rising in Dublin's city, now not many weeks away.

21. No Place for a Lady

Exactly how or when they had found themselves making their way down Merchant's Quay, Margaret Kingston could not remember.

She and Declan had drunk their way halfway down Old George's Street, through Pembroke into Patrick Street. They made their unsteady way past the Father Mathew statue: Father Mathew, the pious apostle of temperance, standing solidly on his plinth in the middle of the street, a figure of hope to the abstemious, while the consumption of alcohol rose ever higher about him. A prophet without honor in his own city.

Porter and Paddy whiskey had alternated in their glasses as they made their unsteady way. Sometimes Declan would sing, his voice rising above the uproar:

> *I met oul' Napper Tandy and he took me by the hand,*
> *Said he, How's poor oul' Ireland and how does she stand?*
> *She's the most distressful country that ever you have*
> *seen,*
> *For they're hanging men and women for the wearin' o'*
> *the green . . .*

As his powerful voice filled a bar Margaret would sit in a corner, silent and admiring, a little proprietorial, feeling as she did sometimes when she took a prize bull to a cattle show.

No one offered to speak to her, for her clothes marked her out as a lady, and ladies did not enter public bars; therefore she could not be a lady. Therefore she was an oddity, and it behooved a man to be cautious about an oddity.

Also, of course, she was with Declan O'Donovan, and it behooved a man not to be too familiar with a girl who went with a roaring broth of a boy like Declan.

Margaret took in her surroundings with a sort of fuzzy clarity. Most of the earlier pubs they had visited were strictly respectable. Shopkeepers and their better-paid assistants, clerks, senior artisans, farmers—these made up the custom for the most part, drinking steadily, talking soberly, enjoying the antics of the wild man from Kilcroom but not sharing them.

All respectable, all dull. All far too dull for Declan.

And thus at some time he set the pair of them in motion toward the quays.

The quays of Cork were like the quays of any other big port: a rambling area of wharves, docks, warehouses, public houses and small hotels. Sailormen have but a little time ashore, the more so in war, and that they like to enjoy. A quick, hard drunk, a woman—and back to the ship with their pockets empty and the hope that the next trip will bring no torpedo; that was their life then.

The whole quay area was designed to facilitate their desires. A man could leave his ship, get drunk, get a woman, get his pocket picked and his head shoved in, all without walking a hundred yards from his ship's side. So it was with the Holy Ground.

Any time Declan came to Cork he gravitated inevitably to the quays before the night was out. And since he had had a great deal to drink already, the gravitation was made despite his companion.

In Rooney's public house a great roar greeted Declan as he entered.

"The bucko himself! Come in then, Declan, boyo. Give's the song and I'll stand the first call."

A fat-bellied, short man with an immense breadth of shoulder stood at the battered bar drinking rum. He wore a greasy sailor's peaked cap, though in fact he had never been to sea. This was Mick O'Hara, one of the leaders of the dockers in the port. It was people like Mick who fixed rates and said who worked and who did not.

Once he had tried to stop Declan's taking a few days' casual labor—and had failed. The memory of the fight was still green about the docks.

Now, as Declan advanced to the bar with Margaret at his heels, O'Hare, following in the path Declan shouldered through the crowd, saw the girl for the first time. His eyes widened in the scar tissue that made up most of his lumpy, amorphous face.

"Oh, you're the purty fellah right enough, Declan," he cried. "Most of them come here to get a girl. But you, by Jasus, you bring one with you."

He paced slowly around Margaret, eyeing her as if she were a prize heifer at a show. He stood no higher than the girl, but his squat body radiated an immense power. Margaret, despite the drink she had downed, felt her face begin to flush at the frank, appraising scrutiny. The flush flamed as he patted her appreciatively on the bottom.

"No call for a bustle there, eh, Declan, boy?"

"None o' that now, Mick, none o' that," Declan growled angrily. "Leave her be. She's not that sort at all."

O'Hare's mouth twisted in a meaningful grin. "Is there another sort then? Sure they're all one, the lot of them. But she's yours and I'll leave her so. Now what is it you're drinking—"

Margaret was sobering fast as she gazed around the long, low-ceiled bar, lighted by gas and thick with the smell of

206

drink and the fumes of pipes and cigars. Down one wall was a row of little snugs, their walls about shoulder-high and their privacy secured by sprung-hinged doors. There were no tables or chairs in the main body of the pub, and there was no room for such fripperies. Men stood everywhere, drinking, smoking, spitting and carrying on a continuous shouted conversation in a babble of tongues. The sound was a continuous roar.

There were Lascars there from India, big Negro firemen from American ships, a few Scandinavians from timber ships, some French, some Dutch—and a great many Irish.

"Get that down you," Declan ordered abruptly and thrust a glass of whiskey into her hand.

She took it, and as she did one of the snug doors opened and she had a brief glimpse within. Her face flamed again as she turned away. Within the snug had been four or five men—and a woman.

A woman with her skirts drawn up, spinning slowly before them with a fixed smile on her face.

Nor was it entirely the mechanical lubricity of the sight that shocked Margaret, she realized.

She's old, she thought with horror. *She must be forty at least*.

There was a roar of laughter from the snug whose door had now closed, and she could only imagine what new obscenity went on there.

She sipped at the whiskey and felt her throat afire. This was not the relatively mild, disciplined drink of the previous houses. This was raw spirits, straight from the still of some poteener. She felt suddenly sick and tired. She wished with all her heart she had not come. At any rate, she would go. Now.

Turning, she looked for Declan to tell him her wishes. And a cold hand of panic clawed at her.

Declan was not there. A moment before, he had been talk-

ing with the squat man. Now both were gone. She was alone
in this frightening place.

Declan had not left Rooney's. He was at that moment in a
tiny back room with Mick O'Hare.

"Look, Mick," he was saying. "We need the guns. It'd be
easy as kiss-me-arse for you to get them in. We'll see to the
transport and all. Just you get them ashore."

"Go way ow dat, Declan, boy. I could be shot for the like."

"If you were caught. But sure how would you be caught?
Don't you slip in many a bit of a load that the customs don't
know about?"

"No guns though. I never had part in guns. . . . And me
own brother in France with the British Army, too. Ah, now,
Declan, it's not sensible you are."

"I thought you were a patriot," Declan taunted. "Don't
you get up there on the dockside and make the great speeches
to the boys about getting better conditions, better wages, a
better life, a better country? Sure I've heard you meself.
Didn't you drill with Connolly's boys too? What sort of an
Irishman are you at all, at all?"

"I'd beat the bloody ears off you for that, Declan O'Donovan, was I not afraid you'd maybe beat mine off first. I'm as
good an Irishman as you are. But there's too many damned
spies and traitors about now."

Declan sighed and said, "We'll be paying."

Mick O'Hare's body shook with wheezy laughter. "Now
you're talking! Why didn't you say that at the start? When
do they come—"

It was at that moment that Declan heard Margaret Kingston scream.

The American was a big man, about thirty and a little gone
to seed. He had long, greasy hair and wore only a checked

shirt above his dungarees. His fat lips were wrapped around the stub of a thick, unlit cigar, and he stood in front of Margaret with his thumbs tucked into a thick leather belt, swaying backward and forward on his heels, eyes appraising her carefully.

"My," he said at last. "You're a nice bit of tail, too. You'll do, sister. The end box."

She gazed at him uncomprehendingly.

He seized her arm suddenly and thrust her toward the nearest cubicle, where half a dozen other sailors eyed her with naked hunger.

"Wait! This is all wrong—" she started to protest. "I'm not what you think!"

"You ain't?" someone chuckled hoarsely. "Then, boy, does that sea air do something to my eyes? You sure as hell look like a woman to me! Show us, baby, show us!"

She stared at the sweating, hungry faces, her mouth dry and eyes wide in slow understanding.

"We'll pay, honey chile," drawled a slow, Southern voice. "We'll pay real handsome. Now, let's see you operate—"

Margaret's mouth opened and closed soundlessly as she gaped at the men. The smell of the sea, of unwashed bodies, of cigar smoke and alcohol, wafted around her.

"Maybe she don't trust us," grunted the one who had brought her in. "Show her some money, boys. On the table—"

Dollar bills began to flutter down on the table.

"Okay, now give. Let's be having you—"

And hands reached for her skirt, hands pawed at her legs and ripped at the white cambric of her blouse.

Margaret Kingston began to scream.

She was still screaming as Declan O'Donovan bulled his way across the bar and into the snug. Her clothes were in disarray, and the hands of the sailors were moving on her.

Declan said nothing, but he surged into the cubicle with the swift, efficient destructiveness of a reaping machine.

His first punch took the big man on the nape of the neck and dropped him unconscious to the floor. In the same movement a big boot was lashing at the jaw of the next nearest man. The crack of breaking bone was very loud.

But now the Americans were roused, and they were still five to one.

With a wild yell the Southerner hurled himself across the table with his fists swinging as he leaped. One of them caught Declan a tremendous blow on the side of the head. The Irishman reeled for an instant, shook his head and struck back with a sudden tornado of short, hooking jabs to the head and body, brutal, massive blows that had the Southerner down with blood pouring across both cheeks and from his mashed nose.

But there were three to take his place, one ducking low to grab at Declan's legs and the other two snatching at the bottles on the tables, swinging them wildly.

Declan ducked one bottle, but the other smashed against the side of his head, shattering and spraying the cubicle with rum. He swayed, and as he swayed the ducking American grabbed at his leg.

Yet even as he fell, Declan was twisting, jerking his knee across to pound it in the face of his nearest attacker.

And he was down for only the instant it took him to gather his legs beneath him and dive headlong at the other two.

His massive head took one man in the stomach, and the two fell together.

Margaret Kingston started to scream again. The remaining American had drawn a bowie knife and was poised to strike as Declan rose.

Then Margaret realized that her scream would only distract her sole protector. And instead of screaming she grabbed at the last bottle on the table and brought it down with all the force of her strong, fox-hunting wrist on the man's head.

Declan's fighting glare softened slowly into his brilliant smile as he rose in the same instant that the other fell. He saw the knife in the American's hand and the bottle in Margaret's.

"Aren't you just me darlin' girl," he breathed. "You Proddies can brawl with the best of 'em."

And abruptly he gathered her to him and kissed her.

It was the briefest of kisses before he stood her on her own feet again and then began to hustle her from the pub.

"Some bloody eejit will have called the shore patrol," he explained as he bustled her through the dark, winding mesh of alleyways. "And if not, there'll be more Yanks about. So it's us for Kilcroom."

His forecast of the shore patrol was almost instantly fulfilled. The tramp of marching feet came from ahead, and in the flickering light of the streetlamps they saw a little file of military—half naval police and half soldiers—marching toward Rooney's pub.

"Right now, my sweety," Declan ordered. "The road's clear the whole way home. Let's to it."

Almost at a run they started down the road the patrol had just left. But Declan had erred in one point. The road was not quite clear.

Two hundred yards behind the patrol sauntered a tall, familiar figure. Major Thomas Greyson, still smarting from the encounter at the Victoria Hotel, had come to see his men at work.

There was all the inevitability of fate about it, and not for anything could Margaret have stirred her legs into a run to avoid the encounter.

With Declan at her side she stood motionless as Greyson

approached. For an instant it seemed he would pass them by. Then he paused, and his gaze took them both in, took in the bruised face of Declan O'Donovan and the disordered dress of his own fiancée.

For an instant his nostrils pinched in and the heavy ashplant walking stick in his hand twitched. Margaret waited for the outburst. It did not come.

Instead, with the briefest and most frigid of nods, Greyson walked on. The pair gazed after him, eyes marveling.

"What sort of a man is he at all?" Declan breathed as the clubs of his fists unclenched. "Just to walk on like that? Is he a man at all, at all?"

He could not know the wild, inarticulate fury that was surging through Major Greyson, a fury so great that it strangled his voice and made him clutch at every vestige of self-control lest the slightest loss of it should drive him into irremediable frenzy.

But as he walked on, pace quickening, the fury subsided into a cold, hard hate that sought reinforcement from the subtleties of the mind rather than the emotion.

If that is the kind she is, he thought, *then that is her kind. But who would ever have thought it? Who would have thought it?*

His mind went back to other girls he had known, and he nodded sagely. He remembered India and the effect of the heat. He remembered officers' wives who had developed a taste not only for other ranks of their own race but even for Indians. These things happened. Ladies ran off with grooms. Yet Margaret—cold, hard, hands-off Margaret Kingston?

That bloody Irishman!

When Rooney's had been cleared of what had now developed into a general free-for-all—not really the shore patrol's business but that of the Royal Irish Constabulary, nevertheless tackled by the military with zest since a few soldiers were also involved—he beckoned Rooney to him.

"A rough place you keep here," Greyson said coldly. "I think in the interests of good order I will have to issue a closure order."

Rooney's face, pale and sharp-featured, sagged in on itself.

"Ah, now, Major, sure you wouldn't do the like! Sure I'm only a poor publican and I have no chance at all with the likes of them ones. How could I keep order when they come in fightin' round me ears?"

"This isn't the first time," Major Greyson went on. "You're getting a bad reputation, Rooney. Yes, I'm afraid I'll have to close you down, unless—"

Rooney's small, dark eyes brightened fractionally.

"Unless, Major?"

"Perhaps you'd like to assist me a little. You'd like to insure that good order was kept and—your license. I'd like a little information from time to time. You follow me?"

The publican gave a slack-lipped smile of relief.

"Information, is it? Ah, now, Major, sure I'm your man. Would there be, maybe, a bit of money for the information?"

Major Greyson's eyes frosted.

"You'll keep open. That should be enough."

Rooney sighed and shrugged. "Well, I suppose—" He fell silent, eyeing Major Greyson watchfully.

"For a start," Major Greyson began, "there was a man in tonight. A man called O'Donovan—"

"Big Declan! That bastard! It was him started the row over some bit of a whore he brought in."

Greyson's lips compressed at the reference to Margaret, but he nodded.

"Declan O'Donovan," he said. "Tell me what you know of him."

*　　*　　*

213

Greyson was immersed in his own thoughts as he left Rooney's. The tap on his arm came without warning, out of nowhere. He started, swung his back to the wall and clawed for his pistol butt.

"Major, sir, would you be sparing a minute itself?"

He peered into the face looming up toward him.

"Oh, it's you."

"Meself. The dirty wee man from the gutter—the one ye owe the money to."

Unlovingly the gombeen-man stared up into the major's face. A few paces behind, lost almost in the shadow, loomed the bulk of Big Teague, silent and watchful.

"Money! You'll get your money."

"Oh, I'll get it. One way or the other."

Greyson cursed the moment when he had first seen Raymond McCarthy. It had been the gombeen-man who had approached him, sidling up to him at a gate when he was out for his solitary morning ride.

"Could I speak with you, Captain?" he had asked (for this was before Greyson's promotion).

Ordinarily Greyson would have driven the horse on past. But McCarthy had chosen an arresting way of catching his attention. He was idly fingering a great wad of treasury notes, several hundred of them, flaunting them in Greyson's face. The morning air had been heavy with the scent of honeysuckle, but Greyson's nose was inhaling the smell of money.

"What is it?" he demanded brusquely.

"Well, I've heard some talk in the village that Captain Greyson has had a little misfortune over the matter of horses not running as fast as they should. I've heard the captain would be glad to have the use of some money for a bit of a while. It's what I've heard, and if there's no truth in it, sure you've no call to wait longer."

He smiled in his curious way that stretched his lips like rubber bands across his face without ever revealing his teeth—which was perhaps as well.

Greyson's eyes could not stray from the tempting money held out so casually.

"What are your terms? What security do you want?"

"Just the captain's note. Isn't the word of an English officer and gentleman good enough when it's down on paper with a signature and a witness' signature? For all the little you'll be wanting you can pay it back when you're married to Miss Kingston there. As for the interest, usually I get ten pounds on the hundred—"

Ten percent seemed more than reasonable without security, and it was only after he had gone back to the big house and scanned the paper more carefully that Greyson realized it was ten percent per month. He had raged at himself then for a purblind idiot, but that was not a lot of use. He had not returned the money and canceled the agreement, he could not afford to. The money was needed for even more pressing creditors.

Instead he had paid his ten percent per month, for a few months at least. Horses recently had been running badly. A crop of bills had come in. And the gombeen-man had become a little pressing.

Now Greyson glowered down at him. "I've no money!" he snapped. "There's no blood to be got from a stone."

"Ah, now, Major, did I ever say a word about money? Sure who'd ever worry about your credit and you engaged to Miss Kingston and all hers to fall to you. Did I ask you for money?"

Greyson frowned at the man. "What do you want then?"

The gombeen-man glanced up and down the street.

"I've had a bit of thought, and though there's money in it,

it won't be your money. Now it's a known fact that you have dealings with informers about the country. It's known too that you pay them money—and why not indeed?"

"What I do on duty is no concern of yours."

"I could make it. . . . What I was thinking, there's not too many in this countryside better placed for informing than myself, traveling the way I do the length of the land to do my wee bit of trading. So why wouldn't you put me on your list, eh? Why wouldn't I bring you the bit of news now and then that would help His Majesty and bring me in what's denied me by your good honor's self?"

Greyson stared. Then dryly he began to chuckle.

"By cracky, you've got a nerve, McCarthy! All right. I'll put you on the list. But any money you get is to be set against my account."

"Just so, Major, just so. And may your wedding be soon and you in a position to settle all with no bother."

"For a start"—Greyson ignored the remark about the wedding—"find what you can about a man called O'Donovan, Declan O'Donovan."

22. *Night Without Fireflies*

There were roses in the silver holders within the soft, leather luxury of the rear compartment of the Rolls. Their scent mingled with the richness of the leather and Margaret's own scent as the big car wound its way westward toward Kilcroom.

The driver's compartment was open. Coachmen had never been sheltered, so why should chauffeurs? The windscreen was a concession to safety, not to the comfort of the driver.

Behind Patrick Coughlin a heavy plate glass window cut him off from the passengers, and communication could only be by the speaking tube that ran to a trumpet at his ear.

Coughlin could hear nothing of what was being said behind him, but he could think a lot. He could wonder just why it was that scruff like O'Donovan rode with Miss Margaret. What exactly was going on?

With anyone else he would have made his own deductions. But not Miss Margaret. She was no flighty flibbertigibbet like some of the young ones he had heard of in the other big houses. Not Miss Margaret. He had known her since she was a baby. He had taught her to ride on her first pony. He thought he knew her through and through. No, she could not be like that.

This would be some little play of her own. She would have some prank in mind maybe, for she was a pranksome lass at times, apple pie beds for the guests, mustard sandwiches, dressing up and the lot. Also, from what he'd heard, this O'Donovan was a wild boy himself, full of jokes and jollities, and yet without much harm in him.

They would be hatching some sort of devilry together, no doubt. His seamed, weather-beaten face eased into premonitory laughter lines. It was not fitting for Miss Margaret to have that fellow riding with her. But if it was a prank they were planning, that was different altogether. There were no class barriers in the world of the prank.

"Come up there, lass, up with you now," he ordered as the Rolls neared a sharp bend. "No jibbing, or I'll beat the bloody daylights outa you."

Declan had taken great lungfuls of the rich scents of the car, and they were stirring him like an aphrodisiac.

Yet with the driver's black outline before him he felt a rare inhibition. In Margaret he was sure he sensed complicity, yet because of the car and the driver he could not reach out to her and take her. Was it then to peter out into nothing, this night which had made such a good beginning?

They had driven in silence, and the nagging of his desire was almost unbearable. He felt a hot, swollen surge of constricted power within him, and he racked his brains for some means to compass his wishes.

Ahead the few lights that still glowed in Kilcroom this late began to glitter through the trees.

"They're like fireflies," Margaret said suddenly. "The lights of the village, I mean."

"Fireflies. Ah, now, I doubt you'd not see fireflies this time of the year," Declan answered. "It's too cold for them, much too cold. They like the heat, do the fireflies, and I wouldn't blame them one little bit. And yet I don't know . . . in a sheltered place . . ."

"You mean you know where there might be some? Oh, I'd love to see that! That would be a wonderful end to the night."

"You'd have to cross a few fields. The car could hardly get there—"

"No matter."

She pulled the plug from the speaking tube. "Where do we go?" she asked Declan, and when he had told her she passed the direction to the driver. Coughlin raised his eyebrows and shrugged.

A few minutes later he had halted the big car beside the end of a narrow path.

"You might as well go home, Coughlin," Margaret said. "I'll walk back across the fields. It's a beautiful night."

"Yes, miss."

Carefully Coughlin avoided Declan's satiric eye as he put the Rolls into gear and moved off down the road.

Anyone else but Miss Margaret, he was thinking, and he'd have wondered a bit. But, no, not Miss Margaret. . . . Anyhow, he would keep silent about this matter. He would not be the one to loosen his tongue and spread scandal about the girl.

The night was clear, and Declan could see Margaret's face plainly as they wound along a narrow path. He had taken her arm by now, and a flow of mutual warmth had begun between their two bodies.

Inwardly he exulted. He could sense the mood that throbbed in her; he could feel the heat of her body and note the way she swayed toward him sometimes when there was no need to from the narrowness of the path.

In a dell among beech trees he came to a halt.

"Here we are," he said slowly, looming above her, his hand still on her arm.

"I don't see any fireflies," she said quietly.

He laughed hugely. "Sure there aren't any fireflies in Ireland," he chuckled. "You knew that, didn't you?"

For just an instant he felt unsure of her. Had she after all been really interested in the insects?

"You knew," he insisted.

She said nothing at all, but her eyes were on his and in the night they seemed to glitter from great pools of shadow.

"There aren't any fireflies in Ireland at all, and never were," he said, grinning, his other hand now on her other arm and both hands traveling up the arms to the shoulders, resting there for a little, no weight and no grip in them.

"No fireflies at all," he said and smiled impudently down. "So we'll have to make our own. If we're to have fireflies they'll be our own fireflies—"

And abruptly he drew her to him. There was a fraction of a second's resistance in the shoulders, and then she came to him and her own arms went around him as his head stooped and his lips came down in what was almost a blow to her lips.

It was a long, breathless kiss, and during it his hands played up and down her spine, across the firm arch of her buttocks, across her hips.

Then the kiss ended and they broke a little apart.

"Oh, you're the dotie girl," he crooned. "Sure you're the most beautiful girl in the County Cork, in Munster—in all Ireland."

There was a bank of short, mossy grass at the dell's edge, and she let herself be led to it, her eyes so wide she was almost blind, and there he seated her, hand on her breast.

"The fairest one of all," he murmured. "The loveliest hair, the loveliest face . . ."

And inevitably he laughed. "The loveliest backside, too, as you showed me when I was in a badger's hole."

There are women who hate laughter with love, but Margaret Kingston was not of these.

Soft laughter gurgled out of her, and slowly she let herself lie back on the mattress of the turf, laughing softly as one of Declan's hands crept over her.

Laughter and love, she thought. That was the way the world should be. There were too many terrible things and terrible deeds. There should be more laughter and love.

"And fireflies," she said aloud as Declan's right hand stirred up excruciating pleasure in her loins. "There should be more fireflies dancing in the trees."

23. Sorts and Kinds of Traitors

Peadar Casey always liked collecting. This was a strange trait in Old Man Silence, for collecting was more a job for the glib, swift-tongued boys, for men like Declan who could charm the coppers from a widow's purse. But Peadar's method had no charm.

Peadar would come to a back door, in the dusk as a rule, and stand there until the man of the house was brought to him.

"I'm collecting," he would say brusquely.

And then there would be the instant protests: "Sure I gave to the Capuchines only last week . . . and the League . . . and the Redemptorists. I'm not made of money."

The protests would vary in a more or less direct ratio to the length of the man's purse. And Peadar Casey would listen to them in silence with a faint, sardonic smile on his hard, thin lips. There was not a single excuse in the world he had not heard. And when all were finished he would repeat: "I'm collecting."

His shoulders would hunch a little and his eyes go a bleak, gray blank. This would be enough most times. But there were some men so mean or so unconvinced of his cause that he would have to speak seriously to them.

These were the ones he enjoyed collecting from the most. Especially if he knew they gave generously to the Church.

For it still gnawed in him, the hatred that had been born when Liam died. Nominally he remained a Catholic; occasionally he even went to Mass. But when he did so it was not to worship but to despise, to hate the richness of the priest's robes, the gold and silver about the altar, the very size and solidity of the church building.

In his mind he would compare this richness with the poverty of those who came there. In his mind he would appraise the cost of the building and its caparisons and allocate the money to the poor. How many could feed on what it took to keep one church and its priest and its parochial house?

Rich, rolling phrases from Marxist philosophy would tumble through his mind, drowning the Latin of the service.

The opiate of the working class, he would think. *The leeches on the body politic.*

Which made it all the more enjoyable when he came across a really stubborn "client" on his collecting rounds.

"An Irishman! You call yourself an Irishman? What sort of an Irishman is that—to grudge a few miserable pennies for Ireland's freedom! Do you want the English to ride their horses roughshod over us for another thousand years? Do you want to be subject to a foreign king all your life? Do you want to see Irish men and women ground down in slavery forevermore? Is that the sort of Irishman you are?"

The harangue would continue until the contribution was forthcoming, and the longer it lasted the more it would veer from the lines of pure nationalism.

"The working man won't stand forever to be the slaves of the rich. Remember the French Revolution? Heads rolled then, and maybe heads will roll in Ireland yet. The working people of Ireland are on the march, friend. To an Irish Socialist Republic. The working people have been denied too long what is theirs by right. Soon they will take it."

And then came the veiled threats.

"When that day comes Ireland will remember her friends —and her enemies."

223

A bleak, ophidian smile could follow from his thin lips, and there were very few who refused to contribute.

Especially did Peadar Casey like to collect from the bigger farmers, the ones who rode to hounds, aping the English and clinging to their coattails. A hunter grazing in a field was a real spur to him, drawing out every subtle nuance of menace.

"I hear there was a fire over at John Driscoll's place last night. He lost the whole yard of hay, poor fellow . . ."

There might have been a fire and there might not. In any case, the fire would have been a pure accident, for the Brotherhood had not yet embarked on coercion, whatever they might do in the future. But the implication was enough.

Peadar Casey collected.

Terence McKeon looked at Mrs. O'Donovan with some bewilderment.

"You want to warn me against Declan?" the schoolmaster echoed. "Warn me?"

Declan's mother had aged abruptly in the last year, lines deepening and darkening around her eyes and beside her nose.

"Master McKeon, it should not be a mother's part to miscall her son. Yet I know what it is you are doing in this town, and my heart is with you. I would not have any miscarriage of your work. It is Ireland's work and needful. Which is why I will say the things that should be said. For yourself, for the other boys, for Ireland itself."

"But, Mrs. O'Donovan, Declan is a fine lad, full of spirit, daring and strong. I'd go so far as to say he's our best."

Her clothes were neat, dark and new, for McGregor, the sawmill manager, was dead now and had left her all he had—a fair little pittance, enough to keep herself and Declan too, when Declan was not working, which was most of the time.

"That's what Mr. McGregor used to say, God rest his soul, the good man. He used to say Declan was a 'braw lad' and he'd go far . . . even when the boy was stealing the whiskey out of the decent man's cupboard."

"You'll know he's done a lot for the Movement," McKeon pointed out. "You must have heard."

Mrs. O'Donovan smiled sourly.

"There's not much I don't hear about Declan, good or bad. There's some about here like to pass the word, you know. Especially the bad word."

"All the same, Mrs. O'Donovan, he really has been most valuable."

"When things are going right, master, when things are going right. But they won't always go right. It isn't when things are going right and it's all gas and garters you have to worry about. Sure his father was the same. A fine great man when things were going right, but he ran when the trouble came on me, and that's what I'm afraid of: that Declan might run on you when the time comes and do you all a harm."

Her lips twisted almost painfully.

"He's never been hurt, master. Nothing has hit him deep— not even his fancy woman at the castle—and when he's hit deep I wouldn't answer for it. I don't know how he'd stand to be hurt. And I thought you should know."

Her hand dived abruptly into her bag and came out with a little paper bag which jingled.

"I've been saving for you, a penny here and a shilling there. That's why I came. To bring you the money, and what got into me to talk of Declan I don't know. My own flesh and blood. You'll think it strange."

She bustled from the room, leaving Terence McKeon with the money still in his hand and thoughts trying to arrange themselves in his head.

He was remembering the ambush at Gilligan's Corner and the way Declan had drawn off the British reinforcements. Had that been his intention—or had he been running, in fact?

Mrs. McKeon came into the room then, limping a little because rheumatoid arthritis had begun to immobilize her leg joints. Her knuckles too had grown great, and the skin on them had the powdery, chalky look that was characteristic of the disease.

"Was that Mrs. O'Donovan I saw going down the garden?"

"Another contribution." McKeon smiled briefly.

Thoughtfully he eyed his mother. Arthritis might be crippling her body, but her mind was as lucid as ever and her eyes as bright.

"Mother—how well do you know me?"

"Through and through," she chuckled. "Every nook and cranny of you, my son. Why? What is it you've been up to?"

"Me? Nothing. Would every mother know her children's natures?"

"Who better? Why, what's worrying you? You've something in your mind—"

He shook his head and smiled affectionately at her.

"Just a thought," he answered. "Just a thought. I was wondering . . ."

"At Easter," Terence McKeon said quietly. "That's the word now. That will be the time."

His voice was as flat and unemotional as ever, but he saw the wave of enthusiasm that swept through the meeting, the glow in the eyes, the tightening of face muscles.

"At last!" said Peadar Casey with sudden fervor. "At last! Ireland will be free at last, and the English and their bloody capitalist despotism will be gone at last. We'll sweep them into the sea, and their horse-riding friends after them."

And there was a hubbub of eager questioning, of promises and threats.

Declan O'Donovan burst suddenly into song, into "The Wearing of the Green," and McKeon did not try to stop him, even though his great voice was probably carrying out into the streets beyond. McKeon gave them all their heads for a few minutes, knowing that they needed this break, that their taut-strung nerves had to have relief.

It had been a hard winter, and it was not over yet. From the Volunteers, he knew, many had already dropped out—because of the weather partly, but more because of the news from France. Several Kilcroom lads lay dead in France by now, and for many of the families in the town the schizophrenic internal struggle had been too much. They loved Ireland, but there was also the war. That was the dichotomy.

"Right, lads," McKeon said quietly at last. "Let's take it easy a bit and think what's to be done. Now I've told you it's Easter. But I haven't told you that it's definite. There's time to go yet, and before then the plans may have to be changed. This time everything has to go absolutely correctly. There has to be timing, there has to be training and more training . . . and we have to have more arms."

"The Volunteers have arms in plenty," Declan put in.

"You're right, Declan," Tomeen Brennan agreed. "Sure they could let us have some—the way they're not all together now."

"You know what their arms are like," McKeon snapped. "We want something a little better than that. And we're getting them."

He smiled at the expression on their faces.

"They're ordered already and they're on their way," he said. "From Boston. Two cases of new rifles and four crates of ammunition. Declan, you'll make the arrangements for getting them in, with Mick O'Hare in Cork. Right?"

"Right it is," Declan beamed. "He'll need to be paid, mind. That's the sort he is."

McKeon nodded. "He'll be paid."

From the back of the room Margaret Kingston spoke up:

"Does he have to be paid? I mean, do the rifles have to be brought in through Cork? Wouldn't it be safer to land them along the coast, away from any chance of interference?"

She flushed suddenly as every face in the room turned to gaze at her.

She was still not quite used to being "Declan's girl." And the group was far from used to her presence. She was an alien, an intruder. And though she had given proof of her loyalty, they still suspected her a little.

She was there only because Declan had said she had to be there—and because McKeon agreed with Declan on the issue. McKeon had sized her up, realized that though her infatuation with Declan was the primary cause of her presence, yet she still had, dormant but growing, their own ideals and aspirations.

Also, she was especially useful to the group. She had time and again brought them information from her friends of the "other crowd" which had been tremendously useful.

In particular she had brought them the list of Greyson's informers, and the assistant provost marshal's spy network was now being used against himself, used to feed in false information that took weary troops out on dark nights to guard against nonexistent ambushes.

Useful indeed—but not accepted yet. Especially by Peadar Casey.

Casey now said sourly: "Is it right or is it sensible to have that woman in our midst listening to all our plans? Sure what's to stop her going off to her castle friends and that Major Greyson with every word and scheme that's in it? I'd say it'd be wise to put her out now before worse comes."

"Peadar Casey," rumbled Declan, "you are going the right way to have the nose of you put where you'll blow your hat off every time you sneeze!"

Which brought a laugh, and a frown from Terence Mc-Keon.

"Miss Kingston is one of us," he said sharply. "We've been through this before. She's taken the oath and she's proved her worth. So leave it, Peadar, leave it."

"We'll have our heads in a noose through her," Casey continued to protest.

"My neck will be in it too," McKeon snapped. "Now, we'll continue with the planning. That is an order."

And it was obeyed.

In her seat at the back Margaret marveled at the complete assurance of the dry little schoolmaster with his prim mouth and his quiet, knowledgeable eyes. She marveled too at herself, at the way she had thrown herself into the work of the organization, the completeness with which she had cut herself from the past.

Nor was it all, she assured herself, entirely due to Declan, whom she could not think of without a sort of inner flush and a wriggle of ashamed ecstasy.

Life had, she told herself, purpose now, reality. It was not merely a matter of maintaining the estate, of enjoying herself, of various frippery follies with her friends.

This was truly rebellion as far as she was concerned. The apostate and the turncoat are always the most devoted to their cause, having the feeling, as it were, that they had invented it. So it was with Margaret Kingston. Now that she was fairly in the Movement she was more violent, more eager for action, than any of the men.

And yet she contrived still to remain a part of her own world at the same time, hugging herself with an inner glee as she attended race meetings or dances, thinking: *If they only knew!*

Also, of course, there was Declan. Above all, there was

Declan. There were frenetic secret meetings in which her body learned a whole new code of sensation. At the summerhouse below the long lawns of the castle they sometimes met. On other nights she would drive to Cork and stay at a hotel, Declan entering by the back door to stay until dawn.

About it all there was the delicious thrill of conspiracy and the even livelier sense of sin.

Yet there had been also a profounder emotion involved. Margaret had never known anyone like Declan before; his mingled knowledge and ignorance touched her with the same thrill that his hands sent racing through her body. He was not just fulfilling a physical need. He was real. He was, indeed, more real to her than Tommy Greyson had ever been. And, of course, they were joined in this bright new Cause that was Ireland.

Peadar Casey disapproved, of course, and so did Tomeen Brennan, because the castle woman had taken Declan from him for so much of the time.

For the rest, apart from Terence McKeon, the group was rather overawed by her presence and support. Probably none of them mistrusted her. Indeed, she could almost have taken over the group if that had been her wish, for though they were fighting against her kind they still had centuries of subservience behind them that would take years to throw off. If she said she was on their side, that was good enough. God knew they could do with all the help they could get.

When Declan had first suggested her membership there had been a surprising lack of opposition—Casey and Brennan were soon talked down, and the girl was welcomed to the meetings. It was odd, it was anachronistic—but it happened.

Didn't history show that Protestants were usually the leaders of Irish rebellion back through the centuries? There had been Wolfe Tone, Grattan, Sarsfield, Emmet, Parnell and others.

It was contradictory—but it was Ireland.

And Terence McKeon, for one, was glad of Margaret Kingston's presence. She had a good mind which had pointed out flaws in plans more than once. And she had the contacts that made her so very, very useful.

As he finalized the plans for the landing of the arms he was more glad than ever to have her in the group. Especially, he thought, since she had a moderating influence on Declan. He was drinking less now, though his spirits were as ebullient as ever.

If only he could be just a bit more reasonable, less liable to fly off wildly at a tangent!

There had to be reason in this business. If there was no reason, there could be no organization. And without organization, there could only follow failure.

Though he might sometimes envy Declan's gift for impromptu oratory, Terence McKeon still placed all his faith in the dictates of reason, the acts of a sensible man.

The Cause was just and right. Reason indicated that. So what more was wanted?

Yet still, sometimes at the back of his mind, nagged this faint envy of Declan and his ability to raise men's spirits at a word.

24. Checkmate

The Rolls-Royce was, of course, the perfect vehicle for the job. A Rolls was the guarantee of respectability. Few sentries or policemen would bother to halt a Rolls or search it. And the vast back seat would accommodate the arms with room to spare.

Coughlin, the chauffeur, had been left behind, not so much because Margaret feared he might talk—of his family loyalty she was sure—but because an emergency might arise in which swift, daring driving would be needed.

Terence McKeon himself was at the wheel. He had never driven a Rolls before, but in his methodical way he had decided years ago that driving would be a useful art for the Cause and had learned that art in various vehicles about Kilcroom.

Now, in the fog that seeped from the River Lee and made the night perfect for their purpose, he coaxed the big car down the winding maze of back streets behind the quays. Navigating in the fog was far from easy, but he came at last to the big double gate that said: O'HALORAN, COX AND MOORE, IMPORTERS AND EXPORTERS, and brought the Rolls to a halt.

"On time," McKeon said with satisfaction as he glanced at his big pocket watch. "I just hope the others are too."

Margaret Kingston, in the seat beside the driver, looked down the gray, fog-wispy street and shivered a little. They were not far from Rooney's pub, and the very smell of the quays brought back memories of that night there.

"Will Declan be all right?" she asked.

"He hasn't much to do," McKeon answered. "Just find Mick O'Hare and give him the money. Then O'Hare will hand over the guns to our boys and they'll bring them through this gate and into the car. Then it's all plain sailing back to Kilcroom. Declan should be all right."

And yet, despite the assurance of his words and the knowledge that this plan should be foolproof, he felt just a shadow of doubt in his mind. He did not have the arrogance of the real planner who *knows* that all will be well. He was only too well aware that even the best of plans can go astray. Yet reason told him he had done everything he could.

Margaret pulled the fur collar of her coat higher about her blond head and shivered a little. She too knew the plans were as perfect as they could be.

But she knew also that she was afraid. Intuition, perhaps, precognition—or simply the chill of the night and the dreariness of the sordid street—sent a shiver up her back, and she wished that she could find the right words to pray. She wished she had the simple uncomplicated faith of the others who had crossed themselves before they left Kilcroom and seemed content to leave their future in God's hands. But what would her own local rector, Mr. Babbington, say if he knew of her actions this night?

And if anything should happen to Declan—

At that point in time nothing was happening to Declan O'Donovan except that he was enjoying himself. He was in the heat and smoke of Rooney's, drinking hot rum with Mick O'Hare.

"It's all right, then, eh?" Declan asked. "All ready for us?"

"Ready as it'll ever be," O'Hare nodded. "You brought the money?"

233

"I did—but you'll hardly want a sight of it in here? Hey, Rooney, another rum for us—"

The nightly roar of the bar was about them, the rumble of laughter, the polyglot gabble of a dozen tongues, the shrill laughter of the girls in the cubicles. Rooney pushed across the drinks, and they sipped them slowly.

Deliberately, Declan was keeping a rein on his appetites this night. There would be time enough for drinking when they were safely back in Kilcroom with their cargo—time for drinking and time for Margaret. When he saw the women in the cubicles and compared them with the woman who was his, his heart swelled within him and he felt a wild pride.

"Take another," Mick O'Hare offered.

They did. And then Declan glanced toward the stained face of the clock behind the bar.

"Time we went," he said.

Outside, the fog had thickened and the other side of the street could not be seen as they moved swiftly down the road toward a side entrance to the quay.

Four more Kilcroom men were waiting there—Casey, O'Dwyer, Driscoll and Haggerty, the silent man from Kerry. In the cold they were shuffling and kicking their heels.

"Right," murmured Mick O'Hare as he fitted a key to the lock. "Just follow me, boys, and say nothing at all. A voice carries far in the fog."

The well-oiled gate opened silently, and they found themselves within a narrow alley between the two warehouses. Here they were joined by others of the group. O'Hare led the little column at a swift, silent walk that was not completely emulated by those behind.

Twice he halted to hiss silence at them, and they tiptoed along in a grotesque parody of secrecy. There were watchmen on the quayside, and though they could deal with watchmen they had no wish to leave any indication afterward that anything untoward had happened in the place.

O'Hare halted abruptly at the edge of a wharf where packing cases made a mountain whose peak was lost in the fog.

"There you are," said Mick O'Hare softly. "There's your stuff."

The arms were in long crates marked: FARM MACHINERY—WITH CARE—THIS SIDE UP. The ammunition was in smaller wooden boxes, roped about.

O'Hare waved them to silence as a little murmur of delight began among them. His posture stiffened as he listened intently. But there was only the gurgle of the water and the distant clatter of a ship's winch as she unloaded. Slowly the stevedore relaxed.

"Thought I heard someone—but it's all right. Well, get loaded and get out."

He looked meaningly at Declan and rubbed thumb and finger together.

"You get the money when we get out," Peadar Casey said harshly.

"I'd like a sight of it," Mick O'Hare answered impudently.

Casey glared and then beckoned to Declan to show the money. It stung Casey that the money had not been entrusted to him. He was second in command of the group, and it should have been his job to handle the money.

McKeon had decided otherwise. McKeon had made it plain that since Declan was known to O'Hare, Declan should handle the organization of the landing. The decision still rankled with Peadar Casey, the more so since Margaret Kingston was also involved. Margaret was horse people, and he would never, could never, trust her.

With a broad smile Declan brought out a wad of notes, displayed them to O'Hare—and stowed them back in his pocket.

"Right, let's be going then," the stevedore sighed.

The crates were heavier than they had expected. It took two men to each of the rifle boxes, and that left only Declan. He flexed his muscles and gripped the roping of the ammunition boxes, one to each hand. There was a full hundredweight to each box, yet he lifted them with scarcely a sign of effort.

"Lead on," he grunted.

The little procession moved slowly through the fog and through the piled heaps of merchandise of every kind. Twice they had to stop to give the rifle carriers a breather. Then at last the other gate was before them, the gate beyond which lay the Rolls and the open road to Kilcroom.

"Now isn't that the lovely sight?" Declan murmured.

And in the same instant there was the sound of feet shuffling close by. It was followed by the sharp metallic click of a rifle bolt being slammed shut.

"Halt!" roared a voice. "Halt in the name of the King!"

And from before and behind them the bright beams of torches cut yellow paths through the fog.

"Ambush!" Declan roared. "We've been bloody well ambushed!"

For one long instant the group stood where they were, pinned down in the glare from the torches. The ambush party had been in the shadows on either side of the gate. They were also behind them. They had walked into a perfect trap.

Then, almost in unison, the crates dropped to the cobbled surface of the wharf.

"Stand where you are! Stop or we fire!" roared the voice again.

And this time Declan recognized it. It was Major Thomas Greyson's voice.

In the light of the torches the glint of rifle barrels could be seen as the trapped men glanced wildly to each side.

"Put your hands up, you damned scum!" Greyson ordered. "And the first man who makes a move will get a bullet."

The hands of the Kilcroom men crept upward slowly, a paralysis of fear gripping them—all save one.

In Peadar Casey's heart there was a furious rage. They had been betrayed. That was certain. Someone had talked of their plans. Someone had given them away to the Englishman. And he was sure who that someone was. Margaret Kingston had betrayed them to the man who was still her fiancé, for all her capers with O'Donovan.

And that rage was so great that it overcame whatever fear was in him. He was not going to let himself get caught. He was going to escape. He was going to see that the Kingston bitch got what she deserved.

And even as his hands went high, he was turning on his heel, shouting aloud: "Scatter, boys, scatter! Run for it! Run like hell—"

And with the word he dived off to the side. There was a khaki-clad soldier right in front of him, rifle leveled.

But the soldier was a youngster. He had never fired a rifle in anger in his life. His finger hesitated on the trigger. Casey grabbed the rifle barrel and swung it aside. With a push he sent the man staggering into his companion, then he rushed headlong into the darkness.

His orders had spurred his companions into the same instant action. Like the separating atoms of an explosion they burst outward. Declan's fist smashed into a soldier's face. He leaped across a barrier of crates.

The first shot cracked out in the fog, and a moment later every soldier was firing wildly at the scattering figures of the rebels.

The Kerry man went down with a bullet ripping into his spine. For a moment his toes drummed on the cobbles before he was still.

Another bullet hit Mick O'Hare in the belly, bringing him to a jerking halt. Stupidly he looked down at himself, clutching with his hands at the hole. He felt the fire of the bullet within him, the curious chill of the dock air following it so that it was as if he had a dagger of fire and ice in his belly.

"You bastards!" he screamed in a voice that was unnaturally high. "You've killed me! You've killed me!"

And he hurled himself at the nearest soldier, his hands reaching for the man's throat, gripping and squeezing with all his ebbing strength.

Still the bullets whined and ricocheted in every direction.

"Cease fire!" Greyson roared angrily, ducking as his own men's fire nearly felled him. "Cease fire, you bloody fools! Cease fire!"

In him was a sickening sense of failure. He should have had the whole gang in his hands by now. Instead, he had two dead men and the rest God knew where. And this would be counted his fault, he knew. He had placed his men badly. He should never have put them where their own fire could hit their companions. Already he had seen two of his men go down from their comrades' shots.

"Cease fire!" he shouted yet again, and only now did the nerves of the men, tautened by their long wait in the darkness, ease enough for them to obey his orders.

Greyson was pale and angry when he stood erect again. His trap had been perfect but for his own misjudgment.

Now it was failure—partial failure only, since he had got the arms shipment. But it was failure nonetheless, and trouble—endless trouble—loomed ahead.

25. A Broken Engagement

The Rolls had begun to move before the first shot was fired. In the instant that the order was shouted Terence McKeon understood that someone had betrayed the plan. How many troops were behind the barrier of the gate he did not know. But it would be folly to wait and find out.

Dispassionately he knew he must cut his losses, abandon the others. No possible benefit could be gained by waiting. He could only be grateful that he himself and Margaret Kingston were still free.

"Wait!" cried Margaret. "Wait for Declan—"

"We can't do a thing for him," McKeon said quietly. "Nor for any of them. We'll be lucky if we get clear ourselves. If they know the car is involved they'll have the roads barricaded."

But miraculously the roads were clear. Through Warren's Place, over the bridge, into Union Quay. Despite the powerful engine the car almost stalled on the steep incline of Barrack Street. But it recovered quickly as they came out into the flat.

McKeon put his foot down hard on the accelerator as they roared down the Glasheen Road, heading for the open country. As they passed through Bishopstown a policeman saluted the car's gleaming bonnet.

"They can't have known about the car," McKeon said, "or they'd have grabbed us. They could have taken us before the others got to the gate, or else have blocked the street against us. That's something, anyway."

239

"Something!" she cried. "Something! Declan must be either captured or dead—and the others. Something!"

She longed to cry, and yet her eyes were as dry as they had ever been. She felt the need for tears, and tears would not come. It was the end of everything.

Yet Terence McKeon was even smiling a little. For he had reasoned out the matter of the betrayal.

Margaret Kingston could not be involved, or he, too, would have been captured in the car. That made it virtually certain that there was no traitor in their own group. Betrayal had come from outside. And the only outside was Mick O'Hare. There would be a reckoning with Mick O'Hare, he thought.

The water of the River Lee was icy, but Declan scarcely felt it as he swam downriver and sought a ladder at the far side on Penrose Quay. The first terror of the ambush had gone, and now he was filled with a mingled rage and laughter —rage at the traitor and laughter at the way he had, after all, escaped the ambush.

He clambered up the ladder and made his way back stealthily to the same gate he had entered with Mick O'Hare. Now his teeth were chattering and he could think only of hot rum.

He lurched into the nearest pub, and as his hands went to his pocket he felt the sodden bundle of notes that should have been Mick O'Hare's.

"Hot rum!" he roared at the barman. "Make it a glass—and make it damned quick!"

He glared around the room, daring anyone to comment on his soaking clothes. No one did, and he gulped down the rum in two swift swallows.

"Same again—"

He thrust a pound note on the counter and loosened his sopping shirt. His mind had been working swiftly the while.

He would have been recognized in those damned torch beams. The major knew him, and the major would be on the lookout for him. He could not go back to Kilcroom.

Dublin, he thought. Dublin would be the place. No one knew him in Dublin, or not many at any rate. Dublin would be the place, and he had the money to go there, all right.

He beamed around at the bar as the rum glowed warmer through his veins. He would have himself a time in Dublin.

"There's a fine, tall, strong man," a girl's voice said from below his shoulder. "There's a man would grace a bedroom rightly while his clothes were drying."

She had red hair and a pert nose, and Declan's eyes warmed as he gazed down at her.

"By God, you're right!" he cried. "Is it far to walk?"

"No distance at all. Near Summerhill—"

Declan's eyes traveled over the girl again. He liked what he saw.

"Righto, mavourneen," he said, a slow grin spreading over his face. "Let's be on our way." His right arm slid around the girl's slim waist.

And no thought of Margaret Kingston came into his mind then.

Hatred is also a corrosive, and in the heart of Peadar Casey the acid had been working all through the night and the next day.

He had always known it was a mistake to bring in the Kingston woman, and he had been proved right. She had betrayed them. All the time she had had Declan on the string she had been betraying them. Major Greyson would have every one of their names by now, a favor from one of the horse people to another.

But she would do him no more favors.

He patted the handle of McKeon's Mauser as he edged through the trees of the castle demesne.

Peadar Casey knew how to deal with traitors.

"I know you were there," Major Greyson said bleakly. "I let the car go to save you . . . embarrassment."

They were in the summerhouse, and to Margaret it did not seem the same place where she had spent so many hours with Declan. The broad chaise longue was still there, the faded carpet on the floor, the few pictures on the walls. But without Declan it was a different place entirely. Greyson's brooding shape threw a chill over it, corrupted it.

"That was very kind of you, Tommy," she answered coldly. "Or it would be if I knew what you were talking about."

"Don't be a fool, Margaret!" he snapped, gripping her shoulders. "I know what you've been up to, you and that damned O'Donovan. Well, there won't be any more scented hours with that fellow. We'll lay him by the heels, never fear."

Her heart leaped. So Declan was still alive—alive and free.

"Really, Tommy, I simply don't understand what you're talking about."

"You and the Sinn Feiners," he growled roughly. "You and your Republican friends. I'm talking about arms and plotting and treason. Even women hang for treason, you know."

She said nothing, but her lip twitched in scorn.

"I may be able to save you still," he said heavily, "if you give me the names of the others, help the government to run the rascals down—"

She laughed in his face and said nothing.

Her laugh stung him into anger, and his reasoned tone vanished.

"So that's it," he growled. "They've all had you, and you don't know which you want."

The color rose violently to her face, and she did what had been in her mind for months. She clawed his engagement ring from her finger and threw it to the floor.

"If that's what you think—you can have this back. Anyway, you'd have got it soon. I couldn't have gone on with the pretense any longer."

White lines sharpened around Greyson's mouth, and his nostrils pulled almost closed.

This was for him the moment of ruin. Even if there were no court-martial over the ambush failure he would be in dire financial trouble the very instant the news of the broken engagement leaked out. Yet he felt he had to make one last desperate effort to save himself.

"Margaret," he begged. "I love you. I want you. I. . . . Well, I'm a reasonable man. I can forgive. Marry me right away and we'll try to forget the whole rotten business."

Incredulously she stared at him.

"You know—or you think you know—that I've been the lover of another man. Yet you'd still marry me?"

"We all have our faults," he said. "I'm not perfect myself. Now say the word. Give me those names, marry me—and you'll see. We'll have a fair sort of life, after all."

And once again she laughed in his face, laughed helplessly and long, her whole body shaking with her amusement. And now at last his anger exploded.

"That's enough! No more of that, do you hear!"

He gripped her shoulders and began to shake her.

"Stop it! Stop it!"

The feel of soft flesh under his hand turned his anger into a new channel. Roughly he pressed her back until the chaise longue struck her behind her knees and she fell backward.

"All right, you bitch!" he growled. "I don't know how many of your dirty Irish friends have had you—but once more isn't going to make any difference."

243

His left forearm pressed down across her throat, and as her hands clawed at it, trying to force it away, his right hand, slowly and deliberately, began to pull at her clothes.

Outside, Peadar Casey had listened intently to everything that was said. Now, as he heard the rhythmic drumming of the chaise longue's springs, the whimpers and the grunts, he debated within himself what to do. He knew now that his suspicions of Margaret Kingston were false. She had proved her loyalty.

He should, he thought, go in there and help her. And yet he stood outside, silent for a little and lost in thought. At last he went as he had come, quietly through the trees of the demesne.

For when all was said, they were both horse people and this was a matter between horse people.

More important was to find the traitor who had betrayed them—find him and destroy him.

Which was a matter Terence McKeon was already dealing with. Carefully he had gone through the list of people who could have betrayed them. Then he had eliminated those whose presence at the ambush would have placed themselves in jeopardy. Even Mick O'Hare had been cleared by his death.

For a little while, Mrs. Donovan's warning in his mind, he had thought of Declan. But even if Declan had turned traitor he would scarcely have taken the chance of being shot at the quayside.

Only one person was left, and it should be simple to prove his guilt.

The dark-haired serving girl tugged at Rooney's sleeve.

"There's a man at the back door wants to see you."

"Can't he come in then?" said Rooney. "Isn't there plenty seeing me this minute?"

244

He was spiling a fresh barrel of porter on the rack behind the bar.

"He says it wouldn't be fitting for him to come in," the girl answered.

Rooney gave the spile another two knocks with the mallet and nodded. This would be another of Major Greyson's men come crawling for news, he thought. Well, he would have nothing for him this time.

He wiped his hands on his apron and stumped out to the rear of the building, where an unlighted lane gave access to a grimy yard.

"I'd have thought I'd done enough," he grumbled to the shadowy figure waiting. "Didn't I tell you about the guns and all? Is it my fault you didn't get your man O'Donovan? Anyway, I've got no more for you, and you can tell the major that."

"I'm afraid that won't be possible," said the quiet voice of Terence McKeon. "The major and I aren't on speaking terms."

Rooney's eyes widened and his mouth gaped, for now he saw the pistol muzzle leveled at him.

"Who . . . who the hell are you?" he gulped.

"A soldier for Ireland," McKeon answered softly and pressed the trigger.

He walked away swiftly down the lane, noting with satisfaction that his hand was still steady and his pulse beating at the normal rate.

Rooney had convicted himself out of his own mouth. And his death should serve a useful purpose. It would serve as a warning to other potential traitors. It would let the people know that this time they meant business.

And yet, he thought dryly as he neared the lights of Patrick Street, it was a strange occupation for a schoolteacher, killing people.

Part Three

Oh, Dublin City, there is no doubtin',
Is the finest city upon the sea
'Tis there you may see O'Connell spoutin'
And Lady Morgan makin' tea.

—Dublin street ballad

26. Ends Meet

IT was on Good Friday that Major Thomas Greyson was sent under escort to Dublin to await court-martial. A formidable list of charges had been piled up against him. Most of them concerned his ambush of the gun party.

There was no doubt at all that he had far exceeded his duties. Martial law had not been declared, yet he had taken armed troops into a civilian area; they had opened fire, and people had been killed. Worst of all, some of those who had been killed were his own troops.

"Think yourself damned lucky," the provost marshal had told him, "that you're not being dealt with by a civilian court on a murder charge. They'd hang you without a doubt. As it is, you've got a very faint chance of getting off on some of the charges. Excess of zeal is always a good excuse. I doubt if it'll wash this time, but you might just avoid cashiering . . . or you would if it wasn't for the other matters."

His pug-nosed face registered intense distaste as he gazed at the sheet of paper which listed a vast number of defaulting checks, overdue bills and various other misdemeanors which would certainly be deemed conduct unbecoming an officer and a gentleman. News of the broken engagement had brought all his long-overdue debts rapidly home to roost.

In the Dublin train his escort, two officers from a service corps base unit, tried on occasion to draw him out and put him at his ease. They failed utterly. His replies were curt and often coarse.

In fact, he heard scarcely anything of what they said. He was sunk in a muggy slough of despair. He was certainly ruined now, his career utterly shattered. If he kept out of prison he would be fantastically lucky. Even if he knew the President and all the members of the court like brothers, it was hardly possible that they would acquit him.

And as the train click-clacked its way northwards toward the city he came to a decision.

He would attend no court-martial. He would stand no trial. Not in Dublin or anywhere else.

No hint of his intention appeared on his face as he sat in sullen silence. But when he reached Kingsbridge station he headed for the lavatories, followed by his escort. He heaved a little sigh of relief when he saw the cubicle he wanted was not occupied. It was the only one in the row with a window.

And two minutes later, after he had bolted the door behind him, he was out of the window and walking swiftly down the street, into the teeming life of Dublin, into a city where officers were ten a penny and no one at all would notice him, into a city where a whole multitude of shops were waiting eagerly to cash his checks.

The Volunteers had come separately to Dublin, little groups percolating into the city unnoticed. The group from Kilcroom had come singly, scattered along the length of the train. Their arms, too, had come separately, stowed in a fish lorry beneath cod and haddock. Now they were stored in the cellars of a school which was closed for the Easter holidays and whose caretaker was a Brother.

Terence McKeon's first care had been to take Peadar Casey and Tomeen Brennan into the cellar to clean the arms. He left them at work while he went off to seek his own orders— and check that the scattered men of the detachment knew where to meet. In the back of his mind was the thought that it was as well Easter had been chosen for the Rising. For once in his life he had forgotten to give his pupils any homework.

All the way to Dublin a quiet confidence had filled him. He knew what his own men could do. He assumed that every other detachment was in the same state of readiness. And, more important, he had assumed that the higher command knew their business.

His confidence was rudely shattered by the time he left Liberty Hall. A cold, resolute anger began to burn within him at the sheer chaos and indecision he had found there. No one even knew whether the Rising would take place or not. No one knew if the Germans were landing. No one knew how many men would come in from the country.

No one, it seemed to him, knew anything at all.

And worse, what little he had heard of the battle plans seemed to indicate that the leaders had taken utter leave of their senses. To try to take Dublin, to attempt to hold a fixed position against better-armed, better-trained and more numerous regular troops seemed to him the height of insanity.

His own men, like the others, had been trained for guerrilla war, to strike and melt away into the country. His own thinking had been dominated by the tactics of the Afrikaner troops in the Boer War. Only thus could a smaller force hope to maintain itself against a greater.

He had time in hand to make his way to the suburbs where Professor Martin, the man who had first sparked his patriotism while at college, now lived in retirement, frail in body but with a fiery spirit still blazing behind pale blue eyes.

"It's going to be like all the others," he said bitterly. "A few shots and surrender and then the hanging parties. God almighty, haven't they learned anything at all? Nothing from Wolfe Tone, nothing from Emmet? If I'd known this was the kind of war they'd planned I'd—"

"You'd have come out just the same," the professor said

251

shrewdly. "You've a bit of the fanatic in you, Terence, for all the logic I drummed into you. But you're right about the strategy. This one is lost before it's begun—but it can win the next one."

Fingers together, he expounded gravely as if in some tutorial.

"One of the principal causes of failure in the past has been that the country was always divided against itself. This in fact is the case today. There will be no popular support for this Rising. Make no mistake about that. Not half the people of Ireland want it, and a good deal less than half the people of Dublin. You will find that some of your Volunteers and your Citizen Army will melt away before the battle. You will find the crowds revile you and the shawlie women mock you."

McKeon listened in silence, intently.

"Inevitably the British, by sheer force of arms, by weight of numbers and superiority of equipment, will crush you. And afterwards there will be hangings.

"But—and make no mistake of this—if your Rising can last two days, and if the British reprisals are sufficiently brutal, you will have laid the foundations for a real war of freedom. And the next war you will surely win."

He lit one of the long, thin cigars which were his sole luxury and continued deliberately: "The war in Europe still hangs in the balance. I think it inevitable that the Allies will eventually win—especially if the Americans can be lured to their side. If they lose, you will have German masters in Phoenix Park and your position will be little altered. But I doubt very much if the Germans will win. Weight of numbers is against them—and is already beginning to tell. When they were halted in nineteen fourteen, I think they had already lost.

"Assume then that the Allies win. They will be tired of

war. England will be filled with men who never want to hear another shot fired in anger in their lives. Then will be your time to strike. Then will be the time for a proper war, for a war waged throughout the country and not in a single city, a war with no mercy, with shots in the back and bombs by night.

"I doubt very much if it will last long. Especially if English repression after the failure of this Rising has unified the country. You will have martyrs and heroes then who will not be vague figures from the past but real people whom others remember. . . . Or have I extrapolated overfar?"

"I think you're right, sir." McKeon nodded thoughtfully. "It's not a cheerful prospect, is it?"

"Reality rarely is," smiled the old man, stroking with one hand the long silken fur of the fat Persian cat in his lap. "There is a good deal of difference between splendid speeches and actual shooting—or so I have been informed. Of course, there does remain the distinct possibility that on this occasion it will not come to shooting at all. From what you have told me, there is a good deal of indecision at the top. John MacNeill and Patrick Pearse are at loggerheads. But MacNeill is a pretty sensible fellow. He might manage to postpone action until it has more prospect of success. On the other hand, he may not. . . . How do you feel about being killed?"

McKeon was startled at the casual question, then he smiled gently. "In a way I hadn't thought of it. Not as a real happening. I don't think I'm . . . afraid. No, I'm almost certain I'm not afraid. If it's necessary I shall die."

"That is a quite exceptionally foolish statement," he was rebuked. "A dead man is of no conceivable use to anyone— though his death may, of course, be used as an exemplar for his fellows and the basis of future heroics. Nonetheless, it is almost invariably better to live than to die. Kindly remember this, if it comes to a matter of warfare. As the jingle has it: 'He who fights and runs away lives to fight another day.' "

"I'll remember, sir," McKeon promised, "though I won't guarantee to take your advice."

They talked on for some little time, drifting at last from the subject of the Rising to memories of old friends, of classes long before and books read in the past that seemed incredibly unrelated to the present.

When Terence McKeon left at last, his mind was more at peace and he saw the future in a sharper, clearer light. It was a future without any hint of glamor, he thought, but what had to be done would be done.

In Peadar Casey's heart there was no thought of failure. They would win because they had to win. Ireland had to be free. The people had to throw off the burden of the native gombeen-men and the alien horse people. It was as simple as that. They would win because they had to win.

After the Rising had been successful, then would come the real revolution. An Irish Socialist Republic would be proclaimed. Out with the nationalists and the gombeen-men and the holy Joes. All *they* would do would be to replace one form of tyranny with another. The Irish working people would simply have two sets of masters instead of one: the gombeen-men in Dublin and the priests in Maynooth. What sort of freedom was that? Was it for just that that Irishmen were expected to give their lives?

No. When Ireland was free of British rule there would be a reckoning. . . .

He had left the others from Kilcroom, and he walked alone down Sackville Street, staring into the brightly lighted windows of the great shops, reviling them in his heart, promising them the fate they deserved. His thin face was tense with eagerness and his eyes were hard and hungry as he paused at the Gresham Hotel, watching the carriages and cars halt to discharge the wealthy for an evening's pleasure.

Enough on her back to keep a family for a year, he thought angrily as a fat woman in a fur coat dismounted from a Rolls and teetered on high heels up the steps of the hotel, to be saluted deferentially by the uniformed doorman. *But she'll not be wearing the like of that much longer. No, by God. We'll have that off her.*

In his mind it was almost as if she lay on the ground at his mercy while he stripped her of furs and jewels. Not that he would take those for himself. Or for anyone. Real people had no need of those fripperies. Furs and jewels would go to buy real clothes and real food for the starving masses in the slums.

He strolled to the general post office and gazed at its imposing façade. Soon, he thought, there would be a different flag flying above the entrance. Soon there would be a different kind of postage stamp to be bought at its counters.

There had been some talk among the Volunteers that the G.P.O. would be battle headquarters, and he thought that would be very fine and appropriate. Also it would be sound planning. Situated in the middle of the rich city, the British would never dare to attack it with all their force. They could never attack here without damaging the nearby property. And they would never do that.

Capital, he had been taught, never destroys itself. And the shops were capital. They were wealth. The British would do anything to save their wealth.

"Give's penny, mister," whined a snotty-nosed urchin.

Casey gazed at him with compassion.

"Land of the noble Gael," he sighed aloud. "Is this what you've come to? A dirty-faced boy begging in the streets?"

"Who're you calling dirty?" howled the boy. "You mean sod!"

He spat on the pavement at Casey's feet and ran down the street with the skin of his backside flashing white through a hole in his trousers.

Peadar Casey walked on with a little less enthusiasm.

27. Waiting

Margaret Kingston was staying in the Gresham. The hotel was packed, and a good many of her friends—or acquaintances, rather, for now she wondered if in fact she had any friends—were also residents there. With a meeting at Fairyhouse, there were visitors to Dublin from north and south as well as the usual sprinkling of army officers.

"Too bad about Tommy," Ivy Blakeston consoled her, the half-kindly, half-malicious smile of the gossip on her lips. "But there—we never could understand what you saw in him."

The long, elegant bar was quite full, and Margaret had seen the interested eyes turn toward her when she entered alone. It was unusual for a woman to enter even a bar like the Gresham's unescorted, and even those who did not know her turned to look.

Ivy's husband, whose prewar genteel poverty had been quite removed by some very successful dealing in horses for the British Army, bustled up with drinks. He had been a slim, lively youngster only a few years before, but now he was quite fat with a creased face and watchful eyes that had almost vanished into the puffy flesh. He echoed Ivy's condolences, and his pudgy hand held hers unnecessarily long.

Margaret, as she sipped her drink, could hardly restrain her laughter. She knew very well the kind of thought in his mind. She was fair game now. A broken engagement was like a divorce—rare though that was. It made a girl "available."

There was an open season on her now, as she had already learned even in Kilcroom.

Margaret did not stay in the bar for long, only long enough to wonder just what the reaction would have been if she had shouted aloud the truth—that she had cast in her lot with the Sinn Feiners, that she was mistress to a wild Fenian boy.

There would have been incomprehension, shock and disbelief, she reflected. Would anyone at all have understood? Looking at them there, she decided not. Hunting, dancing, racing: that was all they seemed to understand. That, and grumbling about taxation.

There was no reality left in them, and that was what she was really rebelling against. A lack of life, a lack of reality.

There was a secret smile on her lips as she left. For there was no lack of life in Declan O'Donovan, no lack of reality.

Declan O'Donovan had enjoyed himself since the failure of the quayside fracas in Cork. He had found lodgings in a pub near King Street, and with money in plenty in his pocket, life had been sweet.

To McKeon and Margaret he had written carefully worded letters that were unsigned. To McKeon he gave no return address in case it should be intercepted. But he had informed Margaret that he could be reached at McGaffigan's Corner House, reasoning that Margaret's mail at least would not be examined.

It had not taken him long to establish contact with the Brotherhood in Dublin, and he knew of the plans for the Rising even before McKeon. Yet though he knew the plans, knew the date and time of action, it was not of rebellion he was thinking. He could not dismiss Margaret Kingston from his mind. For a man like Declan there were plenty of women in Dublin. Yet even when he was coupling with one the thought of Margaret would flash into his mind, almost ruining the moment. The rich clothes, the silk, the scents—these had had an aphrodisiac effect that could not be matched by a common girl's body.

And now she was in the city.

Hungrily he watched the clock and waited. First Margaret —and then the boys from Kilcroom. It would be a weekend to remember, even if the Rising did not take place as the ever-stirring sea of rumor now indicated.

He nodded to the barman for another drink—porter only, since he would soon be seeing Margaret.

For once he was being quiet, restrained, not drawing attention to himself. Which made it seem utterly unfair when he recognized a face in the mirror behind the bar—the face of Major Thomas Greyson.

Declan recognized him instantly, though he was now in civilian clothes. And recognition was mutual.

Sacred heart, Declan thought, *he has me!*

He had no doubt in his mind that Greyson had followed him, tracked him down from Kilcroom. Perhaps he had even somehow traced him through his letters to Margaret. He had no knowledge at all of Greyson's disgrace or that the recognition had been as great a shock to the Englishman.

Declan knew only that here in the same bar was a man who could send him to prison.

He drained the pint and strolled to the lavatory—and out through the back door. He would intercept Margaret on her way to the rendezvous, warn her about Greyson.

But first he would get clear.

Greyson's hand was shaking as he put down the glass of whiskey.

Declan O'Donovan, he thought, a man who knew him, a man who could inform the authorities of where he was, who could send him to face his court-martial.

Flight was his first thought—until he began to consider. O'Donovan was certainly not a man who could afford to go to the authorities. Nor would this be his nature. No. O'Donovan would steer clear of the authorities. But what was he doing in Dublin?

Margaret was the answer that sprang immediately to the officer's mind. He was here to meet Margaret. . . .

The sour taste of anger came to his mouth at the thought. To think that Margaret would come here to meet a yokel like that! To think that she had—

His hand trembled more than before as he picked up the glass and forced the spirits between his teeth. He made up his mind very quickly. Margaret always stayed at the Gresham. He would find out if she was now there. And then?

There was little humanity in the ideas that swirled eagerly through his mind.

All about the city, among those in the know, there was talk about the Rising and whether it would really take place. The wiseacres were quite certain that nothing at all would happen.

"Sure it's always the same. A lot of talk. A lot of parades—and nothing at the heel of the hunt."

Even in Dublin Castle, headquarters of British power in Ireland, where they should have been well informed, no one really believed anything would happen. Or if they believed, no one was willing to act.

The chief secretary, Augustine Birrell, was in London as a member of the Imperial Cabinet; the undersecretary, Sir Matthew Nathan, lacked the authority for the wide sweep of arrests which was the only action that could now halt the Rising.

And in any case, Fairyhouse Races were on. Officials and officers of all grades were on leave. It was unthinkable that anything should actually happen during a race meeting.

Major Thomas Greyson put down the telephone with a rictus of ultimate chagrin on his hard mouth. Margaret had left the Gresham some few minutes before. She had left no number where she could be reached.

And his call to Dublin Castle itself had met with complete frustration. There was only a junior duty officer present, and to him Greyson had not disclosed what he knew or suspected—or his own identity.

For in addition to O'Donovan, Greyson had also seen Terence McKeon and Peadar Casey. They were seated in a tea shop only a hundred yards from where he phoned. With them were other men from Kilcroom, men whom he knew vaguely by sight and men who he was quite certain were part of the Cork rebel force.

The spies he had set to work in his provost job had learned a little of what was afoot, and before he left Cork he had studied the probabilities seriously. In his own mind he was sure that the presence of the Kilcroom men in Dublin indicated imminent rebellion. Why else should they have come to the city?

And if he could provide the warning that saved the state from civil war, surely his minor peccadilloes—as he thought of them—would be forgiven. But how could he give the warning if there was no one there to listen? It was infinitely infuriating.

This detached fury held only a little lease in Greyson's mind. Leaving the post office from which he had phoned, he saw across the street the ominous bulk of Big Teague and in his shadow Raymond McCarthy, the gombeen-man.

Quickly he turned and prayed that they had not seen him. Yet if they had not, what were they doing in Dublin? Had they had word of the court-martial? Had the gombeen-man come to try to enforce his own claim? Had he followed Greyson?

Or was McCarthy there about his own business? If there was really to be a rising, then McCarthy was the man to know it. And if there was a rising, was he not exactly the kind of man to be at the center of things, to take advantage of disturbance to line his own pockets?

Certainly Raymond McCarthy, once enrolled on Greyson's list of informers, had provided good enough value for the money the provost marshal was able to give him from the secret funds. Through McCarthy two rebel ambushes had been aborted—though the ambushers had escaped—and arms had been seized. So had a small, portable printing press.

Greyson had seen the gombeen-man only once since the rupture of his engagement to Margaret Kingston. He had paid him money then, and McCarthy had said nothing about his own debt. But there had been a shrewd speculation in the man's eyes that had left Greyson uneasy.

And yet. . . . A sudden fantasy gripped Greyson. Suppose the gombeen-man was not at all what he seemed? Suppose that instead of being the crude moneylender, the shabby dealer in inconsiderable trifles, he was really a man of importance among the Fenians? Why not? It would be the ideal disguise for a leader, an organizer moving all the time about the country. . . .

The idea grew in Greyson's mind until now it seemed that McCarthy was the *éminence grise* of the rebels, the man whose capture could prick the whole bubble of Fenianism.

And if he himself laid the man by the heels, what credit must come to him! All his peccadilloes could be excused as a painstaking plan to ingratiate himself with the gombeen-man.

Greyson's lips allowed themselves to smile. McCarthy was not a danger to him. He was a danger to McCarthy.

He paused at a shop window and was disappointed not to find the gombeen-man anywhere in sight behind. It was some moments before he realized that the window belonged to a funeral furnisher and that he was glaring fixedly at a tasteful representation of a memorial stone with a white granite border filled with black and white marble chips.

In fact Raymond McCarthy had no foreknowledge of Greyson's coming court-martial or, indeed, of his presence in Dublin. His own presence in the city was purely commercial as he sought out the dockside warehouse of Pritchard Brothers.

John Pritchard was not especially proud of this side of the family business. The big shop with its Grafton Street locale suited him much better. He liked the smells that mingled from confectionery, bakery and pharmaceutical departments, rising like an incense to his sedate, solid office. He liked to walk through leather goods and finger a nice wallet or a dressing case.

He liked the customers who came to the shop, the gentry and the middle classes and even those few of the poorer kind who had carefully saved their shillings and would buy goods over which he was always prepared to stand guarantor for quality.

The shop, he felt, expressed something of himself, not as gaudy as Clery's or Noblett's, not flaunting itself, but just as good in its way.

The shop was his life.

But there was no denying that this warehouse was his money. It was gaunt and a little decrepit, and the smells that wafted about its poorly lighted interior had none of the richness of the shop. But they represented money, more than ever now that there was a war on.

A whole floor was given over to rags. There were thousands of tons there, sorted, baled, ready to be shipped out. Mostly they were woolen rags. They would go back to the woolen mills of Yorkshire where so many had originated.

There they would be ripped apart into their basic fibers and machines would card them and spin them and weave them again into cloth.

Mostly the shoddy which they would make would clothe the backs of soldiers, but some might come to Ireland again, and he wondered how often that journey would be made. Old wool into new cloth into new garments into rags into shoddy into new cloth into new rags. . . . It satisfied him, this basic conservation of material, and since the war had just shot the price of rags up twopence it pleased him too to know how much was awaiting shipment.

Clorinda would get her motorcar this year all right.

"The gombeen-man from Cork would like to see you, sir," said Price, the warehouse manager. "He won't say why. Will I give him his marching orders?"

"Send him up," Pritchard reproved. He liked to feel himself accessible to all customers, all staff. Besides, McCarthy was almost a protégé of his. Pritchard had given him goods on credit when McCarthy was no more than a spindly youth.

The gombeen-man almost genuflected his way into the warehouse's bleak little office.

"Ah, now, yer honor, oh, you're looking awful well. And the house well stocked too, I saw—"

"I haven't had much from you for a couple of months."

"Ah. But I have it. In me own wee shed down in Cork I have a few ton baled and ready for the train. I was thinking maybe there would be a rise in price what with the war and that."

John Pritchard concealed a faint smile. So McCarthy wanted more money. He would get it too. Prices were still rising and would continue to do so until the war was won at last—by England, of course.

"Well, I think I can promise an adjustment shortly. As you say, prices are rising."

He waited for the bargaining to begin. But McCarthy remained silent, his eyes taking in everything about an office that was already familiar. His gaze went out through the glass window to the stacked bales beyond.

"What about your insurance?" he asked. "Are you covered well?"

"Oh, yes. I've got a policy covering the warehouse and contents. Why? Do you think it looks like a fire risk?"

He was jocular, but something in the other's manner disturbed him.

"Fully comprehensive?" McCarthy insisted.

"Of course."

"What about civil disturbance, acts of war—"

Shrewdly Pritchard eyed the gombeen-man. "I doubt if I'm covered for riot. Do you think I should be? You know something?"

"The rebellion's coming. I think in a day or two. There'll be a lot of damage."

"Oh, come, McCarthy! That's not the government's view. And the Lord Mayor told me only yesterday—"

"The Lord Mayor won't be leading the Rising," McCarthy insisted. "It's almost here, Mr. Pritchard."

He gave his tooth-covering, rubber band smile.

"There could be a lot of money in it, Mr. Pritchard, for those with good warehouses to store goods—"

Two minutes later he was scuttling down the open wooden staircase with Pritchard shouting his wrath from above.

"And don't come back either! What d'you take me for indeed? A receiver of stolen property?"

To Price he explained: "He says there's going to be a rising. He says there will be a lot of looting, and he suggested buying the goods from the looters and storing them here. Did you ever hear the like?"

"Sure he's only a gombeen-man when all's said," Price answered philosophically.

"The very idea!" Pritchard raged.

But he paid a call on his insurance broker on his way to luncheon.

"Pearse says that Easter Monday is definitely the day." McKeon smiled thinly around at the others. The quiet, unassuming tea shop was a strange place to pass news like this. "No matter what you hear over the weekend—and there'll be rumors aplenty—it's Monday. You all know where to meet and when. Any questions?"

They gazed back at him in silence, eyes introspective, faces a little tense. They had known, of course, when they left Kilcroom that this was the time. Yet to have a fixed day, a fixed time set on the start of it all—to make a dream reality, that was something else again.

And to have it done in this cold, clinical way, a quiet passing of information with no more drama than a man asking the result of the 3:30 race—that was no way to start a rebellion.

McKeon himself felt the tension—and the disappointment. They were all looking at him, seeking something from him.

"The most sensible thing now would be to split up," he said. "Each of you go off to where you're staying. And don't gather in groups or talk about the matter. Keep quiet and sober."

"Sober!" roared Declan suddenly. "My God, Terence, is this a time for being sober? You do what you like, but if I'm to die for Ireland I'll enjoy myself first!"

Terence McKeon frowned and threw an alarmed glance toward the nearest waitress. Then he saw that the others were chuckling and smiling.

266

"Oh, Declan's the boy all right," wheezed Tomeen Brennan. "Dow-cha, Declan boy! Where'll we be drinking?"

O'Donovan's big hand came down on his shoulder.

"Tomeen, me bucko, this night you'll drink alone or with the others. I'll be drinking sort of privately myself, if you follow me."

And the huge wink he gave indicated plainly what he meant. Tomeen might have been disappointed, but he concealed it in the laughter of the others.

Sensing the tension dissolve, McKeon was grateful to Declan, grateful and puzzled.

Why should the big man's easygoing vulgarity have more effect on the men than his own careful reasoning? He would have to think it out some time. Meanwhile he could continue grateful that Declan had restored heart to the men.

"Well, that'll be all then. See you when we meet again."

They broke up and went out into the streets, where the uniforms of the Volunteers and the Citizen Army mingled with the khaki of the British troops.

It seemed impossible that the outrageous rebellion was only a few hours away.

Peadar Casey spent the weekend with an old aunt, or rather great-aunt, who was living in a small hovel not far from James Street.

"You'll not be here much longer," he assured her. "Ireland will know how to honor its old."

Since she was almost stone-deaf the assurance did little for her. And though she was pathetically glad to welcome him and to inquire after such of her relatives as still lived in Kilcroom, conversation was almost impossible.

He soon wandered into the streets, contrasting the poverty of the district with Sackville Street and Grafton Street, promising himself personally to see that the old woman was among the first to be rehoused when socialism came.

The slums depressed him and exalted him at the same time. In Kilcroom there were people living in the same abject poverty, but there were not so many of them and their plight seemed not so bad because around them there was at least the countryside.

When he returned at last, the old woman had gone to bed, having forgotten him in her dotage and locked the door.

It took half an hour of hammering before he finally got in.

Tomeen Brennan went with the other Kilcroom men and drank for most of the evening before they retired to a cheap lodging house. He did not enjoy the evening. He never really enjoyed an outing without Declan looming at his side to bring security and the guarantee of pleasure.

Yet he felt no anger or even indignation at Declan's abandonment of him. Was Declan O'Donovan not a law unto himself? And wasn't he entitled, anyway, to his pleasure?

This was the soberest night Declan had ever spent with Margaret, and in the shabby hotel room which was such a contrast with the Gresham's rich luxury they made love with a desperate fury, body thrusting at body, hands clawing, mouths seeking in an endless heat of desire.

When they lay in silence at last, Margaret rose on one elbow to gaze into the man's face.

"I've something to tell you," she said quietly. "I'm pregnant."

Declan did not answer. It was a statement with which he was familiar. But this was the first time he had ever heard it said with such an absence of hysterics.

"Did you hear me? Are you asleep? I said I'm pregnant—"

"I heard you," he answered.

He fell silent for some seconds, then went on: "So there'll be an O'Donovan in the castle now? That's not a bad joke, either. Damned if that doesn't beat the rebellion. There's a fine taste of justice in that."

She frowned a little, wondering what was in his mind, wondering too what was in her own. This was a moment of drama, and there should have been a stronger reaction from him. Then she saw that his chest was heaving a little, and for an instant she thought he was sobbing.

"An O'Donovan in the castle!" he cried aloud. "A good start to the Revolution!"

And they were not sobs at all that racked him but the strangulated convulsions of Homeric laughter.

28. Showdown

"It's a hell of a way to run a revolution," Declan complained. "Not a bloody shot have I fired in anger yet, and me with the seas of fire lapping up over my gullet like porter in a belly-burp."

The rear of the G.P.O. was just about the quietest place in Dublin, and the Kilcroom detachment had grown steadily more restive as the sounds of distant battle grew louder.

"You'll get fighting and in plenty, Declan—don't worry about that," McKeon tried to soothe him. "It's coming, it's coming."

"So's Christmas," Declan said. "But it's a hell of a way away too. Could we not get out and do something while we're waiting?"

Distantly came the irregular thump of the heavy Howth Mausers. Even at the foot of the G.P.O. itself there was an occasional shot as a Volunteer spotted a distant target farther down Sackville Street. Only in the waxworks and the adjacent parts of the G.P.O. was there silence and inaction.

McKeon frowned a little as he sensed the spirit of his men. Without action soon the tension of their nerves would relax. Already one man had come to ask if he could go home and milk his cows. He had asked the question seriously, ignoring the distance to Cork, ignoring the sheer fact of rebellion.

"I never knew it would take this long," he had complained. "And the wife, she's no hand at all at the milking. Sure I might as well go. We're doing nothing here."

270

That was the mood of many of them. Elsewhere, men were getting on with the Rising, killing the English, fighting for Ireland. But they sat there at the back of the building and did nothing. To none of them did it seem very glorious.

"If we're not careful," Peadar Casey growled sourly, "the Germans will have the city took and the whole thing will be done with before we get a crack at all."

That fifty thousand Germans had landed in Bantry Bay and were now marching on the capital was a persistent rumor which had been fostered by the commanders, both political and military. As far as they knew it could have been true. Communications had been bad throughout the action, and they did not even know that Sir Roger Casement had been captured at Tralee, or that the *Aud*'s cargo of German arms now lay at the bottom of the sea.

Despite runners and the few telephones that still worked they did not even know very much of what was happening within the city itself, a massive ignorance which McKeon could only hope was shared by the British. He felt reasonably certain that it was, since the confusion in the city was by now almost total.

McKeon had paid a few visits to the front of the building, but he had not remained there. He did not care to leave his own men for long—and he did not like the increasing gloom that the chaos cast on him.

The professor, he thought, had been right. Though he could not have known just how it would work out, he had surely been right in predicting defeat. It was not reasonable that this confused group of amateurs could affront the professional soldiers of Great Britain. And though from the outposts tales of heroic defiance against overwhelming force were brought in again and again, heroism was not and could not be enough.

Already the distant sound of firing had grown closer. And

271

now it came from all directions. A ring of steel was being thrown about the city, a ring that would draw steadily tighter until it was a noose about the rebels' necks.

"Margaret! What in hell are you doing here?"

Declan stared in blank astonishment as the girl, whose clothes were dusty from her passage through the hole in the wall, walked across the waxworks floor. A figure of Charles the Second stood behind her and seemed for an instant to leer down at her.

"I had some news for . . . them." She shrugged a shoulder toward the front of the building. "Then," she smiled suddenly, "I thought I'd come and see how you were doing."

From under the volunteer nurses cloak she wore she brought a medium-sized basket.

"I brought some food for you too—a little better maybe than your rations."

The basket held bread, butter, some tins of meat and fruit. There was also a bottle of whiskey.

"Ah, you're me lovely, dotie girl!"

Declan held up the bottle and made love to it with his eyes.

"Put that away," said Peadar Casey brusquely. "It's not fitting."

"What in hell do you mean, it's not fitting?"

"We're not fighting a revolution for drunks. You'll not disgrace Ireland—"

Declan spun around, gripped the second in command by his shirt front and lifted him slowly from the floor.

"You're telling me now what I'll do and what I'll not do? Is that it? Drunks? A bottle of whiskey! Jasus, Mary and Joseph, do you know how many bottles I have sunk in me time? Do you think I alone couldn't drain it dry till there'd be no more juice in the hobs of hell? Drunks? And only a toothful apiece for all the decent men here."

He threw Casey backward so that the man fell against a tumbled waxwork of Brian Boru.

"Jasus, man, this is an Irish revolution, not an English one!" The lights of mischief in his eyes, he called aloud: "Who's for a drink, me buckos? Who's for a drop of the hard stuff?"

Peadar Casey picked himself up slowly, cold hate in his eyes, hate that was directed perversely at Margaret Kingston rather than at Declan O'Donovan. For was it not the Kingston girl who had brought the bottle into the place? And was she not of the horse people?

His hand fell on to the butt of his holstered Mauser.

"O'Donovan, I'm in command here while Captain McKeon is at headquarters. I am ordering you not to drink that whiskey."

"It's orders now. Would you listen, men? The great Lieutenant Peadar Casey is giving his orders. Next thing he'll be going through and telling James Connolly how to run the Rising."

Slowly and deliberately he took the foil from the bottle's top and drew the cork with an easy twist of finger and thumb.

Margaret, watching, knew she could not interfere—and berated herself for her folly in bringing the spirits. It had been impulse, pure impulse. She had taken whiskey, bread and butter from the smashed front of a looted shop which had not been completely gutted by the swarms that surged up from the combe. The whiskey had seemed a sensible gift to bring.

And now Peadar Casey was drawing his pistol because of it.

"Disobeying an order in the field is punishable by instant death," he said. "Put that whiskey down."

"Kiss me arse!" snorted Declan, unable now to back out with the eyes of all the detachment on him, and especially the eyes of Margaret Kingston. He no longer particularly wanted the whiskey, but he had to drink it.

The neck of the bottle touched his lips.

Casey's pistol leveled, and his finger began to tighten.

Neither man would back down now, and in the tension no one in the room could move, not any of the men, not the woman with the basket still under her arm.

Death was very close.

Then Terence McKeon strode in, face abstracted, moving quickly to the center of the room.

"Put the gun down, Peadar," he said quietly. "We want no playacting here. Declan, you'll get drinking when it's over and not before. Two men stand on sentry. The rest gather around. We've got work to do now, work at last."

Declan glared at Peadar Casey with a look that said: *If it hadn't been the captain speaking I'd have drunk it.* Casey's returned glare indicated that he would certainly have fired. And stiffly, like dogs which have not quite come to battle, they gathered close to Terence McKeon.

"They're bringing up artillery," said McKeon briskly. "Margaret here saw the guns and reported to the commandant general. He has given us the honor of seeking out the guns and destroying them before they can open fire. He'll be sending some of the lightly wounded to take over this place. Then Margaret will direct us to where the guns are being sited . . ."

Crisply he began to give his orders.

"You'll obey orders," growled Major Thomas Greyson. "I tell you to come with me."

The group of British soldiers, who had been scurrying down the street when he saw them, eyed each other for a moment in doubt and then let discipline enfold them again. They had been ambushed and lost their platoon commander and sergeant.

A dozen of them were left, youngsters for the most part with two months of training behind them. They were utterly bewildered by this strange kind of war which was so completely different from anything they had been trained for.

In their training camps there had been marching, a little musketry, bayonet drill and the rudiments of trench warfare. It was enough to fit them as cannon fodder for the western front, no doubt. But not for this weird warfare in which shots came from nowhere and every house could be a fort.

They did not even know where their company headquarters or their battalion was. They were lost and frightened, and the voice of authority that Major Greyson represented was the one sure thing in a nightmare world.

"Fall in!" rapped Greyson. "Who's the senior soldier?"

A wizened, evil-looking little lance corporal stepped forward and saluted smartly.

"Five ocht nine Lance Corporal Macnee, sirr!" he croaked in the accents of Glasgow's Gorbals.

"Right, Macnee. I want five minutes of drill before we move off. Open order arms drill."

"Aye, sirr!"

Macnee turned smartly and began to drill the men in a way that gave Greyson his history almost as if he had written it down. He would have been promoted to sergeant times without number, Greyson thought. A regular who would always be in trouble with the regimental police when he was drunk. A good soldier sober, useless when drunk. Probably deserted a few times. But he would always come back to the army because there was no place else for him.

In which particular he was exactly like Captain (acting Major, awaiting court-martial) Thomas Greyson.

For Greyson had realized when the shooting started that he still had one last chance of retrieving his career. He had pulled on his uniform again in his hotel, sent off the girl he had been bedding with and made his way out into the streets of the city. A bold stroke at this time, a stroke which would be both showy and effective, could make the authorities forget all that had happened before.

He had prowled through the city, sizing up the situation. Sometimes he was sniped at. In a doorway he had found a dying officer and taken his Webley and Scott revolver—for his own, of course, had been confiscated on his arrest.

Only one thing had he lacked, and now he had that too—a unit to command. Seventeen men, he thought, seventeen raw, frightened youngsters, not counting the lance corporal and the one or two older men who made up the numbers to twenty. It was not a lot . . . but Napoleon had started with less.

"Right. That's enough, Macnee. We'll move off now."

"Vairy good, sirr. . . . Platoon—close order march! Forrm . . . fowers! Smartly there in the rear rank. . . . Platoon ready to move off, sirr."

As their heavy boots clattered down the cobbled street, Major Greyson felt hope rise again within him. With men to command and action all about, surely there would be some way to redeem himself.

There had to be a way.

29. The Big Guns

Peadar Casey came to a halt as he heard the first shell whistle overhead. The blast of the explosion came from the direction of the City Hall. And he did not believe his ears.

They were shelling Dublin. They were turning the big guns on the city. Capital was destroying the capital. The English were smashing their own creation.

It did not make sense. Everything he had been taught, everything he believed, had indicated that property was its own protection, that the horse people would never damage their own wealth.

And yet they were doing it.

In Sackville Street the fires had begun to blaze as the rebels themselves burned the buildings near the G.P.O., the buildings that could give cover to the ever-tightening ring of British khaki.

The sky reddened behind the little column as Margaret Kingston guided it to where she had seen the guns. She had to guide them, for her knowledge of the city was not enough for her to give directions.

They wound their way in and out of buildings, across backyards, down lanes, avoiding always the chance of a clash with the military. Only once did they come under fire. As they darted across a street a machine gun opened up from a distant rooftop and splattered its bullets off the cobbles.

Margaret saw fear on some of the faces around her, but no one stopped, no one tried to back out. In herself she felt no fear, only a strange, wild elation as she walked at Declan's side. Had any of her friends, she wondered, spotted her as she left the G.P.O.? How many would know? All of them, she hoped. She wanted the world to know now what she had done.

The guns had settled down to a steady rate of fire, and now the blast of their muzzles was closer than the explosions of the shells as they pounded into the City Hall and the buildings beside it.

Eighteen-pounders, Terence McKeon thought. They would be eighteen-pounders. There was one troop of four eighteen-pounders at Athlone in the Reserve Brigade. They must have been rushed to the city. And they must be destroyed. As far as he knew—and the Brotherhood was well informed—this was the only available artillery in Ireland.

Destroy these guns and the Rising still had a chance. Or—reason told him—if not a chance, at least the possibility of leaving such a scar on English memories that the next time . . .

The professor had been right, of course. Logically, this Rising had no chance. But the next time . . .

It took a determined effort to keep his mind on the present, not to let his imagination roam ahead into the future.

"Round the next corner," Margaret told him quietly. "When I left them they were digging up the square setts of the road."

Field artillery required soft ground for the spade at the tail end of the carriage to dig in and hold the gun against the force of the recoil. But the British gunners had not had time to dig out the road properly. The guns were firing off their wheels, and at each shot the gun would drive backward across the road, carriage and spade driving showers of sparks from the cobbles.

Sweating gunners had to manhandle the weapons back into

position for each shot. And the gun had then to be relaid on its target. Accurate shooting was impossible, and the firing rate was slow and unsteady. More shells were crashing over and to either side of the target than were hitting it.

Terence McKeon prowled through the buildings alone until he reached a window where he could look down on the gun site. Standing well back inside the house so that he was not seen from below, he took heart from the obvious confusion of the English.

They're no better than ourselves, he marveled as he listened to the conflicting orders in the street below.

A mental picture of a grim, supremely efficient race of militarists quietly collapsed. They could be beaten, he assured himself.

They would be beaten.

He hurried back to his waiting men.

"Margaret, you've done all you can now." He smiled briefly. "You'd better leave before we go into action."

Margaret did not move.

"I'm a nurse," she said. "Not a very good one, but a nurse. You'll need me."

Terence McKeon eyed her for a moment and nodded. "If that's what you want. . . . Right, men! That is what we're going to do . . ."

The poet McMahon was in very poor shape indeed. He was, of course, drunk. It was a good many years since he had been totally sober, probably not since he left—or was expelled from, rather—Maynooth College. He had been designed for the priesthood by his mother, and he put the story about that the clash between religion and literature had caused something of a mental breakdown.

In fact he had already discovered the pleasures of strong drink by then, and his expulsion from the college had come after his being discovered one morning in the larder where the sacramental wine was stored. He was piously and paralytically drunk.

He did not go home to the farm in Galway where his mother would be waiting with a frozen face and the offer of long years of expiation in the potato field. Instead he made for the forbidden splendors of Dublin, where a man with a glib tongue could always earn a living of sorts. There he had written pieces for the newspapers and a volume of verse which had been published but had sold no more than four hundred copies. Mainly he spent his time in bars talking about being a poet and carrying out various minor and discreditable enterprises on the hairy edge of the law.

Presently he was living with an aging prostitute who was flattered to have even a spoiled priest under her roof tree. Or rather, he had been living with her until the previous night. There had been a disagreement over a matter of a sovereign missing from the lady's purse.

"For God's sake, it's not that I grudge the money. A man needs money in his pocket if he is a man at all, and I'd be the last to say you nay were you only to ask for it. But poking and prying and taking out of purses. . . . I'll not have you, so you may go, McMahon, and stay gone at that."

She being bigger than he was, he did not argue. He gathered up various scrawls he had made which he called his poetry and also two copies of his book. He walked out into a night lively with rebellion and in various hostelries contrived to get more than his usual ration of spirits. In the looting he came by some bottles of whiskey, and these were a good enough substitute for a roof over his head for one night.

Now, with all the fiends of hangover rattling his brain and a desperate sickness in his belly, a total dissociation from reality was in his mind. More than anything he wanted more to drink, and he prowled through the city seeking it in vain.

Once he came on a scattered group of bodies lying casually behind a barricade with a new flag on a broken staff fluttering in the gutter.

"Boys!" he cried. "You're worse than myself. Oh, you've dirled the bottles to be lying there so sound! Up out of it, you rascals. Up before the peelers come and lift you—"

He kicked one of them and saw him turn slowly under the impact, revealing a bloody concavity where the face had been.

Owlishly he stared, and then it came to him that there was a rising on. He remembered there being a rising now that he saw the bodies. He felt ill as he looked down at the bloody face, but it had been so long since he had eaten that he could only retch painfully.

"Dead men everywhere," he muttered. "Oh, what a desperate day for Ireland!"

There were five men lying there, and it seemed to him that these five men would no longer need whatever money might be in their pockets.

"Sure you'd not grudge a poet the price of a drink," he placated their deadness. "A drop of brandy or rum or whiskey or the like. Now forgive me, men, but you'll have no more call for it."

As an afterthought he picked up the flag, bright and new, sewn by loving hands somewhere in the country. A flag like this should be of value somewhere. He held it up and watched its folds flutter bravely in the breeze.

"What a desperate day for Ireland," he intoned. "When her sons lie in the streets and their blood the gutters greets. What a desperate day for Ireland—"

At the street's end there was a public house, and joyfully he headed for it, flag fluttering and pockets jingling. It seemed to him he saw the pub's door open and then close again.

"Wait!" he cried. "Wait there, man of the pub. Wait for the poet McMahon. I have money, money . . ."

In the pub a frightened English soldier, cut off from his unit, saw a charging man and a fluttering flag; plainly he was being attacked.

McMahon fell with the flag about him, hardly comprehending the pain of the bullet in his chest, not realizing how truly poetic was his end or how he would feature in the legends of the future: the poet McMahon dead with an English bullet in him and his country's flag about him.

"What a desperate day for Ireland," he moaned. "Shooting a man for wanting a drink."

"Shoot him," Major Greyson said briefly and turned away to gaze out through the window of the drawing room of the house he had just taken. There were more rebels across the road, firing down from the rooftop in through the windows. Two of his callow youngsters had already been wounded in their assault on this house, which they had taken through the back door in a sudden surge across the yard.

In the bedroom upstairs two rebels were sprawled dead. There had been three in the house, and the third now hugged a smashed arm as a Kentish lad with a fresh face and rather bulging eyes pointed his wavering rifle at him.

"He was in the bathroom, sir, in the airing cupboard," said the Englishman.

"All right. Now shoot him."

"But he's a prisoner, sir. He surrendered," the private protested. Six months before he had been at school, studying with the intention of becoming a plant biologist.

"Shoot him," Grayson repeated. "I can't spare men to look after prisoners."

He continued to scan the other side of the road, planning his next move. If he moved down the street he could cross behind an overturned streetcar that had been partially burned and work his way up behind the other houses.

When he turned, the prisoner was still alive and the private was staring at him with an expression of hypnotized horror on his pale face. The prisoner was his own age, a dark-haired youngster in the Citizen Army's uniform. Tears were running down his face, but he said nothing and he was not even sobbing.

"Shoot him! That's an order. On the command fire you will fire. . . . *Fire!*"

His face working, his finger jerking in a conditioned reflex, the young private pulled the trigger.

The prisoner slammed back against the wall, stood erect for an instant and then sagged slowly, clutching at his belly. On the floor he lay writhing, dark blood spreading outward from beneath him across somebody's drawing room carpet.

"Bloody young fool, you haven't killed him. Again. Another shot. Through the head—"

The private was weeping now as he shot again and the man on the floor died.

As Greyson left the room he could hear the private retching violently. His lips twitched in something of a smile. They had to learn, he thought. They had to learn.

He called Lance Corporal Macnee and found him in a room to the rear of the building, stuffing his pockets with silver from a sideboard. A half-empty decanter of whiskey was on the sideboard.

"Sirr! All correct, sirr!"

"I'm sure it is."

Major Greyson took the decanter and poured a great swig of neat whiskey down his throat. Then he explained his fresh plans.

Macnee nodded his understanding and called the rest of the platoon from their positions on the upper floor, where they were still firing at the rebels on the rooftop.

Some of the youngsters were like the Kentish lad—sick and

bewildered—but in most of them by now the thrill of battle had conquered other feelings. There were hard smiles on their young faces and a curious bleak glint in their eyes.

The streetcar was reached safely, and though a few shots whined down the street they reached the other side without casualties. Greyson worked his men up the long, tall terrace, sometimes on the roofs, sometimes flitting from back door to back door.

Some grenades began to explode as they reached the rebel-held house, but they were homemade grenades and did little damage.

Greyson reached the house next to the rebels and paused while his men gathered.

"Any building workers among you? Good man—find me the weakest spot in this wall."

A huge, gangling lad thumped at the wall with his fist.

"Mostly plaster here, sir," he announced in a Devon brogue.

"Right. Four men—take that table and use it as a battering ram. I want the wall down in one blow if we can do it. Two more men ready to open fire—though I think all the enemy are on the roof. Macnee—get your best shots at the back door ready to shoot up at the roof as we go through below here."

In moments everyone was in position.

"Right!"

Four strong men with a heavy refectory table in their grasp thundered across a dining room. And with a crash a great polygonal rift appeared in the wall. A flap of wallpaper hung over it for an instant and then dropped to the floor.

There was no one in the room beyond, and Greyson darted out to the foot of the stairs. Above, someone had heard the crash and rushed out onto the landing to investigate.

Carefully Major Greyson aimed his Webley and saw a face vanish above. From the garden came the sudden crackle of the Lee-Enfields of his own men mingled with the slower thump of the single-shot Mausers above.

"Fix bayonets," Greyson ordered quietly. "Right! Up the stairs."

He led the rush, and it was his own Webley which blasted away the first man to come to the door of a bedroom and gape in an instant's terror. But it was one of the older men of the platoon—a gray-faced ex-miner—who led the charge into the room.

The rebels swung from the window. The miner's bayonet sogged home hard into the belly of one. A shot from a young private smashed into the other's face.

There was a trapdoor above with a hoisting ladder leading down from it. And above, on the roof, the Irish were still firing. They had heard nothing of the inrush of the military and had probably accepted the shots from below as from their own people. Outside, Macnee's men still kept up a covering fire.

Greyson motioned to his own group for silence and started up the stairs. From the trapdoor he was looking down on seven men spread out behind the parapet. Even in that instant he marveled at the firepower those seven had produced with their antique arms. He had been sure there were at least twenty men in the house.

Quietly he ducked his head down and beckoned six men forward. By signs he indicated what they were to do and led them up onto the roof.

In complete silence the men spread out along the roof, and even when one of them slipped and his boots clattered on the slates, the rebels did not look around.

The covering fire from the garden continued steadily, with the rebels returning it, until the moment when Greyson lifted his revolver and quietly and deliberately aimed at the spine of the nearest man.

The blast of the explosion from behind brought the snipers turning around with one instant jerk. And as they were turning, the bayonets went to work, driving into unguarded, unsuspecting backs or the bellies of men who had turned.

"Finish them off!" Greyson rapped as his men stood above the writhing bodies. "We've no time for prisoners or casualties."

From one man Greyson took a pair of binoculars and seated himself on the parapet to scan out the area and decide his next move. Behind him the soldiers were chattering eagerly, almost hysterically. They talked as if they were drunk. They had come a long way in experience since their platoon commander had been shot.

Two streets away the eighteen-pounders were blazing the air, and Greyson could see a little of their position. His nose twitched in contempt. Their commander was certainly a fool. He was wide open to enfilade, and he did not seem to have set out any pickets at all. He could lose those guns.

Greyson's eyes narrowed abruptly.

"My God, he will lose them!"

His eyes had picked up furtive movements behind three isolated houses to one side of the gun position. Carefully he refocused the glasses and then with incredulous delight picked out one and then another familiar face.

"The Kilcroom gang!" he breathed. "And right where I want them!"

And an unholy glee rocked him as he saw Terence McKeon make his careful dispositions and prepare to attack.

30. Dublin's Burning!

The center of Dublin seemed all ablaze as Terence McKeon completed his battle plan.

It was simple enough. From the cover of a house behind the artillery half of his men would give covering fire while the rest charged the guns. The charging party would be carrying grenades, and they were to thrust these into the breeches or down the barrels of the eighteen-pounders. Any grenades left over were to be thrown among the guns' ammunition.

"Speed's the whole thing. They don't know we're here. When we attack they'll panic. I expect the gunners will run. Let them. The important thing is to put the guns out of action. Right? When I give the word then, and God go with us all."

He eyed the British position once again, confirming the incredible truth that they had put out no outposts, that there were only the artillery officers and their men there and that there was no lurking party of infantry anywhere to guard them.

A youngster slowly twisted his head to look at the blaze behind them, at the sky red with Dublin's agony.

"There was a song we had at school—'London's burning'— only now it's Dublin burning . . ."

The battery blasted off a salvo, and as the sweating gunners manhandled the weapons back into place and sponged out the reeking barrels, Terence McKeon stood up from behind the cover of the garden wall that hid them all.

"Righto, boys," he said in an almost conversational tone.

287

And as he ran forward he began to fire the Mauser pistol.

On the gunners' faces were ludicrous expressions of surprise as the bullets sang among them and they swung around to see the thin line of charging men.

The rebels were outnumbered by at least two to one, but the sheer shock of surprise carried them forward and began to scatter the gunners from about their breeches. From behind came the steady hammer of the Howth Mausers.

Declan O'Donovan was at McKeon's right hand, whooping aloud as he ran, swinging his rifle in one hand like a club. Peadar Casey, on the left of the line, was firing his pistol.

Only the officers offered any real resistance. One drew his sword, still incredibly worn as if this was a peacetime demonstration, and called on his men to follow him. They had already scattered to the far side of the road and into the houses where their small arms had been stacked.

"Right, me bucko!" Declan roared. "If it's a fight you're looking for—"

His clubbed rifle smashed the sword from the officer's hand, and his left fist swung in a wild blow that took the man behind the neck and felled him.

"Get up and fight!" the disappointed Declan yelled vainly. But the man was unconscious.

The other officer had darted behind the nearest gun and, using it as cover, was firing his Webley with good effect. Two of the rebels were down.

McKeon halted and took careful aim. His Mauser slammed out one round and the officer dropped with a head wound.

"The guns!" McKeon roared. "Smash the guns!"

He thrust one of the homemade grenades into the breech of the nearest eighteen-pounder and ran on to the next. Vaguely he heard one and then another muffled explosion.

In sight there was no one standing, no one to fight. Declan

roared his rage and charged for the nearest house toward which he had seen the men running like rabbits into a warren.

He burst into a hallway as the first of the British started out, carrying their rifles. He hit them like a tidal wave, and afterward the same men swore they had been overwhelmed by a dozen rebels.

Declan swept through the house and out of the back door in pursuit of two running men. There was a yard beyond the back door, and Declan felled the first man as he crossed the yard, his rifle butt catching him in the kidneys and dropping him in a convulsive, moaning heap. The second was over the wall before Declan could grab him.

The Irishman followed in a bound that put one foot on a dustbin and the second on the wall's crown. Beyond was a lane, narrow and cobbled, access for emptying the dustbins.

The soldier had already vanished. Declan chose quickly and turned right—wrongly, as it transpired. He ran down the lane, found that it ended in a blank wall, cursed and turned back.

The lane brought him out at last into an open street but not the one he had left, not the one where Kilcroom was fighting. He chose quickly and again wrongly, turned toward the sound of fighting and in a minute or so ran into an irregular riot where a group of the Royal Irish Constabulary were swinging batons and carbines to clear the street of looters pillaging a terrace of big houses.

Declan paused to draw breath and to assure himself that this was the wrong battle. He was turning back, turning to look for the Kilcroom men, when across the crowd he saw a familiar shape. There could not be in Dublin two other men like Big Teague and the gombeen-man.

Raymond McCarthy had progressed beyond his ass cart now. From somewhere he had obtained a motor lorry, and he was urging the mob to throw loot into its back while Big Teague stood impassively at his shoulder, holding a leather satchel full of half crowns.

The gombeen-man was not bargaining this day. Half-a-crown was his price, whether it was for a brocaded curtain, a Sheraton dressing table or a case of Sèvres china. Half-a-crown. And the looters had so little knowledge of the value of what they stole that they were taking the money gladly.

The police were fighting a losing battle. They were under a gray-haired sergeant whose years of service had inhibited him against the actual use of the carbines as firearms. One volley would have cleared the street. But the police force in normal times made such a fuss about the loss of a single round of ammunition that the sergeant could not bring himself to give the order that would leave a dozen rounds to be accounted for. Perhaps, even, the thought of shooting did not come into his mind.

The whole detachment was driven around the corner and out of sight.

And Declan forced his way through the throng toward the gombeen-man and Big Teague.

In his throat was a dryness which could almost have been fear. But it was counterbalanced by memory and a gorgeous bloody mist of rage. The memory of that humiliation was suddenly bright, dug up from the grave-house of the past. He could remember the sound of Big Teague's horny hand on his backside. He could feel again the sting of pain.

And yet it was the gombeen-man he really hated. Teague was no more than McCarthy's instrument.

"Right, you bastard," he growled and leveled his rifle. "Right, McCarthy, you twisting—"

The gombeen-man's face went waxlike when he saw O'Donovan, and for a moment his mouth opened enough to show its ever-hidden teeth.

"O'Donovan," he croaked at last.

Then his eyes bobbed like black cherries in a fruit cup.

"Teague," he ordered. "Teague, get him."

O'Donovan aimed carefully for the gombeen-man's belly and pressed the trigger.

But the rifle's use as a club had loosened the bolt. There was no shuddering kick of recoil. Relief loosened the muscles in McCarthy's face and he swayed for a moment.

Teague lumbered forward, hands spread to grab Declan. He was big, Declan thought, just as big as he remembered. The memory of that terrible strength which had humiliated his own youth came back and almost succeeded in paralyzing his responses.

For a moment the two circled, and some of the crowd gathered curiously, for a fight was as interesting as looting.

Teague thrust out a hand and O'Donovan swung at him with the rifle. Teague's other hand flew up, caught the weapon and jerked it from Declan's grasp in a reflex gesture. The strength was still there, Declan thought. He felt a heart-cramping instant of terror, of memory. He lashed out with his fist. It was not a full-blooded blow, for he was off-balance, punching as the rifle was yanked from him, but it was a good enough punch to have felled most ordinary men.

Big Teague hardly blinked as the punch exploded on his jaw. His left hand pawed at Declan's shoulder, half grabbing it, tweaking the flesh painfully as Declan wriggled clear.

Teague had dropped the rifle as soon as he had seized it. He had never in his life needed a weapon other than his own strength. He shuffled closer to Declan, trying to back him toward the lorry, to pin him against it.

Declan looked into the flat, expressionless face, as like a weathered knob of granite now as it had been when first he saw it. He evaded the attack and lunged swiftly with a rain of blows to the giant's body. There was fat on Teague, but under the fat was the impermeable layer of muscle that absorbed every blow.

"Why'n't ye stand up til him and fight?" jeered a voice from the crowd. "It's not a dancing match."

Declan tried to dance back as Teague's hand swung. But suddenly his head was held. Teague's fingers were locked in the curly length of his hair. Almost casually the big man forced Declan's head down and brought his own knee up. Declan felt the impact, saw blood spurt, but felt no pain.

He threw himself back as the knee rose again. There was a new pain. Teague did not free his hair. A patch of Declan's scalp was left dangling bloodily in the big man's blunt fingers.

And still Teague was coming at him, the satchel of coins clinking at his side and his face still totally without emotion.

Declan O'Donovan felt the taste, the incredible, acrid flavor of defeat in his mouth. His face was a mask of blood from his nose. More blood poured over his forehead from the raw patch on his head.

"Hurry up, Teague!" the gombeen-man ordered.

And for an instant Big Teague's gaze left Declan O'Donovan.

Declan seized the instant, and as he plunged forward he knew what he must do. Again he evaded the swinging arms and with his own speed got behind Teague, grabbing at the leather strap of the money satchel.

There was a silence in the crowd, and then a roar of approval.

He had turned the tables now, turned them with a vengeance. He rode the big man as a horsebreaker rides an unruly colt. His legs gripped the man's waist. His body strained back against the reins. His knuckles were white with the strength of his grip on the leather strap that was around Big Teague's neck.

Big Teague clawed up and backward, but Declan was beyond his reach. The strap bit deeper and still deeper into his skin. Air was closed off from his lungs. Blood pressed in vain to pass up his carotid artery into his brain.

Big Teague swayed, and as Declan clung mercilessly, heaved the strap still tighter. Big Teague fell.

The gombeen-man found his tongue. His creature was destroyed. But O'Donovan should not escape.

"Who's paying you?" he demanded of the crowd. "Get that Fenian bastard there. Get him!"

But now O'Donovan was on his feet again, teeth shining through the mask of blood. He held the satchel.

"Paying you? I'm paying you, me merry boys. I'm paying you!"

He was roaring with laughter as he scooped great handfuls of silver coins from the satchel, scattered them across the street, threw them high into the air. A silver shower fell among the crowd, and if they had been planning to help the gombeen-man, the thought was no longer in their minds.

Declan threw the satchel high and at an easy lope started in the wake of Raymond McCarthy, who was running ahead with a high-kneed, jerky action like a flustered hen.

There was no hurry, Declan thought. He would certainly catch the little man.

John Pritchard sat halfway up the first flight of stairs in his home with a double-barreled shotgun in his grasp. It was a good London gun, by Churchill's. He had ordered it two years before when he had been invited to a pheasant shoot at a wealthy customer's home.

Now he sat on the rich pile of the carpet, the cold steel a comfort to his hands and an atavistic male pride filling his heart. Upstairs his women were in their rooms. He was protecting them as a man had the fundamental obligation to do.

So it must have been with those Pritchards long ago, he

thought. The men who came out in '98, the men who followed Wolfe Tone and Henry Joy McCracken, those dour, freedom-loving Presbyterians. They had not scrupled to take up arms to defend freedom and family. Nor would he.

But there was no denying a certain difference between the situations. Those ancestors had been "out," taking positive action in the fight for freedom. He was definitely in.

Just the same he was fighting, or ready to fight. And the women had been splendid. Clorinda especially. She had shown no fear at all.

"Mama," she had told his wife, "we should not be in Papa's way if they come. It would distract him."

She would certainly have her motorcar when this disturbance was over.

Through the transom of the door he could see down the front steps of the house. He could see the redness in the sky as Dublin burned, and it was some comfort to know that he had varied his insurance cover to include riots and acts of God. The expense would certainly be worth it, for fires were evident in the dock region. He had little doubt that his own warehouse would dissolve in the flames as soon as they touched it.

When McCarthy came staggering toward the steps, Pritchard was first startled and then indignant. Once McCarthy had had the effrontery to visit the house and Pritchard had made his views very plain on the subject. Now the man was coming again.

Did he still hope to persuade Pritchard into joining him in his plan to buy loot? What sort of a man did he think he was?

Then, as the second man loped along in the gombeen-man's wake, another thought struck John Pritchard. McCarthy was out for revenge. Deprived of the use of Pritchard's warehouse he was egging on the mob to loot Pritchard's own house.

For a moment John Pritchard had a vision of the ragged, stinking scum bursting in through the door, trampling with their rough boots across the polished floors, ripping down the curtains, smashing the furniture. He saw his wife and daughter mishandled.

Through the transom Pritchard saw McCarthy's mouthing, but he could hear no words. In any case, they would be threats.

No man threatened John Pritchard.

There was thundering on the door. They were trying to break in, out of sight now, so close to the door—

Tongue too big for his mouth, heart pounding audibly, John Pritchard paced down the steps with the shotgun in his grasp.

Declan O'Donovan laid the gombeen-man's body on the top step and stiffened slowly. He felt cheated. McCarthy had put up scarcely a fight, staring at him like a rabbit in front of a weasel, mouth working silently, eyes huge and wide. He had struggled so little that Declan thought he was shamming when he released his grip of the man's throat.

When he put him down on the step he was wary of treachery, for surely the man who had walked in his nightmares so often could not really be so fragile that a grip of the neck could kill him?

And yet the gombeen-man's head lolled on his skew-turned neck. There was no rise and fall of the chest. Declan spat on the dead face as he had once spat on the live one and turned to go.

Then, as he gazed up and down the wealthy respectability of the street, an idea struck him. He laughed aloud as he lifted the heavy iron knocker and thundered on the door.

He wondered what respectability would do when it found

a dead man on its doorstep. He could not know how like a break-in attempt his thundering sounded or the courage that despair would give to the mildest of men.

He did not see the letter box open or the gun's muzzle probe out from the slit.

"Jasus!" he cried unbelievingly over the echoes of the gunshot. "I'm hit. I've been shot . . ."

Hand clapped to his arm, he leaped down the steps and began to run.

Terence McKeon was not even aware that Declan had been absent from the battle. Vaguely he was conscious that the big man was clutching an arm, bleeding heavily. But events were moving too quickly for him to be concerned with the worries of others.

Around the guns there was still fighting, and from across the street the soldiers had begun a fire which was inaccurate at the moment but would swiftly steady.

Into this confusion came the shrill sound of Margaret Kingston's scream, cutting the air like a knife. He cursed her silently, and himself for allowing her to come so far. He should have known that she would become hysterical.

But Margaret Kingston's scream was not hysteria.

It was a warning.

Margaret alone heard the stealthy approach of Greyson's men from behind the building. And one scream was all she could give before a hand clapped across her mouth and a surge of khaki burst past her.

Terence McKeon's support group was dealt with in the first furious blaze of Greyson's fire. Then the military had taken over the cover and were firing on the men around the guns.

"Bayonets!" Greyson roared. "Charge!"

It was all over with appalling speed, and afterward Margaret's only memory of Greyson's attack was the sight of one rebel backing slowly away before a British lance corporal.

The Volunteer was crouched a little, hands held out before him pleadingly, and a thin, continuous screaming was coming from his throat, a sound like a snared rabbit's cry.

"It's nau use, sonny," the soldier assured him. "It's nau use at all. Ye've got to get it."

The Volunteer, one of the youngest, came to a halt with an eighteen-pounder at his back, and the Englishman lunged casually with his bayonet, driving it into the Irishman just below the heart.

Margaret never forgot the vivid flow of blasphemy as the Irishman fell and the soldier could not free his bayonet from the bones where it had lodged. His foot was on the man's chest, and he had to lever rifle and bayonet backward and forward until at last the blade came free.

She did not see the care with which Major Greyson insured that neither O'Donovan nor McKeon was killed, or the particular aim he took at Peadar Casey when the second in command's Mauser jammed. Casey's face seemed to shrink into a waxen image of humanity, colorless and lined deeply. Every hair of his four-day beard stood out stiffly, catching the light like a halo. But there was still defiance in his posture.

"Go on then, me gallant captain," he sneered. "Shoot and be done with it. The People's cause will live on even if I don't."

"People's cause!" Greyson replied. "You mean the chance to loot and steal and kill. People's cause! I didn't see too many of the people on your side!"

"The time'll come," Casey growled. "Oh, the time'll come, and all you high-riding people will be swept away and forgotten as if you never existed. You're like one of them beasts in the museum—extinct, only you don't know it."

Behind Casey horses were still screaming, and under the

297

nearest gun a rebel lay crying for his mother through the blood that bubbled from his lips.

"You'll die without a priest," Greyson taunted. "You'll be straight for hell fire."

"I'll keep a place hot for you, then. You'll not be long behind me." Casey's voice came thickly, and somehow he managed to twist a sneer to his lips. He edged a little closer to Greyson. "Anyway, there was no priest there when I came into the world. I can go out of it without their help, too. Priests! Leeches and bloodsuckers, living on the poor. That's your priests—"

Completely without warning his right hand jerked into movement and the heavy Mauser hurtled at Greyson's head. It would have stunned him at the least had it hit. But the major jerked aside, and the metal only grazed his scalp.

But his sudden movement made his finger tighten on the trigger. The Webley barked, and Peadar Casey spun and fell.

For a moment Greyson thought he had killed the man. Then he saw blood oozing from the wound in his back. It was well out toward the shoulder.

Greyson pointed the Webley at the back of Casey's head, again his finger tightened on the trigger. Then his finger eased and he lowered the weapon.

"No," he said aloud. "Not yet. There's plenty of time."

The gunners came out sheepishly from their cover, and Greyson took McKeon's weary surrender.

"What'll we do now, sir?" asked a Middlesex bombardier. "Like with the officers dead—"

"Get on with your job," Greyson said roughly. "You know your targets, don't you? And get your subaltern to a doctor. He's not dead, only wounded."

He felt very pleased with himself. The action had gone off even better than he had hoped. He had saved the guns, and maybe in saving them he had saved Dublin—except, of course, that judging from the look of the sky there wasn't much of Dublin left to save.

Also he had his prisoners. Above all, he had his prisoners. Some of the Kilcroom men had escaped. But he had the ones he wanted. He had McKeon and Casey—and especially he had Declan O'Donovan.

"We've got a room with a lock on it there, sir," the bombardier indicated. "If you want, we could take the prisoners."

Greyson smiled, a quiet brilliant smile that showed all his teeth.

"Thank you, bombardier. I can look after the prisoners. You continue with your target. . . . Macnee, march the prisoners off."

"The young leddy too?"

"The woman too," Major Greyson agreed.

As the doleful procession moved down the street one of the English soldiers began to sing: "Dublin's burning, Dublin's burning. . . . Fire, fire . . ."

And as they marched on, the chorus was taken up by the whole raggle-taggle, triumphant platoon.

"Dublin's burning . . ."

31. *The Cellar*

The cellar had been used for storing junk. There were broken-down chairs, a rump-sprung couch, a sideboard with one leg missing and various items of more or less useless furniture and household appliances.

Inside were Major Greyson, Lance Corporal Macnee, the ex-miner and one of the younger privates who had shown a distinct relish for the bayonet within Greyson's sight. The remainder of the platoon were stationed farther down the street, out of earshot of the house and certainly out of earshot of the cellar.

Also in the cellar were Declan O'Donovan, Terence McKeon and Margaret Kingston. Each man was tied securely, arms behind backs and ankles hobbled. Peadar Casey lay unconscious against the wall.

The soldiers put their guns aside. There was no need for them now.

"Well, my friends." Greyson smiled. "I expect you know why you're down here. I want some information from you. I want the names and addresses of all your gang, the names and addresses of your superiors, any codes you use and any other information you may have which you think might be of use and which might influence me toward some degree of clemency."

Terence McKeon said nothing. He did not even look at the major. As best he could, he was abstracting his mind completely from the present time and place. He was trying to

300

repeat in his mind the whole of Goldsmith's "Deserted Village."

Sweet Auburn, loveliest village of the plain, he recited to himself.

Silence was never Declan O'Donovan's way. Now, bound, he could still rage.

"What sort of dirty traitors do you take us for?" he demanded.

"Do you mean to deny me this information? You're not going to tell me anything?"

"Oh, I'll tell you something all right!" Declan roared.

There was an expectant hush.

"Kiss me arse!" he bellowed. "That's all I'll tell you!"

Greyson did not stir. Rather, he smiled faintly as if this was much what he had expected.

"Your lives are all, of course, forfeit," he said. "You have been guilty of treason against the Crown. Martial law has been declared. I will be quite within my rights in shooting you."

"Get on with it then, you long-winded bastard."

Declan glared at him defiantly, then hawked in his throat for a volume of spittle.

Greyson moved easily aside as the blob of saliva shot past him.

"What an uncouth peasant you are, O'Donovan."

"The blood's as good blood in my veins as in yours!" Declan cried with sudden absurdity. "An English gentleman! Oh, it's fine we know the kind of gentleman you are!"

McKeon said nothing, and Margaret leaned against the wall in numbed horror, not believing that this was happening, that she was here, or Declan or Greyson. Sooner or later she would awaken and the nightmare would be over.

"A gentleman?" Greyson's good humor was impermeable to insult. "You consider yourself a gentleman? Eh? Now that's interesting. Generally speaking, the first mark of a gentleman is considered to be his attitude to the ladies."

McKeon was on safer ground in his mental exercise now, having reached the village schoolmaster. *And still they came and still the wonder grew/That one small head could carry all he knew.*

Was there perhaps a simple vanity in a teacher's mind, a need to show off to the ignorant the knowledge that was his? With utter determination he isolated himself from his presence in the cellar.

"A true gentleman will do anything to avoid embarrassment to a lady," Major Greyson said smoothly. "Anything would include, for example, giving me the information I have requested."

Declan glared at him, his bull head thrust forward and his tremendous muscles fighting vainly with the ropes that held his wrists and arms. In his eyes there was now a faint bewilderment.

"I've told you, I'll say nothing!" he spat.

Peadar Casey lay forgotten. He had been unconscious when they dragged him down to the cellar. But he had been tied too, though not as carefully as the others. Now, despite the agony of his left shoulder, his wrists were twisting, his fingertips reaching for the knot. The frayed ends of the rope came into his grasp, and he began to work at them. He kept his eyes closed as he worked, hoping they would think him still unconscious.

Greyson walked over to Margaret Kingston. His hand slapped hard across her face, sending a trickle of blood flowing from the corner of her mouth.

"Well, O'Donovan?"

He dropped the bayonet, and his left fist thumped into Margaret's stomach.

"Just a few bits of information," Greyson taunted, "and you'll save your doxie a lot of grief."

In his eyes was a wild, inhuman light. He seized Margaret's blond hair, twisting her head back agonizingly, and with his other hand he punched hard at her. Margaret screamed in agony.

The scream was like a trigger that abruptly freed every savage, sadistic element of Greyson's nature. He punched the girl again and again with strong, vicious blows.

And all the while Peadar Casey worked at the ropes, fingered the knot carefully into freedom, drew strand after strand away from its grip. As he struggled, the girl's cries were loud in his ears, louder than they had been that night in the summerhouse. He had gone then to kill her for a traitor. But she had been no traitor. Yet he had left her with this man, left her then at his mercy.

If he had acted then, he thought, this would not now be happening.

One wrist pulled suddenly from the loosened rope. He wriggled it gently to find the use that was still in it, then worked the other one free.

But could he reach down now to his ankles without being seen? Cautiously he opened his eyes a fraction.

Despite the men holding her, Margaret Kingston was doubled up in agony, not so much screaming as retching, a terrible, hoarse sound that should have brought pity to a hunting wolf. But there was no pity in Greyson's heart.

"Over the table with her," he growled.

Declan was howling abuse, roaring every profanity he knew. But no one paid him the slightest attention as he twisted and fought vainly against his bonds.

Now Greyson had a rifle sling in his hand, a long webbing strap with a brass buckle at each end. Slowly, carefully, he wound one end around his wrist. The strap whistled through the air, and Margaret screamed again as the buckle bit into the flesh of her buttocks.

All the soldiers were intent on the work at hand. No one was paying any attention at all to Peadar Casey as he drew his ankles up within reach of his fingers and began to pluck at the fresh knot.

Greyson had to stop to catch his breath.

"Well, Donovan?" he asked. "Ready to talk yet? Or shall we give her some more?"

Declan writhed impotently.

"No!" Margaret's voice came faintly. "Don't. Not a word to them, Declan—"

She was jerking uncontrollably as the men held her across the table. Convulsive waves of pain were tearing her within as the beating went remorselessly on.

Now blood trickled down her legs. And not all of it came from the multitude of strap cuts that had wealed all her back with stripes now swiftly turning from red to black.

Margaret Kingston felt the agony of her womb twisting within her, shedding its burden. It was a greater agony than the blows that still fell. A life had almost been and now would not be. And now she knew there was nothing more these men could do to her but kill her. Her screams began to die.

Peadar Casey was at last free.

And in his heart was a tumult of mixed emotions.

For now he could dart up the steps and away to safety. This he could do surely, for he would be at the door before any of the men would see him. And he could bring help. He could bring others to save McKeon and O'Donovan and the woman.

That was what he should do: get away, bring help—

And yet he could not forget that he had left this woman to her fate once before. Could he do it again? Though she was of the horse people and, by being in the carriage, bore some of the blame for Liam's death, could he abandon her once more?

And even if he brought help—who would be alive to gain from it when he came back? For as soon as he escaped would Greyson not kill the prisoners at once? He had to run—and he had to stay.

Cautiously he stretched his legs, and still no one noticed him. One quick movement and he could be on his feet. Cautiously, steadily, he prepared for movement.

And still the flogging went on, as Declan struggled vainly and McKeon tried to shut out all the present.

Peadar Casey sprang to his feet, and even in that instant did not know if he were going to run or stay.

Then the British lance corporal turned and saw him and the die was cast.

"The prisoner—" he started to gulp.

And Casey was on him, his foot kicking and his good arm flailing. The foot took the miner in the groin and doubled him up. The good fist hit Lance Corporal Macnee and threw him backward across the room.

And despite the agony in his shoulder, Casey's left hand grabbed at Greyson's blood-smeared strap and jerked the officer toward him. As Greyson moved, Casey's head drove forward in a butt that smashed his forehead into the major's teeth.

Then the young soldier left his grip on Margaret and threw himself at Casey, grappling him from behind.

Bodies thrashed around the room. The ancient furniture crumbled under impact after impact. Greyson went down with Casey on top of him, and on top of both was the soldier, clinging to Casey's arms, rendering him almost helpless.

But Peadar Casey had one weapon left.

His teeth snapped and then closed on Greyson's neck.

Greyson was screaming thinly now as Casey's teeth forced into his skin, drove toward his windpipe and his arteries.

I'll kill him, Casey thought, *kill him, kill him* . . .

And with this thought drumming through his skull, Casey died.

For Lance Corporal Macnee had recovered, and with great care he poised himself above the struggling heap of bodies and aimed a powerful kick at Peadar Casey's head.

There was no mistaking the dry crunch of bones breaking or the instant limpness that dropped Casey's head sideways across the major's shoulder.

Greyson dabbed ferociously at his bruised throat with a blood-stained handkerchief and glared at his other prisoners. Then his gaze snapped back to his men.

"All right, let's get on with it!" he said. "One of them's going to talk."

Lance Corporal Macnee coughed apologetically.

"The wuman's fainted, sirr," he said. "I doot she's well awa'."

Scowling, Greyson turned on Declan and shook him.

"Are you going to talk now or are we going to have to bring her round again?" he demanded. "Come on, it's up to you—"

Declan's answer was a scream. For Greyson's jerk had forced his wound against the battered couch and a stab of agony ran through him.

Greyson was suddenly very still and thoughtful. Then, quite deliberately, he punched Declan on the wound.

And again Declan O'Donovan screamed.

"So here's our weak link," Greyson gloated. "It looks as though we've been barking up the wrong tree. Yes, I think we have."

For a third time he struck O'Donovan's wounded arm. And with the same result.

O'Donovan screamed loudly.

"You can leave the woman," Greyson said. "I'm just beginning to understand I misread the situation."

He squeezed on the wound, and Declan's cry rang out again.

"It seems our Irish gentleman, our Mr. O'Donovan, is just a little sensitive to pain. He doesn't mind his doxie getting it. But when it comes a little closer to home—"

Declan was swearing again, a constant flow of expletives and blasphemy flooding his lips. Greyson affected a certain distaste, curling his lip in a sneer while he continued to knead and pound on the Irishman's wound.

And in his own place, Terence McKeon was remembering the words of Declan's mother: *He's never been hurt.*

She had meant emotionally. But it was true, too, that he had never truly been badly hurt physically. He had fought and taken his bruises. But he had always handed out more than he received. He had never been helpless and hurt. He had never really suffered.

Now he was helpless. And pain was going to be thrust on him.

How much could he stand? How much would he stand? Each man has a different threshold of pain. Agony to one is mere irritation to another.

"I think," said Greyson, "we'll see what this great lover boy is made of."

He slid the bayonet down Declan's belly and ripped at his trousers.

"Corporal Macnee, I've always been told that a kick in the private parts is the most painful blow of all. It's one I have not myself suffered. I would like to see if it's true, though."

"A kick would be a wee bit awkward," Macnee answered. "The way he's lying on the sofa. Not but what I haven't rattled a few goolies in my time. Like we're no' too ceremonious where I come from. But maybe a thump with a rifle butt would do as well."

"An excellent suggestion. Carry on, Corporal. But not too hard nor too well aimed at first. Let him savor what is to come."

And yet at the first blow Declan screamed.

McKeon abandoned his abstraction. He had no doubt now in his mind that Declan would talk.

"You'll have no use for any woman by the time we've finished with you," Greyson promised as the brass-shod butt shot forward again. "And this is only the beginning. So why not start talking now?"

"Say nothing, Declan!" McKeon ordered sharply. "Margaret told them nothing. So can you."

Greyson walked over and kicked him in the face.

"I think we can do without your advice, McKeon," he observed. "Another word and I'll shoot you now."

The youngster took over the rifle and pounded it again into the region of Declan's groin.

Declan screamed, and the tears ran down his cheeks in a steady stream.

"Jasus, Mary and Joseph!" he babbled. "Ah . . . ah! Oh, sweet Jasus!"

Greyson smiled. The Irishman was softening up nicely. All the bitterness this man had brought him welled up in the major's heart. This peasant had taken Margaret from him, her fortune, his future. By foiling his ambush of the gun smugglers back in Cork he had even brought his career to ruins.

It was right that he should suffer.

"Hit him again!" he ordered.

308

"Ah, no! No! No more. I can't take no more. Ah, for Jasus' sake . . ."

The tears coursed down Declan's cheeks, and he sobbed uncontrollably. And yet so far he had not been really hurt. The blows had been deliberately directed so that the muscles of his thighs had taken most of the impact, and his wriggling at each blow had made them glance over his body.

"Do you know what can happen to you?" Greyson inquired quietly. "Do you know what a few more knocks from the rifle will do? You'll swell up like a football. It'll be agony, O'Donovan—and permanent. You'll walk around with a football under your trousers."

Greyson laughed. A slow, harsh laugh.

"You could talk, of course. You could tell me what I want to know. And then you'd walk out of here a free man. And a whole man, what's more. Just a few words and it's over."

"They'll shoot you in the back once you've talked," Terence McKeon put in. "Don't trust them, Declan."

Greyson walked over and kicked McKeon again in the face.

"I want to see you hanged," he remarked pleasantly. "But that is only my preference. It is not necessary. I shall not mind shooting you. Be quiet!"

He turned and nodded to the young soldier, and the rifle was raised again.

"Take better aim this time," Greyson ordered.

And now, with the rifle poised for a final vicious blow, Declan O'Donovan cracked.

"No!" he screamed. "No more. I'll talk, I'll talk! No more, no more . . ."

32. No Grave, No Victory

In Terence McKeon there was an infinite sadness and pity rather than anger as Declan babbled out names and addresses, passwords and codes. He had been warned. Declan's own mother had warned him of the hidden weakness in her son. He had chosen to ignore the warning, so the blame, in all logic, must lie at his own door.

Margaret listened unbelievingly. This was not Declan, this was not the roaring boy who would defy the world with a laugh on his lips. This was some changeling thrust into Declan's body by Greyson's torture. She would not believe it. She would not.

Not even when Greyson himself strode over to her and jerked her erect by the hair of her head.

"There," he said in triumph. "That's the bastard you left me for! Now are you proud of yourself, you whore?"

He turned on McKeon.

"A great hero for Ireland," he sneered. "A fine patriot. Blabbing out his secrets—your secrets—before he's even really hurt. Set him on his feet," he ordered Macnee. "Untie him."

"You'll not let him go, sirr?"

"Do as you're told."

Puzzled, the lance corporal obeyed.

Declan's great head turned slowly from his captors and tormentors to McKeon and then to Margaret. His trousers, ripped at the waistband, began to fall down, and he clutched at them.

310

He was a pitiful, shameful figure, standing silent, eyes downcast.

"There's your man now," Greyson crowed. "And nothing so special, is he? Just a slimy, treacherous peasant who betrayed his friends. Well, go on, O'Donovan—get out!"

Declan blinked at Greyson.

"You're letting me go?" he said unbelievingly.

"I said I would if you talked. Don't you believe the word of a gentleman? But then, your sort wouldn't. Here, buy yourself a drink—"

His hand went to his pocket, and he flicked half-a-crown to the floor at Declan's feet. And in an automatic reflex Declan found himself stooping to take it. Only at the last second did his fingers fall short of the coin. He straightened, and his face was a violent, shamed red.

"Get out before I change my mind!" Greyson hissed.

And Declan shambled slowly for the cellar steps. His legs splayed from the ache in his groin, and his hands still clutched at his trousers. His eyes refused to meet Margaret's as he passed her, and he did not ask what was to become of the others. And that was the most terrible thing of all to the girl. Lost in his own abject misery, he had no thought for the rest of them.

For just an instant hope flared in Margaret as Declan neared the rifles leaning against the wall. He could be acting. He could be seeming cowed to get the chance of snatching at a rifle, of swinging around and, in a final blaze of action, atoning for what he had done and what he had said.

The thought was in McKeon's mind, too. Perhaps after all Declan had talked just to get the chance to be free for an instant.

In another step he would reach the rifles, seize one and turn on his tormentors. Even were the weapons not loaded, in the confined space of the cellar Declan could club down the enemy, destroy them with his great strength.

But Declan O'Donovan did not even see the rifles as he stumbled up the steps. He had no thought of resistance, of turning to fight. He was indeed beyond thought now. There was no spirit in him, nothing but a knowledge of his ultimate weakness and of what he had done. Within, he was as numb as if he lay under an anesthetic.

He shuffled to the door at the top of the steps and opened it slowly. And from there it was to Greyson and not to his comrades or his woman that his gaze went. He looked at him silently as if imploring permission to leave.

In the cellar no one spoke until he had gone out into the street. Distantly they could hear rifle fire.

Others still fought.

"And you really thought you could beat us with trash like that?" Greyson sneered at Terence McKeon. "My God, you must have been mad!"

McKeon said nothing. He was thinking of the men and women whose names were now on Greyson's list, men and women who would meet the same fate as themselves. He thought of the long agony still to come and held his peace.

Greyson walked across the cellar and beckoned his men to follow him. He had his pistol in his hand now. As he passed Margaret he looked for a moment into her eyes, and his lips twisted briefly in a smile.

"Your friend has been a great help to me," he said. "I doubt very much if the authorities will want to court-martial a man who has been as helpful to them as I have been. Don't you agree?"

He strode on up to the top of the steps.

"I wouldn't bother untying McKeon," he said. "We'll be back in a minute to complete the matter."

Margaret stood briefly transfixed after the door had closed. Then she ran to McKeon's side and began to work on the knots.

And now at last the tears had begun to pour down her face.

On the sidewalk outside, Declan O'Donovan was trying to run. But his bruised legs splayed out under him and he was swaying like a drunken man.

On Macnee's face came a broad smile of relief as he saw Greyson carefully level his revolver.

"Och, I thought you wouldna' let him go," he breathed.

At the foot of the street there was a sudden burst of rifle fire from the men Greyson had sent ahead. But the officer ignored the distraction as his sights leveled on the Irishman some twenty-five yards away.

With great deliberation he pulled the trigger and saw O'Donovan jerk forward as the heavy slug tore through his body, pulping a kidney and ripping its way out through his stomach wall.

As Declan fell he twisted so that he landed on his back. He was lying there, squirming and clawing at his belly, when Greyson walked up unhurriedly and gazed down on him.

"To think that a piece of filth like you could have nearly ruined me," he said softly.

And in a paroxysm of rage he emptied the pistol straight into Declan's face, five heavy slugs one after the other, smashing through bone and flesh and careening off the stone setts beneath to fly wildly in little fragments of lead and copper.

Greyson stood still, swearing aloud in a thin, high voice, as rifles poked forward from a window farther down the street and roared out revenge.

The soft-lead, broad-nosed bullets of the Howth Mausers were an outlawed missile by the vagaries of international law. The first one caught Greyson just below the knee, and the

313

spreading lead pulverized his shin bone. For an instant he stood there, one-legged, like a toy soldier on its base.

Macnee was already dead, most of his head blown away by another bullet. The young soldier was screaming as he clawed at the writhing worms of his intestines spilling on the pavement.

Only the gray-faced miner was still alive and running. He ran like a snipe, and his darting, stooping run almost took him to safety before a bullet cut his spine in two and hung him across the low railings of a garden.

Greyson fell slowly, fell to his face, the Webley still in his hand. He could see the attackers now, the faces at the window. And as the blood pumped from the severed artery of his leg, he leveled the gun carefully. He would take some of them with him. He would take some of them.

The pistol hammer fell on an empty chamber—and another, as in a last desperate frenzy Greyson pulled and pulled again at the trigger until there was no more strength in him.

"They've got the major!" one of his makeshift platoon shouted. "Oh, my God, they've got the major!"

The panic of the leaderless gripped them, and they fled out through the back of the house and away across the gardens of a burning city.

Margaret followed Terence McKeon from the house. Across the road the Volunteers had also come out. They were standing over the bodies, and as McKeon came up one of them spun swiftly, his rifle at the ready. Then he recognized the uniform.

"Who's this?" he demanded, pointing at Declan O'Donovan. "What was happening? We saw him shot, but—"

As he left the cellar, as he rubbed back life into his wrists and ankles, Terence McKeon had been thinking hard. He felt no relief at his escape, as he had felt no fear in his captivity. But in his mind he was reviewing everything that had happened in one swift, comprehending instant. And deciding how best what had happened could be used for the good of the Cause.

In life, wherever he went, Declan had been a vast, wild, commanding figure, a man to lead men into the jaws of hell. He had had all the shapes and virtues of a hero—until those last minutes of collapse in the cellar.

And Ireland had need of heroes. He remembered the professor's words only days before—yet a lifetime before. Ireland would need heroes and martyrs from this time, men who were known, whose memory would urge other men on to great deeds, whose spirit would live on and hearten others, who would be the inspiration of the next bid for freedom when it came.

Declan would be one of those heroes. That final weakness would not have happened. Already McKeon's mind was editing it out of existence, rewriting the chapter as it should have been.

For a moment his voice was dry and scholarly as he answered the Volunteer.

"Who's this?" he echoed. "This is Declan O'Donovan . . ."

The Volunteers showed little interest, and their indifference was the final spur that was needed to utterly transform Terence McKeon.

For suddenly he was no longer the schoolmaster McKeon, the quiet reasonable man who could persuade men's minds but never, never infuse their spirits.

"Declan O'Donovan," he declared. "You know him now and Ireland will know him tomorrow."

In his voice there was a new timbre, and a strange light sparkled in his eyes.

"There lies Declan O'Donovan, who died for the freedom of Ireland. Go and see the cellar where the English tortured the great patriot that now lies dead before you. See how they used him. See how he was tortured as they tried to make him talk. Listen, and I'll tell you the things that were done in that cellar to Declan O'Donovan. . . .

"Any man may die, but O'Donovan died greatly. And you were witnesses to his death; you saw at the last how they had to shoot him in the back, he who had fought them off by the dozen and despite his wounds went seeking more arms to fight on against them. You who saw him die, listen and remember. For men like this come only once in a lifetime . . ."

Terence McKeon had abandoned the cold reason by which he had lived all his life, abandoned it for a greater reason. And his own heart thrilled now as he spoke over the dead body of Declan O'Donovan and saw how his words reached straight to the hearts of these other men.

This was a small audience, his first small audience, and he held it in the hollow of his hand, playing on the men's emotions as if they were some subtle musical instrument and he was a great musician.

Soon there would be greater audiences and he would play on them as easily. Declan's memory would be a flaming flag to lead other men on to victory. And he, Terence McKeon, would be the standard-bearer.

Margaret Kingston had said nothing at all. Silent and dry-eyed, she stood in the street with the wind blowing chill about her legs and her feet stained with the blood of the two men she had known so well.

She was almost beyond conscious thought. She knew what it was that McKeon was doing, and she neither approved nor disapproved. This she accepted, that the real truth was not useful. That the new truth was useful.

316

But not to her. No truth and no oratory could change anything for her.

No oratory would wipe from her mind Declan's last betrayal or Greyson's cruelty. Those truths would remain with her always. But Declan's was a truth of which she would not speak.

33. *Endings and Beginnings*

Now it was over.

It had ended as it was bound to end—in the defeat of the few by the many.

> In order to prevent the further slaughter of Dublin citizens and in the hope of saving the lives of our followers, now surrounded and hopelessly outnumbered, the members of the Provisional Government present at Headquarters have agreed to an unconditional surrender, and the Commandants of the various districts in the City and Country will order their commands to lay down arms.
>
> Signed: P. H. Pearse,
>
> 29th April, 1916. 3.45 p.m.

The slow anguish of realization had begun. In many an outlying detachment there were bitter disputes before at last the order was obeyed.

But it was over.

Terence McKeon was in civilian clothes again as he stood on a Dublin sidewalk and watched the doleful procession move slowly by, men and youths, some in uniform and some not.

A hostile crowd jeered the rebels, jeered them for their failure, for their disloyalty to other Irishmen fighting in

France, but jeered them more for the discomfort and inconvenience they had brought with their folly.

Irishmen taunted Irishmen for trying to free Ireland, and
this was the bitterest note of all to the prisoners. They had
not fought for themselves, for their own greed, but for others,
for the chimera that is freedom.

Now their own people taunted them and the shawlie
women from the slums pelted them with refuse.

And yet McKeon knew they had not failed. They had lit
a spark which no flying refuse could extinguish, and whatever followed the trials that would come soon, the spark would
become a flame and the flame would light up Ireland.

"Bloody fools," a man behind him commented, a fat man
with a short meerschaum pipe in his mouth. "Bloody fools.
Sure anyone could have told them they didn't have a chance."

"A chance!" McKeon turned fiercely on the man. "What
do we need with a chance? Did Declan O'Donovan have a
chance?"

"And who the hell might Declan O'Donovan be?"

"My God!" McKeon's voice grew louder as others turned
toward him, tired or sickened by the spectacle of defeat.
"Here's a man who never heard of Declan O'Donovan! Here's
a man doesn't know the name of one of the greatest heroes
of our day! Here's a poor, foolish, ignorant man who . . ."

Louder his voice grew, and more confident, as he gathered the crowd and held them.

And as he turned real defeat into imaginary victory, made
a hero from a broken coward, McKeon saw men's shoulders
stiffen and the cynicism of destruction give way to a light of
new hope.